ONE SMALL CANDLE

a full-length novel

by

Cecil Roberts

published by

Hodder and Stoughton

ST. PAULS HOUSE · LONDON EC4

CECIL ROBERTS

NOVELS

Miscellaneous

ONE SMALL CANDLE

Cecil Roberts

FIRST PRINTED · JULY 1942
THIS EDITION JANUARY 1950

Printed and Bound in England for
Hodder & Stoughton Ltd., London, by
Hazell, Watson and Viney, Ltd.,
Aylesbury and London

To

ELIZABETH STABLER

CONTENTS

CHAPTER ONE

MORNING BY THE RIVER

HIS dear Mother, who had a quotation for every occasion, believed that all things come to him who waits. Charles had always scoffed at this, with all the impatience of his twenty-four years. And now something he had never waited for, and had never really planned for, had come with the suddenness of a thunderclap. It had left him a little stunned, so loud was the applause of the gods. With one month's work, snatched from time he should have devoted to his medical studies at Guy's Hospital, he had pulled fame and fortune about his ears. The destined heir of the medical practice of his indulgent uncle, Dr. Wyndham Woodfall, in the charming old riverside town of Henley-on-Thames, he was now confronted with the painful task of revoking a carefully planned destiny.

It was hard on Uncle Wyndham. He was getting old, he was mistrustful of the selfish opportunism of juniors, for three in succession had deserted him for town practices, lacking the backbone required of a general practitioner in a country town. The younger generation, softened with a passion for tennis, and burdened with an expensive taste in motor-cars, had saddened the heart of Dr. Woodfall. "Soft, soft, that's what they are—they object to farmers' wives having babies at midnight, three miles up bad cart-tracks. They want 'em born around the corner, in between week-end parties," snorted the doctor. His look notwithstanding, Uncle Wyndham was as gentle as his forceps. Astute young doctors engaged by Dr. Woodfall soon spotted the destined heir, home from Guy's on week-ends. It was obvious the name-plate would not change on the surgery door.

But now it was going to change, and on this lovely June morning of 1935, when England lay in loveliness and tranquillity on the threshold of a hot summer's day, young Charles knew he was about to throw a bomb that not only would shake the rafters of this early Georgian mansion, but would, metaphorically, cause the Thames to swamp the varnished shells in which young England, young America and young Europe were practising for the famous Regatta.

With over a dozen letters in his hand, all of which he had hurriedly skimmed in the intoxication of success, Charles went out through the rose garden down to the river-bank, collecting Tilly the dachshund *en route*, and sat on the white bench commanding a view of the lovely balustraded bridge, the old bow-windowed inn across the stream, and the castellated tower of the church, which, like the hub of a wheel, sat at the centre of every divergent spoke of Henley's revolving life.

It was a scene, familiar through twenty years, that still gave delight, for here, red-roofed in green shade, by translucent water, the old town lay out in the morning sunshine while, distant, the beechwoods covered the enfolding hills, green footstools to the cloudy feet of heaven. Behind him, the old house smiled beneath a roof warped by Time, its complexion gained from nigh two hundred summers through which roses had fallen and peaches ripened, what time a German George had lost England her American Colonies and a Nelson had thwarted a tyrant. But it was not any historic sense, the fact that horsemen had ridden past its walls with news of Waterloo, or a heated Dr. Johnson, with his Boswell, had called for a drink of mulled ale *en route* to Oxford, that endeared the old house to Charles Woodfall. He loved it not only because it was home but also as the sailor loves the port that sees him embark on new voyages, already anticipating the thrill of his return. For, with this sudden achievement to his credit, he was free now. Spare money in the bank suddenly placed at his disposal all the efficient transport of the era, by road, rail, boat and plane, with which the earth had been vanquished for the traveller's delight.

A punt went by with the Wicker boys in it, probably going downstream for a bathe before breakfast. He looked at them,

Pat, Tony and Derek, and he laughed inwardly at the antics of the law of cause and effect. Those three boys, completely unaware of themselves as the agents of Fate, had spun a thread of escape for him, from the dissecting theatres of Guy's, London, to orange groves in Witterwittee and fabled Hollywood. He remembered how he had laughed, when about their age, on first hearing that fantastic name, Witterwittee. It did not seem possible there could be such a place, or that people could live in it with serious faces. Yet Great-Aunt Woodfall lived there, with a very serious face, if report were true. Great-Aunt Woodfall had been a tradition since his infancy. Was it possible he would see her in the flesh and walk through her Florida groves?

" 'Morning, Pat; 'Morning, Derek! 'Morning, Tony!" shouted Charles to the boys as they drifted by, smiling. They answered his salute with a gay commotion of voices and paddles. He felt tempted to add, waving one of the letters he held, "Do you brats know you've put over ten thousand pounds into my pocket—and no more pills for me!"

He did not shout this. Somehow, later, he would devise a rewarding celebration. Instead, he watched them drift away, and wondered where now was the tutor of last summer's vacation. That tutor deserved a rewarding celebration even more than those boys. Perhaps he would turn up again this summer, for the boys were home prematurely, blessed, at Regatta time, by an outbreak of measles which had disbanded their school for the rest of the summer term. Yes, he owed everything, truly, to that dank-haired, bespectacled tutor, a scholarship-supported product of one of Oxford's lesser colleges. Dash the fellow, he didn't even know his name! What he did remember, as vividly now as when they had provoked much unkind mirth at Henley's garden-parties, were the poor youth's trousers, which were always so short, and so tight in the seat. Those trousers, and the tutor's curious waddle as he walked, had earned him the name of Mr. Duckbottom. It marked a degree of affection for, as well as derision of, the amiable, worthy youth, victim of economic pressure and, as his spectacles proclaimed, chronic myopia. Yes, the humblest of God's creatures had his mission in the closely woven scheme.

Witterwittee and Hollywood, via Duckbottom, reflected Charles on this blithe summer's morning, summed up the young tutor's influence on his own life. Without that vision of tight-trousered, peering young Duckbottom he had never conceived the character of Horatius Blear, the tutor in the comedy that was now convulsing London, and with which, according to the letter in his hand, he had ensnared a film magnate to the tune of fifty thousand dollars. A month's easy scribbling, provoked by a vision of young Duckbottom, tutor to the Wicker boys, had won him, overnight, fame and fortune. The former had flashed upon him only a mere month ago, the latter was beginning to trickle into a bank balance so anæmic by nature that it would have to suffer blood-letting to avoid congestion.

The family had not yet realized the change which had come over his affairs. He had not wholly realized it himself, still ingenuous in the enjoyment of fame, exhilarating at any time, but intoxicating to the swift spirit of youth. He still pored over every press-cutting acclaiming him as 'the famous young playwright' or that 'very promising dramatist'—a little patronizing, this—or 'brilliant young Mr. Woodfall.' There were ten of these cuttings this morning, all worthy of planting in his pleasant garden of praise, with scissor-trimmed edges and paste. It gave his mother such joy, he persuaded himself, not wishing to seem a rank egotist.

Uncle Wyndham was pleased, of course. He knew that, though the doctor said nothing. His hazel eyes had twinkled proudly at the 'first night.' "You're a scamp, poking fun at young Duckbottom like that," he said, shaking his hand warmly, behind the scenes, following the commotion of calls, compliments to the producer, compliments to the cast, a not too fluent speech of thanks, since audiences like their playwrights bashful, particularly if young, and the recurrent curtains. At the Savoy, afterwards, it had been all compliments, champagne, effusive praise scattered like confetti on actors and actresses, loaded with 'darlings' and 'my dears' and 'marvellous' and 'wonderful'—endearments and adjectives all the easier to use in a world given to insincere exaggerations, because, for once, neither insincerity nor exaggeration was necessary to voice the certainty of this success.

Very late, or rather very early, he had conducted his leading lady to her limousine.

"See you at the Ivy to-morrow, lunch-time?" she said, with a radiant parting smile.

"Alas, no—I've a lecture on the poliomyelitis virus."

"The what?" she had exclaimed.

"Sorry—I'm a medical student, you know," he explained.

"Oh—how thrilling! Good night!" And she had drawn off into the quiet of the Strand, wondering, no doubt, at his odd performance, for the Ivy restaurant was the bowl to which everyone went on the morrow to lap up the cream of success.

For a month now he had taken his medical labours faithfully, striving to ignore the significance of this new field of activity. Uncle Wyndham had completely forgotten the play. His mother, on his return home at week-ends, had asked, "You're not working too hard, dear?" meaning, "Are you being enticed out too much, and getting to bed too late?" Odd, but neither of them realized in any way that his whole life was changed. Henceforth he would be more allied with the footlights than with the stethoscope, for, of course, he would write other and better plays. This was only a beginning, a frivolous beginning.

"Charles!"

He started. It was his mother's voice. He got up from the bench and turned to see her coming down the flagged path that cut through the rose garden, with its sun-dial centrepiece. A slight figure, with greying hair, she was rosy-cheeked and dark-eyed, with laughter never long absent from her serene face. Her husband, a cavalry officer, had died four years after the close of World War I, and she had come to live with her brother-in-law, Wyndham, to look after his house, and to fill to some extent the void left by the death of his own wife, a wound fifteen years old and not healed yet. She had found in him a father for her two boys, Charles and Peter, whose education he had planned and financed. Charles, whose memory of his father was now faint among childhood's recollections, knew it was his mother whom he resembled. He had her spare figure, her colouring, dark blue eyes and black hair, unlike Peter, the kid brother, now eighteen, who was a Woodfall.

Peter was obviously his uncle's nephew—large, blond, and with a broad open face and merry eyes. He had the Woodfall mouth too, wide, full-lipped. He had none of his mother's quiet poise or her seriousness. Even thus early, Charles knew how different they were, in temperament as well as mould, brothers only in blood. For Peter was a faun, irrepressible, infectiously gay, a creature of laughter and physical charm, determined to treat the world as an oyster for his dexterous opening. Everything came to Peter, easily, with an eager benevolence towards him. It had always been Peter who had been taken away for extensive Continental holidays, whose presents at Christmas, and on birthdays, had been more lavish and numerous than his own. Charles was certain that throughout life Peter would gather up everything he needed with careless ease.

But Charles knew he was nearer to his mother than Peter could ever be. Perhaps the companionship in her early years of widowhood had bound him closer to her, perhaps he had a deeper nature than Peter's, though in that he might do his brother an injustice, for, as yet, he was a mere boy; but whether by nature or the years of companionship, he knew that whatever was in his life would be shared by his mother, and felt by her in a degree that deprived him of full and thoughtless liberty.

It was this knowledge that troubled him now. Uncle Wyndham would be very hard hit by his decision to break the pattern of life wrought for him. From his early boyhood Uncle Wyndham had seen in him the only successor of the practice, the bearer of the Woodfall tradition for the third generation in Henley. Yet, hard as it would be, it was not Uncle Wyndham who made Charles feel reluctant to announce his decision. The old boy would take it gallantly if sadly, but not so his mother. Her life was built around his own. A communion of spirit had so grown between them that each loosening of the bond would be painful. He looked at her now, conscious and proud of the beauty she still retained, as she came down the path towards him.

"Wyndham won't be back for some time—he was called out early, so we'd better not wait breakfast for him," she said; and nearer, kissing his cheek, "Good morning, dear!"

He kissed her in return and held up the letters.

"I've been offered fifty thousand dollars for the film rights," he cried, exultantly. "And a trip to Hollywood!"

"Fifty thousand dollars—how much is that?" she asked, standing still.

"Roughly, ten thousand pounds."

"Charles, that's an awful lot of money."

"For one so young, yes," he laughed. "It represents a thousand tonsils at a tenner a time, Uncle's price."

"What a horrible thought!"

"What a horrible job!" retorted Charles, linking his arm in his mother's, as they went towards the house.

"Charles—you don't feel superior?" she asked, quietly.

"Superior?"

"Your uncle is a wonderful man, nothing is too much trouble—he wears himself out."

He saw then what she meant.

"You mean, do I take playwriting as seriously as medicine? No, of course I don't. Doctors are essential, I know that, but——"

He left the sentence unfinished, and they walked on in silence for a few moments. A broken delphinium halted them. Mrs. Woodfall tied it back to a stake. Then, satisfied with the rescue, she turned to her son and smiled.

"It's going to hurt poor Wyndham terribly," she said.

He looked at his mother. So she knew what was in his mind, as ever.

"I know that—I'm wondering how I'm going to tell him," said Charles; "but he knows, I'm sure, that I'd never be much of a success as a doctor—I'm not built in the heroic mould. I've always shuddered at the thought of passing my life among sick people."

"Someone has to do it, Charles, and I don't think Wyndham has ever felt heroic. He believes he does it for a living, it's a profession and he earns money by it—that's how he thinks of it, I know," said Mrs. Woodfall.

"And he could retire to-morrow if he wanted. But he doesn't want to. He loves looking after people. He'd die if the surgery bell ceased ringing. I admire him tremendously —and it's because I admire him so, and I'm grateful for all he's done for me, that I let myself be persuaded into studying medicine. I know he wants me to carry on the practice— but——"

He broke off, and looked at his mother.

"I feel very mean about it—what am I to do?" he asked her.

"We must each lead our own lives. I'd rather you were an ungrateful nephew than a bad doctor," replied his mother.

"Ungrateful——"

"That's the wrong word. Sorry, Charles, I know you're not ungrateful."

He pressed her arm. They arrived at the garden door, and went into the square hall, with its old broad staircase, the apse holding a statue of the young Bacchus, which always seemed incongruous in this temperate house, and the heavy Georgian front door and beautiful fanlight.

"When are you going to tell Wyndham?" asked Mrs. Woodfall, depositing the roses she had cut on the hall table. Some letters, addressed to her, lay there, and others for the doctor.

"I'll have to choose my moment—perhaps after dinner to-night."

"You should remember one thing, my dear. Ten thousand pounds doesn't last for ever," said Mrs. Woodfall, "and money isn't happiness—I know that's a trite saying, but it's true, nevertheless."

He laughed and kissed her cheek.

"You don't imagine I'm going to sit back and do nothing more? I'm only beginning. But I must find material, which means I must travel and see life. Don't worry, darling, leave Uncle to me," said Charles, affecting a confidence he did not feel.

They passed into the dining-room and sat down to breakfast. The doctor's chair, at the end of the table, was empty, but Pat, the Irish setter, sat patiently by it, waiting for his master. Tilly lay down by the fender. They were half-way through breakfast when Pat, quick to hear the beloved footstep, gave a sharp bark and went to the door. It opened, and Dr. Woodfall came briskly in. He carried with him an air of cheerfulness, not because it was a professional habit, but because a love of life radiated from him. Nearly forty years of attendance upon the sick and the dying had made no inroad on his zest for life, for had he not started hundreds of healthy infants upon their pilgrimage, and was he not saluted wherever he went by the hale and hearty? Had anyone called him a faith-healer he would have snorted with indignation, for he professed a contempt for cranks of all kinds, yet this is what he was, unwittingly. The poor woman he despatched from his surgery with a bottle of medicine, swallowed it, and had belief in its efficacy because the doctor's assurance of recovery was so positive, so cheerful, that she absorbed the optimism with which he faced life. Cynics asserted that Dr. Woodfall's popularity was based upon his reluctance to send out bills, and the modesty of their charges when they were sent, and that, outside the common run of ailments, he was quite useless as a practitioner.

A very smart young doctor who had invaded the town some years ago had taken all Dr. Woodfall's best-paying patients. A uniformed nurse assisted in the surgery, a uniformed chauffeur drove an expensive car, and the brilliant young doctor took the utmost precautions. He rarely trusted to his own opinion, but called in the expert aid of radiologists, bacteriologists, and outside consultants; he diagnosed diseases of a complexity and rareness that seemed quite unknown to old Dr. Woodfall, who suffered the loss of his better-class patients without a murmur. Three years later they all came back, when the brilliant young doctor, involved in unsavoury divorce proceedings, suddenly fled the scene, leaving behind a mountain of debts. He was more missed at smart dinner-parties than at bedsides.

Dr. Woodfall did not scorn dinner-parties. He was a sturdy diner-out, though he seldom got through any dinner before a telephone call robbed him of a glass of port and a cigar. He had a sharp tongue when the call was frivolous, and recalcitrant patients quailed before the sudden glare of his blue eyes. But his anger was swift and rare. He displayed endless patience under the load of human stupidity. He read souls as much as bodies, and knew well how much disease resided in the minds of his patients. Had he possessed the disposition, he could have complained of that jade, Fortune, in her dealing with him. In the visible rewards of his profession he had not been richly rewarded, but if the instant light of a smile on the faces he encountered, from old cronies to pinafored toddlers, could be measured in gold, Dr. Woodfall was the richest man in the district.

"I'm glad you didn't wait for me—an early call to the Barkers—I'm afraid we're going to lose that boy," he said, sitting down, after bestowing a pat on the dog's head. "Dear me—those Barkers have had a run of ill luck! A fire, foot-and-mouth disease taking his cattle, that scallywag son in trouble, the girl marrying a drunken lout, and now poor little Ralph folding up!"

"Is there no hope?" asked Mrs. Woodfall.

"None, I fear—I'll go back this evening, but I wouldn't be surprised if—— Sorry, my dear, I'm forgetting!"

Dr. Woodfall was always forgetting. Years ago he had

made a rule that 'shop' should never be talked at table, but the rule had never been kept. His patients, after all, were part of Henley's history, and his sister-in-law encouraged him to talk. Last night, at three a.m., he had been called out to a case four miles away, up on the Chilterns, and again at seven-thirty the Barkers had made a desperate appeal. At his time of life this night work was a strain. Thank heaven, Charles, having just qualified, could take over this coming winter.

"Any news?" asked the doctor, cracking an egg.

"I've got Hollywood in my pocket," answered Charles, exuberantly. "They've offered ten thousand pounds for the film rights of *Good Morning, Children*!"

The doctor paused, his spoon deep in the egg, and looked at his nephew's radiant face.

"Ten thousand pounds!" he said, slowly. "Ten thousand pounds—why, that's the end of a hard life's work, with luck!"

He paused again, lifted the spoon to his mouth, and nibbled at a piece of toast.

"Are you really sure you're going to get it? It's one of those things you read about—I've never been able to believe things like that do happen—not to anyone you know," he observed, quietly. Then, a smile spreading over his face: "Why, you'll be able to buy your mother a small car—and perhaps I'll get some new chairs in the surgery! You'll be surprised how many friends you'll have with bright suggestions! And have you to do anything more for that money?"

"Not unless I'm paid extra—they do suggest that I might go to Hollywood to work on the scenario—all expenses and a thousand dollars a week," answered Charles, gaily.

Dr. Woodfall looked at his sister-in-law.

"Mary—it makes medicine seem a pretty poor show. How long did that play take you, Charles?"

"About a month, Uncle. Of course, it's only a piece of fantastic luck. Some folks write all their lives, and can't pay their gas bills," answered Charles, feeding Tilly, who had advanced to his feet.

"H'm—it takes nine months to bring a child into the world —and that's only the beginning of all the work. The pen's mightier than the forceps, I see."

He said it gently, but they both knew the old doctor was shocked by the vagaries of Fate.

"Well, Charles, I'm glad for your sake—it's a wonderful beginning."

The last word startled Mrs. Woodfall. She glanced hastily at her son.

"But no one would for a moment make any comparison between a doctor's life and a—and a thing like this, however rewarding," said Mrs. Woodfall, earnestly. "Think what a doctor means to humanity!"

Charles stirred his tea, uneasily. This was just the kind of conversation that made them all uncomfortable. He wished he had kept his film offer to himself, for some time at least.

"Of course, the two things aren't comparable. I've no illusions about that," he said, a little desperately. "You'll get more by making the world laugh than by curing its pains— but everybody knows which is the essential service," said Charles.

His uncle looked at him with smiling eyes.

"Well, that may be, my boy—but a good comedian may do more for sad folks than a good physician," observed the doctor.

"Wyndham, you can't really believe that!" protested Mrs. Woodfall. "Look what you do for people!"

"Of course not—why, it's ludicrous to get ten thousand for an idiotic thing like *Good Morning, Children*. I shall take it, of course—and know I'm lucky," said Charles.

The maid came in. The doctor was wanted on the telephone—yet one more oft-broken rule. Messages were not to infringe on meal hours. But they always did.

"Excuse me!" said the doctor, rising.

Mrs. Woodfall waited a few moments after he had left the room. She and her son looked at each other.

"You know, it makes me feel the meanest cur on earth!

I begin to wonder if I can do it. I'm sure the old boy scents what's in the wind and is making a brave front," said Charles. "I wish I'd never written that blessed play, or that it had flopped!"

"You couldn't help it, not really, Charles."

"That's the idiotic part of the whole business. I just scribbled that nonsense—and now it's going to smash us all up!"

"Oh, no, Charles—we're all glad for your sake."

"But it has upset everything—damn Mr. Duckbottom!"

"I can't help feeling proud of you—and Wyndham does, I know," said Mrs. Woodfall. "And there's always been a strong connection between medicine and literature—Oliver Wendell Holmes, Conan Doyle, and Somerset Maugham, and——"

"Charles Woodfall. But, darling, my play's drivel!" protested Charles. "I believe that thing'll go reeling round the world—it's found the lowest common mentality!"

"It's really very brilliant—everybody says so. Look at the critics!" said Mrs. Woodfall, proudly.

"I'll write something some day—perhaps something great —and then what will they say? They'll tell me I can't write. You know I'd be much safer here—listening to the surgery bell and looking at little Annie's tonsils, and growing old, at ten shillings a visit—and who knows, I might be much happier, like Uncle Wyndham, the grand old boy. And I'm going to stick a knife in his heart, I know that. Oh, what a mess!"

"It's funny, isn't it?" asked his mother, quietly.

"Funny!"

"You're famous, and you've got more than ten thousand pounds in your pocket, and the beginning of a very interesting life—and you're miserable. Which just proves what you are."

"And what's that?"

"A boy with a good heart—otherwise this would never bother you, and you'd quit Wyndham without a qualm."

"Quit—that's an awful word!"

"Sorry, darling."

"But it's the right word, Mother. I'm quitting."

"I don't think Wyndham will see it like that—however disappointed he is. He would——"

The door opened and the doctor came into the room. In the instant they saw something had happened.

"Wyndham?" asked Mrs. Woodfall.

He sat down slowly, and shook out his napkin. Then he did an odd thing with it. He wiped his brow, although the summer morning was cool.

"Henry Fritten's shot himself," he said, quickly.

"What!" exclaimed Charles. Henry Fritten, the solicitor, came in and out of the house like a member of the family. He was Uncle Wyndham's oldest and closest friend.

There was a shocked silence.

"I can't eat anything," said the doctor, pushing his plate away. "I must go round and see what I can do for poor Alice. It's—it's——" He looked at them stunned.

"But—how—why——" asked Charles.

"In the hut at the bottom of the garden, with a revolver. He got up early and went out—he'd had insomnia, you know. I must go—the police are waiting for me."

They got up from the table. The canary, singing shrilly in the morning sunshine, sounded horribly incongruous.

"Shall I come with you?" volunteered Charles.

"Oh, no, thank you, Charles. Stay with your mother. I may bring Alice and Marjorie back—they can't stay there, amid all that. Poor Henry, poor old fellow!"

They saw the doctor go off in his car, and went into the study.

"I didn't know he had insomnia—he seemed quite all right. He took two sets off us yesterday. He seemed in excellent form," observed Charles, opening the newspaper but oblivious of its contents.

"He's been worried, so Alice tells me, for the last few weeks. She said he's had frightful fits of depression. Oh, it was unlike Henry, he was always so full of life," observed Mrs. Woodfall.

There had been a time when a close tie had been expected between the Woodfall and Fritten families. Marjorie Fritten was one of the beauties of the district. Charles, in common with the local youth, had fallen in love with this tall, lovely creature, and had been shown preference, until, in the spring of his twenty-second year, Marjorie, without any warning, had announced her engagement to a young Austrian violinist, encountered at a Salzburg festival. The Frittens had opposed the match, desperately, but without success. Marjorie fled to Vienna, married her swain, and was now home again, forgiven and 'expectant.' All Henley speculated whether Marjorie's romance had come to an end. Why should she have come home for the 'event,' and where was Fritz Ungar? Marjorie indignantly denied the gossip. Fritz had gone to Buenos Aires to play. It was natural for her to come home for the birth of her child.

Charles, thinking of poor Marjorie now, wondered how he could have been shaken by an event that, only two years old, now seemed to belong to a remote and unreal past. It had been a youthful infatuation that might have led on to disaster but for Marjorie's well-balanced nature.

"I wonder," said Mrs. Woodfall, "if poor Henry has been worried over Marjorie—he told me he thought her husband should not have gone to South America at such a time."

"But he has his professional engagements to keep—I see nothing unreasonable in that. Personally, I think it's all just malicious gossip about Marjorie and Fritz. She tells me she's wonderfully happy, and I believe it."

Charles opened the lid of the writing-bureau and spread out his letters. His correspondence was quite formidable these days.

"I'll leave you to your work," said his mother, always tactful. "I'd no idea authors had so much writing to do outside their work. Will the fans be ringing the bell soon? If they use the surgery entrance it will be quite confusing!"

He took hold of his mother and kissed her. He knew these bantering moods of hers very well.

"If they do come, I shall turn them over to you—but it'll be some time before I get over the thrill. I've seen no fans yet —except Miss Whissitt, who stopped me in Bell Street yesterday, and wanted to know who Mr. Duckbottom was in real life. I evaded the question, but she'll track it down sooner or later."

He worked for a couple of hours at his letters. The one from his literary agent about going out to Hollywood to do the scenario of his play—how should he answer that? Was he really going to desert? Here he sat in his uncle's study, just qualified after those long, expensive years of study. Only a few weeks ago, coming in from the morning round, the old man had paused at the surgery door and, tapping the nameplate, had exclaimed, with a ring of pride in his voice, "Well, we'll have to have another plate under this!" And Charles knew that Uncle Wyndham had seen that second plate, in his mind's eye, for the last five years. It was very hard on the old boy. Why could he not come into the practice, and carry on his writing as an aside? After all, he might not have another success like this. It had been a lucky shot.

Hollywood. The name was a lure and a warning. It was a madhouse set on the Pacific Coast, whose gold and glamour drew men, as Circe had drawn them. Unreal as its sham façades, its love scenes, incredible in all its legends save that of its blatant vulgarity, he felt the pull of it, nevertheless, as strong as any stage-struck girl whose mirror filled her with dizzy dreams.

Still undecided, he put in a London call. A few minutes later he was talking to Arnold Phipps, his literary agent. Charles, sitting at a window looking out on the rose garden, with a sun-burnished streak of the Thames flashing through willow trees, conjured Phipps at his desk, in the grey room above the fruit barrows of Covent Garden. Phipps's 'harem,' as he called it, held half a hundred young women sitting in rooms shaken by typewriters, and littered with magazines, manuscripts, and tea-cups. In his first visit to this agency Charles had suffered a shock. He heard authors' 'futures' being sold like shares or cabbages. They were a rising market. No, Miss Winnipeg was falling—her serial was a flop. No, they couldn't get a Hamish story, he was contracted ahead for three years, and drinking hard. Costock? His cinema rights had gone a month ago. No—Catlins never gave big advances, and twelve per cent. on royalties was their top, unless . . .

A strange world in which inspired genius was lined up in a skittle alley, and knocked down by editors and publishers, wise in the run, or trying to be wise, of public favour. And at the end of the alley, above the rattle of a clean sweep, loomed Hollywood, the goal and death-place of authors, according to report.

"Of course! Why not?" said Phipps, crisply on the telephone. Everything about him was crisp, his hair, his speech, his manner even with formidable and fading lady novelists entrenched behind triple names. Had Charles but known it, at that very moment, smoking a cigarette in an amber holder, Fanny Dodge Howard, for twenty years a front name on every important magazine cover, was seated in a large leather chair listening hard to Phipps's conversation. Her morning, her week-end, and her whole robust temperament, had been shaken by something she should not have seen in the correspondence tray on Phipps's desk. It was a letter confirming the preposterous fact that Annabel Parris Paget had accepted a contract for three more novels at an advance of fifteen hundred pounds each. And that woman's sales were only half of hers! While Phipps recommended Hollywood to Charles Woodfall as "an interesting trip anyhow, and they are unusually interested in you," Miss Fanny Dodge Howard—in real life Mrs. Spear, Mrs. Lowe, and Mrs. Dryden successively— nursed, figuratively speaking, a tomahawk for Phipps, who had shamefully sold her for a mere thousand pounds advance.

Phipps, buoyant, crisp, and insistent, thought it was a wonderful offer from Hollywood. First-class travelling expenses, out and return, minimum engagement of one month ("always extended—they work very slowly, you know"), less ten per cent. split commission, less British and American income-tax, it would not—— Here Phipps paused while his pencil went over the blotter. Five hundred pounds, at least, and an interesting experience. Certainly he should go!

Charles felt somewhat disappointed. *De luxe* travel each way, all expenses paid, a month in the world's most glamorous centre—and five hundred pounds, the last detail seemed a let-down. Anything in Hollywood seemed to be measured in units of fifty thousand dollars.

"We might get the figure up a bit—I'll try, but that's net, you know, commission and double income-tax." Commission and double income-tax, how resolutely they reduced the price of success!

"Well, I'll think it over—no hurry, I suppose?" asked Charles.

"Not for four or five days—I think we should cable them."

"Yes—thanks."

"Bye-bye," said Phipps.

Charles leaned back in his chair and looked out of the window. Why not go, and take in a visit to Witterwittee? A translantic trip, first-class hotels, and all the glamour of going there—and five hundred pounds in hand! His uncle couldn't give him that for a whole year, rising at dawn for childbirths, lancing Mrs. Brown's leg, sounding Mr. Smith's chest, looking down Willie Robinson's throat. And here he sat considering it, the big world calling! What was the matter with him? Loyalty, whimpered the small voice. Sentiment, said a louder one.

The clock between two tobacco-jars on the mantelpiece struck twelve. It was a Saturday morning. They would be gathering at Auntie Janet's. He would consult her. She had the soundest head combined with the kindest heart of any woman in England.

CHAPTER TWO

WILLOW VIEW

I

JANET CHERWELL lived in a large boathouse with a long, river-bordered lawn, a short distance below the bridge. Why she continued to live in a house with ten bedrooms, three sitting-rooms, built over a boat-dock with five boats, a long verandah and a landing-stage, no one knew until after joining 'the Cherwell circus,' as it was called. The possession of three brothers, four sisters, and uncountable cousins, each prolific in ensuring the future generations, taxed to its uttermost on Saturdays, Sundays, and holidays the hospitality of the house. It was a point of honour with Auntie Janet that no one was ever refused a bed, somewhere, and no one came or went without a drink, somehow. It would be unfair to say that the popularity of Auntie Janet waxed and waned with the weather. It was only natural that some twenty relations living in London found it irresistible to come down to Henley on a warm sunny day. They all loved Auntie Janet, and she made this affection stronger with an unfailing table, generously loaded, a bar, well-stocked, established between the pantry and the linen-room, and an unfailing cheerfulness in the face of all imported sorrow and tribulations. If the weather was dull, of course, Auntie Janet could recuperate before the next spell. Through a winter of wind, rain, and fogs she stuck faithfully to 'Willow View,' overhauling the linen, renewing the gaps in the china, and steadily stocking up the bar, ten shelves of bottles, not one of which she ever opened for herself.

At the beginning of spring, when, with the flowering of the forsythia, elderly gentlemen across at the Leander Rowing Club began to appear in pink socks and caps, Auntie Janet had the awning roped down over the iron bars on the boathouse verandah, the Axminster carpet spread across the broad projecting platform, the club chairs re-upholstered and set in position, and, as the last touch in her perfect hospitality, the field-glasses put out on the table. Like the first swallow, an oarsman would go skimming downstream and the field-glasses would come into use.

"Why, if it isn't old Mr. Scarrett," someone would shout from the verandah, having watched a large body, heavy in the midriff, skilfully perched on what seemed only a floating toothpick.

"Isn't he wonderful! And I know he's seventy-two," would exclaim Aunt Janet, borrowing the glasses. "And his grandson stroked the Pembroke crew last year!"

She knew everyone on the river, of course. She had been in it and on it for a large part of her life. She had celebrated her fifty-fifth birthday by diving in and swimming across to the opposite bank and back on a freezing April day. Nothing ever tired her. Three mornings a week she went bobbing along the lanes on horseback, accompanied by some odd niece or nephew or, failing these, alone, except for her ever faithful Whiskey, the Irish retriever.

Willow View reached the apex of its bursting hospitality in Regatta week. No one knew how many slept there, for cousins brought friends, nieces brought young men, nephews brought their fiancées; brothers and sisters, with wives and husbands, all descended on Auntie Janet. Cots were dumped in corridors, mattresses were put down even in the summerhouse. Every window framed a head, a babel of voices filled the rooms. Somehow forty sat down for lunch in relays, and then a calling launch would unload another dozen, who had not really meant to stay for lunch and, of course, stayed. People floating by in punts, in between the races, would look up at the choked verandah loaded with Cherwells and Cherwell offshoots, quite certain they would find someone there they knew, whereupon a waving would start.

"Oh, it's Mr. and Mrs. Brand, and their children," a Cherwell would exclaim, and Auntie Janet, true to form, would lean over the verandah and call, "Won't you come up?" And up they came. Five more places had to be squeezed in at the table.

This was the Auntie Janet that the Regatta and the rowing world knew. There was another Aunt Janet found only in the dull season, when the rains pitted the river and the beech trees stood barren on the hills. She was found there, in the large sitting-room, her armchair drawn up to the brick fireplace, and her needle busy on odd articles. This was the Auntie Janet who listened to a hundred griefs, and all the problems her friends brought her. She had never failed them, and her purse, often sorely depleted, backed up her sympathy. Her round, pleasant face invited confidence. Her physical and mental courage were matched in her robust mind. No one ever wondered to whom she turned with her own problems, she seemed so wholly self-sufficient, so poised above the turmoil of life. Yet to her, as to all the human race, came a horde of trials. Funds, well invested, shrank; properties, once well let, fell empty; and no one stood behind Auntie Janet save a cautious solicitor suggesting retrenchment here and retrenchment there.

"All you've got to do is to see me out!" retorted Auntie Janet. "And you can put that limit at eighty. After that I deserve whatever happens to me, for cluttering up the earth."

Whereupon old Mr. Gannett, sitting in his dark chambers in Lincoln's Inn Fields, would shake his head and say, fondly:

"Janet, ever since I've known you, you've been a rash girl!"

"I only regret the things I didn't do which I shouldn't have done!" retorted Auntie Janet.

She had been a widow for five years, and had no intention of changing her state. Romance was behind her, and she was well aware that nothing in the future could approach the utter felicity of her past. She had an unfading memory of one whose last words, breaking through his fading consciousness, were an affirmation of love. Perhaps this was why she felt she

owed something to life, and gave of its fullness to all who
came to her.

She was putting the final touches to the verandah when
Charles arrived, coming across the lawn. He mounted the
wooden staircase from the boat-landing, admiring the long
boxes of red geraniums and white marguerites that made
festive Henley's river-front.

"Good morning, Janet," he said, giving her a hug, as he
came up behind her. "Getting ready for the battle?"

Next week brought the Regatta. The white booms were all
in place along the course, behind which the punts and the
applauding supporters would be stemmed. The Judges' box
had gone up, the temporary grandstand in the Stewards' Enclosure opposite had reached the draping stage. Placed at an
angle looking up the course, towards Temple Island set at
the foot of its amphitheatre of beechwoods, and fronted with
shrubs in boxes, the grandstand began to suggest an air of
carnival. The itinerant circus was already beginning to spread
over the meadow, roundabouts, helter-skelters, shooting
alleys, and coco-nut shies, and a monstrous, bleating pipe-
organ. Its vulgar blare sometimes jammed the strains of the
military band stationed by the copper beech on the great lawn
of Phyllis Court Club whose brick rampart, facing the river,
was almost obliterated beneath a cascade of rambler roses.

"You do look smart," said Charles, surveying Auntie Janet.

"Yes, I've had the carpet cleaned," she answered.

"I mean you—not the carpet."

She was wearing a flowered silk blouse, with Magyar embroidery on the throat and sleeves.

"A bit giddy for an old thing like me," she laughed,
realizing what had caught his eyes. "But I'm being tactful.
Some Hungarians are coming. I found this in a drawer—I
bought it ages ago in Budapest—so I thought it would be a
nice compliment."

There was the unfailing sherry decanter on the white
wicker table, and glasses and cigarettes.

"Hungarians?" asked Charles, helping himself.

"Yes—Zemzeti—something. They've sent a crew from Budapest, and everyone thinks they're going to win. Eight of the nicest, handsomest young men you ever saw—young gods, but dumb for our purpose. They can't speak English, poor dears!" She banged some of the cushions. "The Hungarian Minister and some ladies are coming here to see them row over the course at one o'clock. Where's everybody this morning?—I asked Marjorie Ungar to meet them. We'll have to talk German to 'em—and I don't know a word."

She glanced at her wrist-watch. A practice crew went down the river.

"Lady Margaret boat," said Auntie Janet. "No. 2's Jack Fritten—a pity Marjorie isn't here."

She picked up the glasses, and surveyed the crew, before Charles could say anything. They swept past with a rhythmical click of oars in the rowlocks.

"Why—I don't see him—surely they've not dropped him!" she exclaimed.

"You've not heard?" asked Charles.

"He's not ill, poor boy?"

"No—not that. I don't think you'll see Marjorie either. Mr. Fritten shot himself this morning."

"Shot himself!" exclaimed Auntie Janet, turning an incredulous face to Charles.

"Uncle was called after breakfast—early this morning, it seems, in the garden-house. It's quite stunned us."

"But I can't believe it! He was so full of life—frightfully excited about Jack rowing in the Lady Margaret boat. Poor Alice—and I can't get to see her until these folks have gone."

Auntie Janet sat down and surveyed the flower-boxes in silence for a few moments. Then, looking Charles full in the face, she said, quietly, "When solicitors shoot themselves it's either trouble at home or at the office. And there was no trouble in that house—so——"

"What do you mean?" asked Charles, though he knew what she meant. Fritten's office was in Reading, but he had many clients in Henley.

"This is going to be a sad Henley for a good many people here," said Auntie Janet, quietly. "He was the kindest man that ever lived—poor Henry!"

"You don't mean he—he——"

"I'm afraid so. Well, this has knocked the sun out of the day," said Auntie Janet, quietly. " But perhaps I'm unjust to poor Henry. He was always so terribly generous and easygoing. Sherry?"

He filled his glass.

"I want to consult you, Janet—before the others come," he said, having sipped his sherry, excellent, as always.

She looked at him quietly, and as if with new eyes saw vividly how very attractive he was, with his black hair and neat head. Nothing that he would do could surprise her, he had always been the brightest of bright lads. She had watched him and loved him through jumpers and short trousers. She liked his even teeth, the set of his head on his flat shoulders, the flash in his eye when animated, which was his usual state.

"Not—not another?" she asked, kindly.

"Oh, no—not that," he answered, hastily, flushing slightly. At least three disturbing creatures had been encountered on this verandah.

"I'm told one of these Hungarian girls is simply ravishing—she's come to see her brother row," said Auntie Janet.

"Not interested, Janet dear, thank you. No, this is business," he said. "I'm on the spot."

"How?"

"This morning I've been offered ten thousand pounds for the film rights of the play, and a trip to Hollywood."

"It's worth every penny of it. I'm delighted."

"Oh, thanks, but—it's not that. You see, I've to decide something—something pretty serious."

He explained his problem. She listened to him without interruption.

"It will hurt the old boy terribly—I should feel a worm,"

he said, coming to the end. "And yet—I want to go, to get away from here."

"Of course you must go," said Auntie Janet.

"You think that?" he asked, eagerly.

"Certainly—you know, loyalty is a splendid quality, Charles, but it can lead to disaster. I can't see you as a doctor, I never could. You can't tolerate idiots and silly females. Medicine, successful medicine, is full of distressed females, and you'd have to diagnose every sickness except the right one—the man they can't have. And if it's not that then it's the man they can't get rid of."

"But poor old Uncle Wyndham——" began Charles.

"I don't want to seem hard—but let's face facts. It's natural for your uncle to want you in the practice, but it's sentiment after all. Medicine's not an hereditary calling, like ruling nations—and that tradition's going—and your uncle, who is the salt of the earth, an angel with a black bag, has really got things mixed up. I'm all for boys following the family trade if they can't make a course for themselves. But you've done that, and the prospect's not intoxicating. You've just qualified, you've got that, if ever you should want it. But you won't, I know that. No, off you go!"

"Janet, you are so comforting!" said Charles, gratefully. "I was feeling mean."

"I'm not comforting you at all, but I'm always for adventure, even at the cost of hurting others."

"You could never hurt anyone," affirmed Charles.

"I hurt my mother when I was twenty and went off with an engineer ten years older than myself, to live in the wilds of Bolivia. I'd known him a month when I married him. Everybody prophesied disaster and heartbreak. I remember standing in the hall, with the cab waiting, and my mother in tears, and I felt a monster of hardness and ingratitude. But I was right—oh, how I was right! You must lead your own life, and if you make a mess of it then it's your own mess. I admire your Uncle Wyndham tremendously, but an archangel's no right to shut a door on a prospect of adventure like yours.

o.s.c.—2

You go to that incredible Hollywood, and find out if one quarter's true that they say of it."

Charles laughed with relief, leaned over, and planted a kiss on Auntie Janet's cheek.

"You know you're splendid! That's settled it. I shan't stay in Hollywood—it's fatal. When I've finished the picture I shall go to my great-aunt at Lake Witterwittee."

"It sounds like your next comedy—my great-aunt at Lake Witterwittee. Is there such a place?" asked Auntie Janet.

"Certainly—it's in Florida and full of cowboys and oranges, with the most terrifying old lady of eighty, and a hush-hush scandal in the family."

"What's the scandal—I feel I want to go to Lake Witterwittee if only to write on note-paper with that address," said Auntie Janet, lighting a cigarette. Another practice crew went by. The opposite bank, with its white marquee used for dressing-rooms and boat storage, swarmed with half-naked youths carrying in and out their boats.

"The scandal—oh, the old aunt ruled four daughters with a rod of iron. Three of 'em are quite flattened out, the fourth bolted, and came to the bad end that overtakes reckless girls. She married a cowboy, or something like that, was forbidden the home, and died in childbirth. The old lady's eighty and keeps Victorian state in the middle of a derelict orange grove on an island. She must be a character. I want to go and see her, she's been a legend in my family ever since I can remember."

The sound of voices came across the lawn. Auntie Janet got up and went to the end of the verandah. The maid was ushering a man and three women towards the boathouse.

"Ah—here comes the Hungarian Rhapsody! I feel a fool in this blouse now," said Auntie Janet, pulling down her skirt. Then she went to the steps to welcome her guests.

II

By one o'clock there were twenty visitors on the verandah, natives of Henley who always dropped in for a pre-lunch

sherry, half a dozen lumbering boys in college blazers, pink
and fresh from their morning row over the course, and the
Hungarian contingent, with two smiling young men from the
visiting crew. Two of the foreign ladies were elderly and
spoke excellent French. Charles found himself engaged with
these and a thickset youth who was addressed as Lajos, a
member of the Hungarian crew. Presently Lajos and Charles
found themselves detached and floundering in German, as
Charles tried to explain various things about the Regatta.
"Ja—ja—ja!" exclaimed the foreign youth, desperately trying to be intelligent.

A moment came when a young woman spoke to him, and
in turn was introduced as his sister. Not a dozen sentences
had passed between her and Charles before he began to marvel
how he had missed her even in this crowd. She spoke excellent
English. She was blonde, with a good complexion. At first
glance she was not beautiful. She had high cheek-bones, and
the broad face had a Hungarian cast. But her eyes, grey Magyar eyes of the utmost candour, looked at Charles until he
felt a finger traverse his spine. He tried to talk to the *ja*'ing
brother, keeping his eyes away from this perturbing sister.
Later, he could recall how she was dressed, in a pearl-grey
costume, with silver shoes, and a military hat with a single
osprey feather that made her look like a young cadet of the
Hussars—at least something suggestive of what he imagined
Hungarian Hussars were like. Her voice was slightly husky,
and confidential. She exhibited no nervousness. Her eyes,
which she played upon Charles as she told him she had been
in England only a week, and for the first time, had a cool,
provocative challenge.

"You know Hungary?" she asked.

"No—alas—but I hope to now I've finished my studies,"
answered Charles. Where had she learned her English, he
wondered, and found his speculation answered by her next
sentence.

"You'd find it cute," she said, smiling. "What have you
studied?"

"Medicine—I'm a doctor," he volunteered. For a moment he thought he would call himself a dramatist, but checked the claim as a little boastful. "Tell me—what part of Hungary do you come from?"

"Oh—Budapest and Tiszatardos—and Tallahassee!"

Her eyes twinkled at him derisively. She put the sherry-glass to her provocative lips and unblushingly coquetted with him. A minx, undoubtedly.

"Tallahassee—not in Florida?" he queried.

"In Florida—now how would you know that? No one has ever heard of it—here—in Europe."

"So that explains the accent!" he laughed.

"Ah—you dislike it!"

"On the contrary, on your lips it sounds delicious. Budapest and Tallahassee—what a fantastic mixture, Miss——"

"You'll find my name funnier than Tallahassee—Kazinczy," she confessed, running her tongue over her lips.

"I don't find either funny," replied Charles. "They are both delightful and intriguing."

"Intriguing?"

"Sorry—we use that word stupidly. I mean, of course, interesting. Now, since you know Tallahassee in Florida, have you ever heard of a place called Witterwittee?"

"Lake Witterwittee?"

"Why, yes—how extraordinary, you know it?"

"I had a school friend come from there—you see, I was educated in the States, at Vassar."

"Oh—I see, you're half American!"

"Not even one per cent," she answered, laughing at him. "Let me explain. My mother, when I was a little girl, married again, an American, and settled in Tallahassee with my stepfather. I went with her—my brother stayed at Tiszatardos with my uncle."

"I begin to understand," said Charles, with a hundred questions in his mind.

"And you—how have you heard of Tallahassee and Witterwittee?" she asked.

"I have a great-aunt lives at Lake Witterwittee. I am always hoping to go there—and to Tallahassee, now," he added, boldly.

Her eyes lingered with his for a moment.

"I never go there now, but I am always travelling," she said.

"How delightful—you like that?"

"I get very tired of it, sometimes."

"Then why——" he began.

"I go with the company—I'm a ballerina."

"Oh!"

"Don't say 'Oh' like that!"

"Sorry—did I?" he laughed.

"Everybody does—we work very hard, and we are very respectable!" she added.

"Of course!" he agreed. "But I'm dismayed." And in answer to her questioning look: "I may have to run all over the world to find you again!"

"What a pretty speech!"

They laughed gaily, and at that moment Aunt Janet sailed in.

"Now, you've monopolized Miss——"

"Kazinczy," supplied Charles.

"He's remembered my preposterous name!" exclaimed Miss Kazinczy to her hostess.

"He's the kind of young man who can remember anything —when he wants to," said Aunt Janet. "Now we're all going in to lunch."

"Oh, no—I'm going, really I must!" protested Charles. There was a mob in the dining-room already. Fifteen, twenty, twenty-five? Even Aunt Janet did not know, nor care. "Don't be silly," she said. "Of course you're staying!"

Later, at the side of Stefanie Kazinczy, he counted. There were twenty-four to lunch. By the time they came to the sweets he was calling her Stefanie, and was dismayed to learn she was not staying in England for the Regatta. "We're dancing in Copenhagen," she explained.

"I hope you come back to London," he said, earnestly.

"No, then Paris, Dresden, and Warsaw."

"And never Tallahassee? I'm going to Witterwittee soon —at least I hope to, and perhaps——" he prompted.

"No—never Tallahassee. My mother died last year. I can't think of anything that would take me back. But you will come to Budapest—everyone comes to Budapest!" she cried.

"Of course," he replied, gallantly, and began to regret his plans for Hollywood and Witterwittee.

That night, undressing and emptying his pockets, he looked at his note-book. She had written in it her name and address. Stefanie Kazinczy, VI ker, Istvan út, Budapest. It looked very puzzling as a clue to a delightful young woman, but it fitted the whole romantic atmosphere. Budapest, a ballerina, Stefanie, and those lovely Magyar eyes. It was not likely he would ever see her again, however.

III

The Fritten suicide shook the district in which the old solicitor had been so widely respected. His firm, established for three generations in Reading, had one of the best connections in the county. The old panelled offices were visited by all the countryfolk. It was here that General Downe stormed about the taxes deducted from his diminishing rent dole. It was here that fastidious Miss More came to ask for "a little in advance," and always got it. Her income was derived from some slum property which should have been demolished long ago, and was so small that, for twenty years, Mr. Fritten had never presented to her a bill for services. Yet she complained bitterly that he was unenterprising and failed to fight the authorities over their monstrous demand that new drains should be installed in her properties. Her visits disorganized the office. She imposed upon Mr. Thale, the chief clerk, a dozen telephone calls which she had saved up to spare her the expense. She was always attended by a Pomeranian that paid visits to all the office stools. She complained bitterly of the flight of stairs to the office. The clerks groaned at her approach, yet Mr. Fritten always received her with patient and exquisite courtesy and, on leaving, escorted her to the foot of the stairs. She had seen better days, he would remark. It seemed to him that most of his clients had seen better days. In his kindness of heart a score of them, muddled in their affairs and troubled in finances, found a refuge from a harsh world of rising taxes and falling revenues.

And now Henry Fritten was dead, by his own hand. He had blown out his brains in the garden-hut behind his pleasant old Georgian house. Silver-haired, sixty-five, benign, a Justice of the Peace, he had been a pattern of respectability and social security. At the inquest it transpired that he had been worried by personal affairs. Rumours began to fly. Within a week of his funeral, attended by every notable in the district, the truth was out. Henry Fritten had every reason to feel worried. The death of one of his clients had enforced a settlement of the estate. For months the winding-up had been deferred, owing to legal complications, according to Mr. Fritten. Then an impatient legatee had brought in his own solicitors, a ferrety, hard city firm, who had pressed certain demands upon Messrs. Fritten & Fritten.

The old solicitor, at the end of his tether, could not face the threatened exposure. Kindness leading to muddle, muddle leading to deficiencies, deficiencies leading to juggling, juggling leading to borrowings, taken from the funds of clients, the first small discrepancy had grown to a mountain at the day of reckoning. A cold-blooded newspaper headline told the world the truth. Henry Fritten, over a space of twenty years, had embezzled eighty-five thousand pounds of his clients' money. Twelve clients were involved. Of these twelve, Dr. Woodfall faced a loss of twenty thousand pounds, the savings of forty years of medical practice. He was aware of the fact from the moment when, in the presence of a police officer, he pulled back Fritten's clenched fingers from the revolver. Happily married, in excellent health, he could have had only one reason for suicide.

Dr. Woodfall broke the news to his nephew one evening after dinner. Charles had heard the rumours, but he had no idea of the extent to which his uncle might be involved. It was clear that the doctor was greatly worried, but the death of such an old and valued friend had produced a shock. For this reason Charles had deferred the announcement of his decision in the matter of not entering the family practice. It could wait a few weeks. But now as he heard the news, and watched the gallant old boy attempt to minimize the personal disaster, he knew he could not add another shock to the one sustained. He could not desert Uncle Wyndham at such an hour of trial.

"So you see, Charles," went on Dr. Woodfall, "it means I must plod on to the end of my days. Of course I never really wanted to retire—you never can retire from this job. But I did hope to take it easier. It was very foolish of me—very!"

"Foolish? How?" asked Charles, filling his pipe from the tobacco-jar between them. "You couldn't possibly foresee that Fritten would do a thing like this. He was such a grand old boy."

The doctor sat silent for a few moments, then he looked at his nephew.

"I—I must be honest with you. I suspected something for quite a time. I knew Henry was worried. Three years ago he asked me for a loan of five thousand pounds. That surprised me."

"You didn't——"

"Yes—oh, quite on business lines, at four per cent. I sold out some War Loan to accommodate him, and he gave me a mortgage on his house."

"So you'll get that, anyhow," commented Charles.

"No," replied Dr. Woodfall, quietly. And, observing the surprised look on his nephew's face: "You see—he'd raised four other mortgages on his house, for other loans."

"Oh—the old villain!" exclaimed Charles. "How could he face us!"

"Well—when men get themselves involved and start things,

they have to go on. I'm more grieved than angry—poor old Henry!"

"Poor old Henry! Why, you can't pity a double-dyed crook!" expostulated Charles.

"Come—come!" said Dr. Woodfall, quietly. "Henry was never a crook. He—he was the victim of his own kindness. I know that. He advanced loans on the flimsiest security. He had a fatal weakness—he was sorry for people."

"But he wasn't sorry for you—he's embezzled your money!"

"Well—my case isn't desperate. I can carry on. I'm worried about Alice Fritten and Marjorie—they'll have nothing," said the doctor. "Alice tells me Fritz makes very little—he gets an engagement here and there. Marjorie drew an allowance of four hundred a year—that's ended now."

"You mean she was keeping the fellow!"

"Well, that's a little harsh, isn't it?" asked Dr. Woodfall.

"People should stand on their own feet!"

"My dear boy—they never do. A great many stand on other people's feet."

Charles was about to make a comment when he suddenly recollected that he had been doing precisely the same thing since he had come into his uncle's house.

"Can I say something to you—without offence?" asked Charles, after a silence in which they both smoked.

"You know you can. What is it, Charles?" asked the doctor. "You think I've behaved like an old fool? Well, I'm unrepentant. I'd have given Henry all that money if I'd really known the truth. Poor old boy—to shoot himself like that, after sixty-five years of life!"

"I've a proposal to make, Uncle."

"Which is?"

"Let me buy this house, and the practice—on a purely business basis. You'll go on living here, of course, just the same——"

"That's not business," said the doctor. "And thank you, my boy—but I can carry on until you——"

He paused and then looked uneasily at the young man sitting before him.

"Unless——" he continued, hesitatingly.

The telephone rang. He crossed the room and picked up the receiver.

"Yes—yes—I'll be along in twenty minutes," he said. Then, replacing the receiver, "I must go to Huntercombe," he said, knocking the ashes out of his pipe.

Charles stood up. The thing must be faced.

"You were saying, 'Unless——' Unless what, Uncle?" he asked.

Dr. Woodfall placed his hand on the young man's shoulder and smiled.

"My boy, I fear I've been rather stupid and selfish."

"You!"

"I've turned you into a doctor, because I've nourished a silly idea about carrying on a tradition. You're standing on your own feet now, and I go on asking you to stand on mine. You must lead your own life—so go on with your writing, travel, go out to Hollywood."

"But you want me here—now more than ever——" began Charles, when the doctor interrupted him.

"Yes—I did. But I was thinking of myself, and your mother, and your own future. And now you've made a future of your own—with much more to it than bottles of medicine, and surgery hours. And you'd be no good here, Charles!"

"No good!"

"No good, my boy. You've broken into a different world—and if you stayed here you would always be wondering what you'd missed, and I'd always be worrying over what I'd cheated you of. No, Charles, it's no good. We must face it. I needn't worry about your mother now—or Peter—or you."

He pressed Charles's arm.

"And thank you for being so considerate, my boy."

"Considerate!" echoed Charles.

"You were afraid I'd be hurt—and that takes the sting away. Well, I must be off."

The doctor picked up his pipe and pouch, smiled, and was gone.

Outside in the summer dusk the doctor switched on the headlights. They made a familiar pattern on the old stable walls as he turned in the drive. Through the window Charles watched the red tail-light vanish through the open gate.

"The salt of the earth," said Charles, aloud, standing at the window and troubled in his heart by this new freedom.

IV

Charles carried the news to Auntie Janet the next morning. It was a beautiful August day, and on the verandah at the noon hour, when the maid brought out the shiny decanter and the glasses, Auntie Janet sat sewing what she called 'the unmentionables.' She was alone when he walked on to the verandah. The river, like glass, glittered before them. Gone was the festivity of Regatta week. The white booms along the course had not yet been taken in, but the meadow opposite was cleared of the Stewards' Enclosure, and the field that had been converted into an amusement park was attempting to recover its turf, after the trampling of a thousand feet in the riot of that closing Saturday night when lusty crews, released from training, had made the welkin ring. Boys, beer and bacchanalia, yawping maidens, blaring pipe organs, strident hucksters at the stalls and shooting galleries, shattered the country quiet. Under a sickle moon the black woods cut the sky-line, woods in which the startled squirrels fled at the sound of low voices and crushed bracken.

But to-day all was peace, beauty, and propriety. Small boys fished from the towing-path, the broad, tree-shaded lawn of Phyllis Court was deserted. A punt glided downstream, and a solitary oarsman skimmed by, leaving a wake like an opening fan. It was ninety in the shade, and the morning newspapers reprinted their stock bathing pictures and spoke of a heat-wave.

Auntie Janet looked up at Charles Woodfall's approach.

"They've deserted me this morning—where is everybody?" she asked, snapping the cotton thread with her teeth.

"Oh, they'll come yet—it's scarcely twelve," said Charles, dropping into a wicker chair.

"And what's your news?" asked Auntie Janet.

"I've done it," answered Charles. "I'm leaving on the 10th of September—for Hollywood first and then Lake Witter-wittee."

"And how did your uncle take it—I'm sure he was generous about it?"

"He made me feel a selfish wretch—he produced an excellent reason for my quitting."

Whiskey came in wagging his bobbed tail, and Charles played with his ear as they talked.

"What reason?" asked Auntie Janet.

"Well—the poor old boy's lost a lot in this Fritten business."

"We all have."

"You?" asked Charles, surprised. It had never occurred to him that Auntie Janet might be involved.

"A couple of thousand pounds—but that's between us, Charles. I've cancelled it—it means I'll have to die a couple of years earlier. And your uncle made it a reason—you've to go out in the world and make money to assure the family's future?"

"It was something like that—a pretty weak reason for a noble gesture."

"The Woodfalls are famous for their gestures," commented Auntie Janet, shaking out an unmentionable. "Pour me a glass of sherry. And before anybody comes—what did you do to that Hungarian girl?"

"What Hungarian girl?"

"Oh, come now!" cried Auntie Janet, diving a hand into the pocket of her skirt and pulling out a letter.

"Oh—you mean—Miss Kazinczy?"

"Stefanie—the same," said Auntie Janet, opening the sheet of paper. " 'After that we shall be in Paris until September the 11th, then Dresden until the 20th, and then, after a week in Warsaw, Monte Carlo for the whole season. Is there any chance of your coming to the Riviera this winter? I have not forgotten your Regatta party. Do you see anything of that delightful young doctor——' "

"Is that me?" interrupted Charles.

"That's you."

"Well, she might remember my name."

"Perhaps she never heard it fully—trifles like that don't matter when you make an impression. 'I wonder if he will go to America to see that old great-aunt——' "

"Good heavens, she remembers that!" exclaimed Charles. "I must have talked a lot."

"You monopolized her throughout lunch and took down her home address."

"How do you know that?" demanded Charles, quickly.

"She says so, here: 'I gave him my address, but I don't suppose he will ever come to Budapest, or that I should happen to be there if he did.' "

"I say, she—well—she rather shows her hand, doesn't she?" asked Charles, embarrassed.

"I don't blame her, after the way you ate her up. When do you sail—the 10th?"

"Yes."

"Those Atlantic liners call at Cherbourg, don't they?" asked Auntie Janet.

"You don't suggest——"

Auntie Janet laughed.

"I'll tell you a story that is a warning. I once knew someone who pursued a ballerina. 'Never—never,' he said, 'take her out to supper after the show. Ballerinas don't eat before dancing, but after dancing, oh, how they eat! And then, being tired and full of food, they fall asleep!' You might remember that."

"Thanks—but I've no intention of taking any ballerina out to supper," said Charles, filling his glass.

"I suppose I'm incorrigibly romantic. If I were a young man I'd love to take out a ballerina, hungry or full—it would give me such a Russian feeling. I always felt sorry for my poor dear Freddie, when he came round to take me out. Being a hospital nurse, I smelt of carbolic and felt heavy on my feet."

"You were never heavy on your feet, and you never smelt of carbolic—you must have been an intoxicating creature," said Charles.

"Thank you—there is a little truth in the statement, I hope."

Footsteps sounded on the staircase.

"The world's arriving," said Charles.

"There's nothing to eat in the place."

"That means at least ten to lunch," prophesied Charles.

Three, accompanied by five unknowns, projected themselves on to the verandah. By one o'clock twelve persons protested they must be going, with no intention of going. A sister-in-law, two nephews with two girls, one niece with two boys, a stout, good-humoured cousin who carried around glasses and always had matches, a Belgian cartoonist with a Turkish wife, and Charles—Auntie Janet added them up. "Oh, my God, we're thirteen!" she muttered. But at that moment more feet sounded on the staircase.

"Lucy, my lamb!" exclaimed Auntie Janet, rushing forward and embracing an elephantine lady who obscured her husband, following.

"We're not staying, my dear. We're on our way to Oxford, but I thought I——" she began.

"Sherry or a cocktail?" asked Auntie Janet, of the lesser half.

"I must say, my dear Janet—it's very peaceful here," he said, sitting down, and surveying the river.

"Fifteen," whispered Auntie Janet, quickly, to the maid, bringing more glasses, "—and open the salmon. There's a cucumber in the basket."

The solitary oarsman returning to the Leander Club glanced up at the verandah as he skimmed past. That was one grandstand that never vanished all through the season, and was never empty.

V

His trunk was roped in the hall, his portmanteau labelled with the berth number written on the Cunard tag. At noon to-morrow he would sail from Southampton for New York, *en route* at last to fabled Lake Witterwittee. The great-aunt had written him a gracious note of welcome. The phrasing of it had raised a laugh in the Woodfall household:

. . . we shall be glad indeed to see you, and to offer you such hospitality as our poor household is capable of. Gaiety may be missing, and that fuller life that our dear England offers, but you will find here a tranquil spirit, some natural beauty, and the warm welcome of myself, my son, and my daughters. It will be for you to set the length of your visit.

From your affectionate great-aunt,

JOSEPHINE WOODFALL.

"That," exclaimed Dr. Woodfall, reading the letter aloud, "is Aunt Josephine herself—and what handwriting at eighty! Not a shake in it. I wonder if she'll send you all to bed at ten as she did us?"

Over thirty years ago, on his honeymoon, Dr. Woodfall had spent a month at Sundown Grove. The impression of that visit had never faded. Aunt Woodfall was already a widow, and ruled her domain like Catherine of Russia. Four daughters and one son silently obeyed the Czarina of Sundown Grove. That was before the great revolt, when high-spirited, lovely Harriet fled the castle, to the amazement of the country-side. Poor truant Harriet, for ever banished, and doomed to die, in childbirth, in Chicago, punished for her folly and disobedience.

Charles knew the legend of Harriet, the rebellious daughter. Reared in strict piety, the loveliest of the four sisters, and the youngest, Fate had selected her as a solemn warning. She had had the temerity to fall in love with James Lanier, a 'rough-neck' who had come on some business to Sundown Grove.

Bold, reckless, with a merry, dark eye and the head of an Apollo, he had wrought swift mischief in the Woodfall household. The truth broke one morning like a thunderclap from a clear sky. On the pincushion before the mirror in Harriet's room the coloured maid had found a note addressed to her mistress. What message it contained, exactly, no one ever knew. The name of Harriet was dead in the house at Sundown Grove.

Ten years later, one stormy night in March, a drunken man swam across the lake and hammered at the door, as Mrs. Woodfall, her son, and daughters, sat at dinner. In vain the servant sought to restrain the rowdy intruder. Later, it was reported that, after a quarrel, the visitor, James Lanier, who had left his young daughter Laura in Witterwittee, had threatened Mrs. Woodfall with a revolver. She had knocked the revolver out of his hand, it was said, and, pointing it at him, had driven him into the storm-lashed lake.

The next morning, two hands working in the groves, on their way over to the island, saw a body floating in the water. They pulled it out and brought it to shore, where they laid it out in the gloom of the packing-shed, and went up to the house with the news. It was the body of a youngish man, poorly dressed, with no money in his pockets, but some letters and bills addressed to James Lanier.

Mrs. Woodfall took immediate action. She telephoned the police, and went at once into Witterwittee. There she obtained the address where Lanier had been lodging. Within an hour she had discovered the child, Laura Lanier, her own granddaughter, whom for years she had refused to see. The child was pretty, but obviously undernourished. Mrs. Woodfall put her at once into the buggy and drove her back to Sundown Grove. When the whole story came out at the inquest there was a movement to march on Mrs. Woodfall and burn her out, but no one seemed willing to lead the movement. They feared Mrs. Woodfall. Moreover, she had taken custody of the child, which had suffered enough, poor thing.

And then the miracle happened. Mrs. Woodfall, holding

three daughters, a son, four servants, and twenty grove hands in absolute subjection, fell under the spell of Laura, a Laura that expanded into a vivacious, lovely, and wayward young lady. Life at Sundown Grove began to revolve around her. Mrs. Woodfall, a martinet, a miser, and apparently inhuman, doted on the brilliant Laura. When, at the age of twenty, this radiant orphan expressed a wish to go on the stage no storm broke. A month later she departed to study at an academy of dramatic art in New York. Two years later, from a smashing hit on Broadway, she had been called to Hollywood. Thus it came about that, one evening in Henley, Dr. Woodfall, Mrs. Woodfall, Charles, and Peter had gone to the cinema. There was a film in which Laura Lanier was starring. If she was one half as beautiful and vivacious as she appeared in that film, then the transition of old Mrs. Woodfall, from the wicked aunt in the fairy-tale into a reasonable human being, was explained.

"Of course, she's terribly made-up—and they always 'shoot' at the best angles," said Peter, the kid brother. "You've got to see 'em in the flesh to get the truth," he observed, with the candour of eighteen.

"And how many have you seen in the flesh?" asked Charles, derisively. "And where?"

"Oh," answered Peter, reddening with embarrassment, "you'd like to know, but I'm not talking!"

It was Peter, who was always talking, who had roped his brother's trunk. He had just come back from a walking-tour in Scotland in time to say good-bye to Charles.

"I think you're a mean beast—don't you want a secretary?" he asked, as they walked round the garden, after breakfast.

"You're to go back to school," said Charles.

"It's my last year—I could cut it."

"Thanks, Peter—but if you'll forgive me, I settled your fate last night."

"Whatever do you mean?" asked Peter.

Charles looked at him as the lad halted on the path. He wore an open white shirt, blue shorts, and grey stockings, and at that moment looked no older than sixteen, with his vivid colouring and crisp, wavy hair.

"We held a conference last night, Uncle and I—on you. We both agreed you should go to Oxford next year," said Charles.

"Who's paying?" asked Peter, quickly.

"I am."

There was a silence. Peter snapped off a Gloire de Dijon and twirled it in his fingers.

"That's jolly good of you, but why should you? Have fun with your money."

"That's having fun," answered Charles. "And there are no strings to it."

"Meaning?"

"Uncle doesn't want you to come into the practice—not unless you wish."

"I don't," said Peter. "But it's tough on the old boy—first you, and now me."

"Don't rub it in, Peter. Well—and what are your plans?"

"If I go to Oxford? President of the Union, then the Bar, Parliament, and a seat in the Cabinet," said Peter, decisively. "England's going to the dogs. It wants new blood. My God, look at the gang that's in now—selling us out all the time!"

Charles laughed.

"Going to the dogs has been our national pastime—we're a dog-loving nation, you know," he said.

"I think we should be serious about it," answered Peter, with an air of reproof.

Charles ploughed his hand through the boy's fair hair and pulled it down over his eyes. In a moment they were in a scuffle. Then, holding him, Charles looked into his brother's flushed face, more than ever aware of the tremendous vitality shining in those eyes, and expressed in every line of his young body.

"Well—is it Oxford or not?" he asked, holding his brother.

"If I can pay you back—sometime, Charles."

"Nonsense—it's a gift, outright. Three hundred a year—will that do?"

"It's handsome—thanks a lot," said Peter, quietly. "And if I turn out to be a bonehead——"

"You! Not a chance!" laughed Charles.

There was another silence. Suddenly Peter stopped in his walk and confronted his brother. He brushed his hair back with a lean, brown hand, holding it above the broad, smooth brow.

"Charles," he said, "why do I always have everything just thrown at me—like this Oxford offer? That motor-boat, holidays abroad, and now this. I get frightened sometimes, I feel it can't last. It's all working up to some tremendous finale."

"You were always an imaginative kid—what finale? A seat in the Cabinet?" asked Charles.

"No—I don't mean that, that's commonplace ambition. No —we're in for something, something we can none of us control—something dynamic—cataclysmic——"

"You know, my boy, you're suffering from a rush of words to the head. To come back to earth—Oxford, or no Oxford?"

"Oh, yes—of course. And thanks. You are a noble and generous soul, one in whom Nature has so——"

Charles caught the twinkle in Peter's eye, and gave him a swift cuff.

"You can improve on the gallant gesture," cried Peter, dancing away. "What about your car? You're not taking it with you—the least you can do is to lend it to me, if you don't feel equal to an outright gift!"

"So that's your tremendous finale—I think it's tremendous cheek!" exclaimed Charles.

"You can't let it rot in the garage."

"I shall want it when I come back, thank you."

"You may never come back. Great-Aunt Woodfall may shoot you!"

"I'll risk that," said Charles.

"I want that car—frightfully. Please, Charles!"

"You'd drive it frightfully."

"That's a libel—I'm a better driver than you are!"

"I admit that," said Charles. There was nothing Peter did

not know about engines and all the mechanical gadgets that bewildered him. Perhaps the car would be better for use, moderately, in skilled hands. "Very well, I'll lend it to you."

Peter flung his arm around Charles, and looked with tragic earnestness into his eyes.

"Brother o' mine, O brother o' mine," he shouted, dramatically. "But seriously, you are fundamentally noble. Thanks a lot. To-morrow—to console myself when you have gone, I shall drive to Oxford, and examine all the colleges to see which has the best plumbing."

"And will you do one other thing?"

"Yes?" asked Peter.

"Get your hair cut—you look like a bad poet."

"I am—but it's a phase I shall grow out of!" retorted Peter.

VI

Auntie Janet was out when Charles called, late that afternoon, to say farewell. She was out walking with Whiskey. Charles knew the round she made, familiar through the years, in fair and rainy weather. She was a steady walker, and three miles just warmed her up and tired Whiskey, whose growing rheumatism made him a poor performer on his legs, and curtailed his passion for jumping in the river whenever some nondescript canine intruder went by in a boat.

Cutting up the beech avenue, towards the Fawley ridge, Charles intercepted Auntie Janet in the elm-lined lane. They knew every one of these monarchs in whose branches, crowning the ridge, the wind sounded like the surf of the sea. They mourned them when they fell, aged victims of the storm, or of road-widening. They knew and loved the green panorama of the folding hills, the dark mass of the beechwoods, the reddish loam, the light yellow patchwork of wheat-fields, the emerald velvet of pasture-land, the dense green copses of fir. Deep in a fold, the Thames ran in silver flood. Afar, the upper slopes of Berkshire caught the evening sun and lay in warm gold under a sky luminous with the last splendour of the day.

"I wonder when we shall do this together again," said Auntie Janet, as they walked on, after rubbing the nose of a mare in the riding-master's paddock. "You'll probably find me in a Bath chair, with visiting hours, like a zoo exhibit!"

"You talk as if I were going away for years. I shall be back next spring," answered Charles.

"Why should you? Go on round the world. Enjoy yourself, you're young, you're free. Go native in Tahiti and come back and tell us what insects make a misery of idyllic love. Why are you writers so silent about the minute pests of Paradise? One mosquito in the net can make a Venetian honeymoon a nightmare."

"That sounds autobiographical."

"It is," said Auntie Janet, laughing.

Dusk was falling when they came to the long elm avenue of the Fairmile, leading back to Henley. The glimmer of something on the roadside caught Auntie Janet's eye.

"Whatever's this? Why, it's a tombstone!" she exclaimed. "I'll swear it wasn't here yesterday—a tombstone, of all things!"

There was no doubt about it. There, by the kerb of the path on which they were walking, was a small stone with a bevelled edge.

Charles stepped into the road to examine this stone so curiously placed. The light was fading rapidly. The stone was not more than a foot high, like the headstone of a child's grave.

"There's an inscription," he said, stooping to read.

"What does it say?" asked Auntie Janet.

"To Peter."

"Peter?"

"Yes," answered Charles, and then was silent.

"Well—the rest?"

Charles stood up, and looked for a few moments' silence in Auntie Janet's face. Then, with a quiet voice: " 'There is not enough darkness in all the world to put out the light of one small candle,' " he quoted.

They neither of them spoke for a time. At last Auntie Janet spoke, resuming her walk, and slipping her arm in Charles's.

"That's true—every word of it," she said, quietly.

They walked on, and the night fell around them.

CHAPTER THREE

SUNDOWN GROVE

I

A SINGLE track led to the dead-end station of Lake Witter-wittee. Three trains a day came in and out, connecting with the main line. To the south of the lake, one of some two hundred in the same county, lay Florida's greatest inland stretch of water, Lake Okeechobee, surrounded by its flat plains, home of the cattle-raising industry. The small town of Witterwittee, taking its name from the lake, sixty miles in diameter, consisted of one Main Street, in detail exactly like ten thousand Main Streets throughout the United States. It had a couple of drug-stores, each with ten stools along a snack counter, behind which a brown-armed young man, in a white athletic vest and round sailor's hat, served ice-cream sodas, Coca-Cola, and ten varieties of double-decker club sandwiches.

Across the road, and stretching to the corner, was the five-and-ten-cent store, with its infinite variety. Next came the local hotel, with a lobby whose plate-glass window exhibited its patrons, in rocking-chairs, spittoon-spaced, to the world. A barber's red and white pole, electrically rotated, signalled the world to be shaved. Down the centre of the wide street, in such shade as a dozen languid palm trees offered from the subtropical afternoon, the local automobiles stood parked, with a blue-jeaned negro sprawled on a bench, in optimistic make-believe that he was guardian of them. Through the open door of the local radio shop the voice of a Hollywood crooner filled the Florida scene with a musical advertisement of its great winter rival, California. A young man, with passion vibrating his vocal chords, proclaimed the soothing joy of love in Laguna.

Two cowboys, in from a ranch to buy a pair of gelding clippers, spat in contempt of Californian love. They were satisfied with the local version found at any Florida crackers' dance. They shuffled their high-heeled Spanish riding-boots over the red-brick sidewalk, and called in at the drug-store for some five-cent cigars. The local doctor went by in his Ford sedan, and waved to one of the boys, father to lusty twins overnight. A truck, full of coloured pickers going out to an orange grove, went clattering by.

A row of twelve palm trees, outside a low concrete building that looked like a fort in the Sahara Desert, marked the railroad station. Beneath them a hedge of blazing hibiscus made a scarlet patch in the parterre where, on a gravel square, half a dozen automobiles awaited the train from Sanford. One exception in this line of vehicles was an open carriage, a faded symbol of gentility. Over it hung a brown tasselled awning. A pair of horses, with straw sun-bonnets that struck a note of levity, twitched their fly-pested flanks as they stood in the hot sun. On the box, Lincoln Robinson, his face as black as his top-hat, dozed in the heat of this January day, his sweat-soaked collar crumpled about his neck. The reins drooped from his ancient hands. He had sat on that box-seat for almost fifty years.

Under the awning, with a gloved hand gripping a lace-frilled sunshade, rarely opened, sat Mrs. Woodfall, bolt upright. She was dressed from head to foot in white, except for a flat, wide-brimmed straw hat, decorated about its low crown with a bunch of cloth violets. A thin gold chain, looped about her neck, held a locket-watch that lay on her bosom. She looked at it now, holding it up with a lace-gloved hand. As usual the train was late, fifteen minutes late, and it had not yet been signalled.

As she sat there, while her son sat in the waiting-room gossiping to a local orange-grower about crop prospects, Mrs. Woodfall speculated upon the approaching guest. He was young, she knew, but it was many years since she had seen her nephew Wyndham, and, even if she had remembered what he looked like, it was no clue to the appearance of her nephew's nephew. She hoped he was pleasant to look at, tall and lean, with good eyesight. She detested young men with glasses and a myopic stoop. That affliction of her own son, Henry, had always infuriated her, and there was no reason for it, no hereditary reason. Her husband had been the best shot in Florida, her own eyesight was still good—she could see now every wire looped around the green glass insulators on the telegraph pole at the end of the station.

This boy Charles seemed to be clever. He had written a successful play, successful enough to make it worth while throwing up a medical career, successful enough to have taken him out to Hollywood where, according to his letters, he had had three wonderful months—if anything really wonderful, without vulgarity, could be found in Hollywood. It was a pity Laura had gone off to Mexico on a holiday. She could have sent a report on Charles Woodfall. He might be an odious young man, and he might stay a month. She had never been fond of visitors. That had been a trial from which she had been relieved by her husband's death. He liked to clutter up the house with parasites. For twenty years now tranquillity had reigned at Sundown Grove, except for James Lanier's intrusion.

A column of smoke rose in the air. At first she thought it came from the approaching train, then she realized it was from a scrub fire, set alight by those idiotic and lazy cattle-breeders. They burned the scrub to produce a crop of grazing grass for their cattle, and thereby ruined the land for all future use. Everybody decried the disastrous habit, but the politicians, being vote-catchers, dared not make a stand. The cattle-breeders were in a majority.

Mrs. Woodfall raised her parasol and poked Lincoln Robinson in the back. He started out of a doze.

"Ask Mr. Henry to find out how late this train is," she commanded.

"Yes'm," said Lincoln, descending awkwardly from the box. He disappeared through the waiting-room door. Five minutes elapsed before he reappeared.

"They says'm it'll be another ten minutes—it's not so slow to-day," reported Lincoln, mounting to the box again.

But it was another twenty minutes before the sound of the approaching train stirred up the negro porter asleep on his hand-barrow. The train, with three coaches and a fruit refrigeration car labelled 'New Orleans,' came noisily clanking in. It pulled up with a great hissing of steam.

Presently the passengers emerged, Floridians chiefly, from stations up the line. Then, with her son Henry leading the way, a young man stepped out of the shadow into the sunlight and stood, hat in hand, at the side of the carriage.

"Charles!" exclaimed the old lady, looking at him openly as he stood there, slim and cool in a light grey suit.

"Aunt Josephine!" he responded.

She had expected him to look young, but not as young as this, with a boy's brow and smooth black hair, glossy and thick. She scrutinized him thoroughly until he felt embarrassed.

"You don't look a Woodfall at all. They're all fair—where do you get your black hair and that high complexion?" she asked. "You're not at all what I expected."

"Oh—I'm sorry if I'm a disappointment," answered Charles, laughing.

"I didn't say that—get in. Henry, have you seen to the luggage?" demanded Mrs. Woodfall.

"Yes, Mama. The boy's bringing it," answered Henry.

Charles repressed a smile. It seemed odd to hear a grey-haired man of fifty say, 'Yes, Mama.'

"Have you much?" asked Mrs. Woodfall, speaking to Charles.

"Two bags—I sent my trunks on to New York."

"That's sensible. How long will you stay?"

"Oh—I hadn't thought. If a week isn't——" began Charles, unprepared for this abruptness. The old lady fulfilled the legend. She was downright.

"A week—it's ridiculous to come all this way for a week! You young people are so restless. I expect you to stay a month,

Charles. That's a polite period. You look healthy," added Mrs. Woodfall.

"Yes—I am," answered Charles. He felt like an exhibit at a cattle show.

Her eyes went over him again slowly. He was quite a handsome young man, she observed, with a good mouth and chin. His eyes were very noticeable, but he was not a Woodfall type.

"Was your mother Welsh?" she asked, as the porter lifted the bags up on to the box and Henry stood by.

"No, my mother is Scotch—she's a Cameron of Lochiel," said Charles, not without a trace of pride.

"I suppose I ought to have known that—but there's nothing to be ashamed of in the Woodfalls. Your father evidently made a good choice. I never saw him. Your Uncle Wyndham came here once, on his honeymoon. I believe he thought us barbarians—he's never been since."

"I'm sure that's not the reason—he's always been so tied down by the practice," explained Charles.

"Has he made money?" demanded Mrs. Woodfall.

"Yes, but he's lost it lately."

"How?"

"A solicitor embezzled it."

Mrs. Woodfall shook her parasol.

"I never understand why people trust solicitors so implicitly. My husband made the same mistake—they swindled him." She turned to her son. "Get in, Henry—how much did you tip the boy?"

"A quarter, Mama," he said, taking the opposite seat.

"I hope that's the truth!"

"Oh, yes, Mama," cried Henry, earnestly.

Charles looked at the man opposite. It seemed preposterous that any human being could be so docile. Aunt Woodfall was a dragon. He decided at that moment that he would not be browbeaten by the old tyrant.

The carriage started, and soon began to rumble down Main Street, aglare in the sun. Henry, sitting opposite, had the expression of a mute.

"I expect you'll find Witterwittee a dull place," said Mrs. Woodfall. "It's only a town of orange-growers and cattle-breeders. Most of them work hard—they have to. But they're lawless when they've liquor in them. They hold a rodeo here once a year. Then it's full of rustlers and quick-drawers—the cowboy element comes in from all around."

"Oh, yes—I've heard about it," said Charles.

He knew he had made a slip the moment he had spoken. The old woman turned a pair of gimlet eyes on him.

"What have you heard?" she asked, watching him.

"Oh—well—my uncle has told me a little about the life here," explained Charles. "He said it was an exciting and delightful place."

"Your uncle knows nothing about it. What he told you, I expect, was that I drowned James Lanier in the lake."

"Mama, I'm sure Cousin Charles——" began Henry, in faint protest.

"Be quiet!" snapped his mother. "Charles will hear the story here, if he hasn't already heard it." She turned to Charles. "They'll tell you I drove James Lanier into the lake and drowned him. He came to me drunk, to make a scene and get money out of me. He tried to swim back across the lake and was drowned. It was really a misfortune for no one, not even for the child, Laura."

The carriage rumbled on as Mrs. Woodfall began to cross-question Charles about his uncle, his mother, and life at Henley. The landscape around them was flat, with wide stretches of land bearing some pine trees and much scrub oak. They had left the town and were journeying down a long straight road, with only a few wooden shacks which seemed too crude and miserable to house the people who lolled on the low verandahs. It was hot, even on this January afternoon, though the sun was already low on the horizon. Presently, from a rise, they had a view of the orange groves. The trees, with their bright metallic-looking green leaves, were almost geometrically spaced. The oranges hung like golden globes among the thick branches, which also bore the blossoms, to become in turn next year's crop. The scent of the blossom in the air was delicious. From the crest of this small hill they seemed to look over miles of these perfectly spaced groves. In the distance a sheet of water gleamed like a mirror, set in its dark green frame of groves.

"That's our lake," said Aunt Woodfall. "We live on an island in the middle of it—we shall be there soon. I expect you are tired. Have you come straight through from Los Angeles?"

"No—I broke the journey at New Orleans. What a wonderful sight these groves are!" answered Charles.

"You are just in time to see the picking. To-morrow Henry will take you through the groves. But we have had one freeze. Another like this, and we shall all be ruined."

"A freeze?" echoed Charles.

"By that we mean several degrees of frost which ruins the fruit," explained Mrs. Woodfall. "We have to keep the smudge-pots going all night—look!" said his aunt, pointing to the foot of the groves. Objects like cannon-balls lay under the trees. "We have to keep those oil-pots burning all night to break the frost. There was once a large English colony here, when I was a young woman and came out with my husband. Now I am the only one left. They were all frozen out, and died of heart-break and poverty."

Charles began to like the grim old lady. It was difficult to believe she was eighty. Her eyes were keen, her voice strong, she sat bolt upright in the carriage. Henry, sitting opposite, did not utter a word. He peered out, through his strong glasses, apathetic and time-bitten. In half an hour they turned off into a sandy track that led through a wilderness of scrub oak. Charles felt they had come to the end of the world. A few turns, and suddenly the lake was revealed. Its water was crimson under the falling sun. It looked about twenty miles long and ten miles wide. In the middle of the lake was an island, densely covered with tall water-oaks, festooned with grey moss hanging from the branches, and dark green orange trees. There was no sign of a house. The carriage pulled up beside a rough wooden stable, and a frame house. A flimsy pier ran out into the lake, which looked like a jungle river amid the dense woods.

"Sundown Grove," said Henry, opening his mouth after a long silence.

The whole place now burned in the lurid light of the quickly falling sun, an enormous disk blazing on the horizon. The place was well named.

Mrs. Woodfall descended from the carriage. Charles was surprised to notice how nimble she was. At the end of the pier a small motor-launch, in the charge of an old negro, awaited them. As they set out its *chug-chug* reverberated across the great expanse of crimson water. Again Charles caught the drifting scent of orange blossoms. Slowly they drew towards the island, where another flimsy jetty ran outward from the shore.

The launch drew aside. The three of them walked up the jetty, the negro following with Charles's bags. They seemed to be entering a dark jungle. The oak trees looked huge and threatening, shutting out all light. The grey moss dripping from their branches gave a macabre air to the scene. It was like an illustration from Gustave Doré's *Hell*.

Mrs. Woodfall marched on. Then, at the end of the slightly mounting path, Charles saw a part of the house. It was built of wood, raised up from the ground on brick piers, with a long wide verandah, shut in with a fine wire netting to keep out insects. It looked ghostly in that tree-menaced place, and its white painted walls and dark windows had a chilling effect. Nothing like the glowing sunshine-drenched Colonial mansion of his imagination was here. Aloof, immense, it stretched away on either side of the wide entrance porch, and Charles felt it might have been an institution, a hospital, or a mental home.

At that very moment demoniac laughter and screeching voices burst forth overhead. Charles started and looked around in alarm. And then it was that, for the first time, he knew Aunt Woodfall could smile.

"That's Darwin and his wives giving you a welcome," she said, with a laugh.

In the branches overhead four monkeys scampered and

screamed obscenely, and then broke into childish laughter.

Charles followed his great-aunt across the verandah and into the dark hall. A negro in a white coat came forward to take the bags from the boatman. In the gloom another figure stood by, tall, silver-haired, in a black tail-coat and white wing collar, with black bow. He might have stepped straight from any house in Grosvenor Square.

"This is Jefferson, Charles. He will take you to your room. Dinner is at seven. You will hear the bell," said Mrs. Woodfall, leaving them.

"This way, please, sir," said Jefferson, the butler.

Charles mounted the wide stairs after him, their feet echoing on the uncarpeted boards. At the top there was a wide landing. A faint light came from a large white globe. It was an oil lamp, of the kind Charles had seen only in old Victorian pictures.

Jefferson led the way, into the darkness again, past several doors, and, opening one, stood aside.

"Pray enter, sir," he said.

Charles entered. At first, in the light of three lamps burning in wall-brackets, he could not see the size of the room. Then, his eyes growing accustomed to the gloom, he saw it was immense. A large four-poster bed, draped with heavy blue curtains, stood on a dais against one wall. The centre of the floor was occupied by a round mahogany table, bearing a lamp. A long pier glass in the corner reflected the lamp. A rocking-chair, upholstered in black buttoned leather, with a white lace antimacassar, stood near it. A triple-mirrored knee-hole dressing-table, with glass-knobbed drawers, occupied the wall opposite the bed. Prominent on the table were two large hair-brushes, with backs of heavy repoussé silver, a hand-mirror, similarly ornamented, and a large white pincushion, with lace fringes.

"I hope you will be comfortable, sir," said Jefferson, as the negro brought in the bags and placed them on the luggage-stand. "The dressing-bell will sound in a few minutes, the dinner-bell half an hour later."

"The dressing-bell? You don't——?" began Charles.

As if anticipating his question: "Mrs. Woodfall always dresses for dinner, sir. I will have some hot water sent for you. There is a bell-rope by the bedside should you require anything, sir," said the butler.

"Thank you," replied Charles, finding voice.

Jefferson withdrew. The door closed. Charles stood still in the middle of the room, looking around him. A large screen with pink, frilled silk panels attracted his attention. He went over to it, and peered over the top. It masked a marble-topped washstand on heavy cabriole mahogany legs, and, on the floor, a large flat bath-tin, like a yellow saucer, with a lip, set on a rubber mat, a towel-horse behind it.

Charles stared, and then, flinging himself into the rocking-chair, burst with loud laughter. Presently he was joined by a more ribald merriment that mocked him. It came from Darwin and his wives, screaming in the trees opposite the window. Silenced by this frightful accompaniment, Charles went to the window and looked out; but he could see nothing except through the upper branches, a sky which seemed afire above the black wood.

II

When Charles, having dressed, descended to the hall, the watchful Jefferson showed him into the drawing-room. It was empty when he entered, so that he had an opportunity of examining this extraordinary room. No doubt, some fifty years ago, when new in its splendour, it had struck a note of stately distinction. It was a long room with six windows down one side, three on each side of an immense Gothic stone fireplace, in which a pinewood fire was now crackling. From the centre of the high ceiling hung a heavy crystal chandelier with candle sconces. The wax candles in the bottom tier of these had been lit and cast a soft light on the polished pine floor. Three large gilt mirrors filled the wall opposite the windows, with Buhl tables under them, cluttered with photograph frames and bric-à-brac. There was a large, cretonne-upholstered scroll-end couch, three easy wing chairs—Chippendale obviously—and a dozen smaller chairs, from the same workshop, with *petit-point* embroidered seat-covers. There were some oil portraits, a colonel whom Charles recognized at once as a Woodfall ancestor who had fought at Waterloo, an excellent Raeburn of a young woman, and a portrait of another young woman in Court dress, complete with feathers, fan, and jewels—a striking composition that suggested Winterhalter. He decided it was a portrait of his great-aunt at about twenty-six. The eyes and the determined mouth had persisted through some fifty years.

A grand piano stood against the wall at one end of the room, a massive instrument smothered under a Persian shawl, and bearing a horde of photograph frames. Charles examined it more closely. The yellow keys were out of alignment. 'Collard & Collard, London,' he read on the gilt-letter inscription above the keyboard. He could not resist an impulse to strike a chord. The result made him grimace. There was a piece of music on the stand: "What are the Wild Waves Saying?" ran the title. He turned away with a feeling of unhappy, far-off things. How odd it was, this setting of Queen Victoria and the Prince Consort—England in the wilds of Florida. A marble bust of Disraeli on the mantelpiece flanked an enormous bronze clock, over which several naked nymphs clambered. Two Roman soldiers, also of bronze, massively sustained candelabra at either end of the mantelpiece. The clock ticked audibly. It was ten minutes to seven.

The opening of the door startled Charles in the act of examining some miniatures in a Sheraton cabinet. It was Jefferson, carrying a silver salver on which were a decanter and glasses. The butler put down the tray on a small side-table.

"May I serve you with a glass of sherry, sir? The ladies will be down in a few minutes. Master Henry is apt to be late," said the butler.

"Thank you," responded Charles. He wanted to ask whether Master Henry was permitted to take intoxicants.

The butler came forward with the tray.

"I don't suppose you drink cocktails here?" asked Charles, unable to resist the question, and anxious to see the effect on Jefferson, whose respect he might thus lose for ever. But to his surprise the old man smiled quietly.

"That would require a revolution, sir," he said. "Not even Miss Laura has suggested cocktails."

"Miss Laura?"

"Mrs. Woodfall's granddaughter—the actress, sir."

"Yes—I know. She comes here a lot?"

"Oh, no, sir, very occasionally—and then only for a few days. She is a very beautiful and clever young lady. Mrs. Woodfall is very attached to her."

"I hope I shall meet her."

"I hope you will, sir. At present she is in Mexico."

"You've been here a long time?"

"A long time. I came out in 1886, with Captain Woodfall, when he bought Sundown Grove. Witterwittee was only a settlement then."

"You are English?" asked Charles.

"Oh, yes, sir, from Exeter, sir."

"And you have never been home?"

"No, sir. I was about to go, when Captain Woodfall was shot in the fighting——"

"Fighting—against whom? The Indians?"

He remembered now that he had heard of his great-uncle's violent death.

"Oh, no, sir. There were some families here, sir. They owned groves, and a quarrel broke out and they began fighting. It was desperate and bloody. Over thirty people were killed, sir, including Captain Woodfall."

"And you saw it?"

"I was in it, sir. When the captain was wounded, across in Ward's Grove, we got him back here, and they marched against the house—to burn us out. These Florida crackers are a desperate lot, sir."

"Crackers?"

"That's a native of Florida—white, or near white," explained Jefferson.

"Did they burn you out?"

"Oh, no, sir, it was this house, which the captain had bought. We defended it. Mrs. Woodfall was a wonderful shot. The wood wasn't grown up around the house like it is now. She could see the men from an upper window. She shot eight of them, and they gave up the attempt. The captain died that night, with the children crying around him, except Master Henry, who was in his cot. We buried him, and the others, down in the grove the next day. You can see their graves now, with a large stone over the captain's."

"Here, on this island?" asked Charles.

"Yes, sir, in the orange grove. But you will excuse me, sir —Mrs. Woodfall doesn't like me to gossip."

"It's very interesting. Thank you."

"Thank you, sir," said Jefferson, putting down the tray, and leaving the room. The door closed softly.

How different the picture of Sundown Grove had become in the last few hours of reality! He had spent three very pleasant months in Hollywood, but nowhere, among all the diversified characters he had encountered in the studios, had he come across a lady of refinement who had shot eight men. The set-up here, too, was more Hollywood than anything he had found on the Goldwyn lot. Jefferson cried out for casting as the traditional butler. Master Henry was almost a comedy role. He had yet to encounter the three sisters.

The door opened, and Charles, turning from the fireplace, saw a middle-aged woman with greying hair come towards him. She smiled as she crossed the floor. She held herself stiffly upright.

"How do you do, Cousin Charles—I am Eugenie Woodfall. It is delightful to have you with us."

He took the outstretched hand, and looking at her he saw she was a gaunt-faced woman of about fifty. Her voice was somewhat hard to the ear. She was tastefully dressed in a mauve evening frock that harmonized with her clear grey eyes. They were engaged in a pleasant conversation when another sister entered the room. He was presented to Grace. She had not her sister's distinction, and had a timid manner. She was the complete spinster, refined, slightly emaciated, shy. She sat stiffly in a small chair, and let her sister carry on the conversation.

Henry was the next to arrive.

"Oh!" he said, advancing towards them, and peering through his strong glasses. His evening clothes fitted him badly. They were old-fashioned, worn, and had long required pressing. His dress shirt was crumpled, and his black bow, a ready-made one, sat askew on his collar. He glanced around him nervously.

"I thought I was late," he said. "You found everything you required, Cousin Charles?"

"Everything, thank you," responded Charles.

He sat down. There was an awkward pause.

"You have a swift twilight," observed Charles, to break the silence.

"Yes," answered Eugenie. "You see, we are in the sub-tropical zone—we are south of the same latitudinal line as Cairo, I believe."

"Oh—that's interesting," responded Charles.

What was the matter? They were all talking and acting like puppets. There was another appalling pause, but action came with Jefferson opening the door, and standing aside for Mrs. Woodfall to enter.

She advanced, erect and without hesitation. They all stood up, and Charles was conscious of the majesty of the old lady. She was dressed completely in black, except for a frilling of white lace on the throat and sleeves of her silk dress. The gold chain and locket again hung on her bosom. She wore a pair of jet bracelets, and a big jet comb with brilliants in her hair.

"Good evening!" she said, as she seated herself in the large winged chair by the fireplace. Then, glancing around, and up at the clock: "Where is Emily?" she asked, sharply. As no one answered her question, she addressed Jefferson, just leaving the room.

"Tell Miss Emily we are waiting," she called to the butler.

"Very good, madam," he said, retiring.

"I hope, Charles, you are punctual—I dislike unpunctuality," said Mrs. Woodfall. "You have had a glass of sherry —or perhaps you don't like it? We haven't the cocktail habit yet."

"Thank you—I like sherry. If I may say so it is an excellent dry Amontillado," he replied.

Mrs. Woodfall looked at him sharply.

"I see you have the Woodfall gift of saying nice things," she said, with a glimmer of a smile.

The door opened and the late-comer entered. She was the youngest of the three sisters, slight in figure, but graceful, with a soft, high complexion and a mass of brown hair. She might be forty and looked thirty. As she smiled, on seeing Charles, she revealed beautiful small teeth.

"Oh, how do you do, Cousin Charles—how wonderful to see you!" she cried, vivaciously.

She advanced towards him and offered her hand.

"Thank you, it is good to be here," he answered, smiling down at her. She had no resemblance whatsoever to her two sisters, or her brother.

"Emily—you are late—five minutes late!" cried Mrs. Woodfall, severely.

"I'm very sorry, Mama. My dress was——"

"We are not interested in your dressing difficulties, Emily. This has happened before. You know I detest unpunctuality. It disorganizes the household."

"Yes, Mama," said Emily, the animation fading from her face.

Why, why didn't they snap back at the old dragon, thought Charles.

Jefferson appeared.

"Dinner is served, madam," he announced.

They all rose, awaiting Mrs. Woodfall.

"Give me your arm, Charles—it is seldom I have the pleasure of being taken in to dinner by a handsome young man," she said, smiling at him.

And at that moment as he offered her his arm he realized how formidable Queen Victoria must have been.

The dining-room, which Charles now saw for the first time, was in keeping with the general style of the house. Had Mrs. Woodfall told him that Mr. Gladstone, Florence Nightingale, and Lord Tennyson had been guests at her table he would have felt no surprise. It was ornate, heavy, and mannered in every detail. Mrs. Woodfall occupied a large high-backed chair which might have been a bishop's throne. Two candelabra lit the table, on which stood a pair of silver epergnes, loaded with fruit. The knives, forks, and spoons were sterling, and of a solidity never again to be seen in an age when scarcity of servants makes the cleaning of silver a thing to be avoided. But clearly Mrs. Woodfall avoided nothing. Under her firm hand Time stood still. Here, in the wilds of Witterwittee, some few yards distant from the burial-ground of those insurgents she had shot dead, in a wood house built by native labour, and not far from those mango swamps in which the alligators still wallowed, Mrs. Woodfall maintained the habits learned in her childhood at Tunbridge Wells. On ivory tablets reared in front of each plate at table the dinner menu was carefully written, in French: *Pot-au-feu, filet de sole vin blanc, côte d'agneau, pommes-de-terre frites, haricots verts, crème renversée, fruits, café.*

Charles looked around the table. Eugenie sat opposite. On his right sat Grace, with Emily facing, and at the bottom end of the long table sat Henry, in a chair scarcely less episcopal in style. The butler had been reinforced by the negro servant who carried up his bags, immaculate in a white coat and wearing white cotton gloves. There was a Sauterne with the fish and a Burgundy with the lamb. Charles had always had the impression that the Woodfalls lived in straitened circumstances. Nothing in the nature of this table, or of the service, bore out that impression. Mrs. Woodfall was a determined stylist. His uncle had told him that the groves had long been bankrupt and no one knew how old Mrs. Woodfall kept the roof over her head. But nothing in this household suggested any severe economy.

The dinner was excellent, but the service proceeded at a funereal pace. Mrs. Woodfall enjoyed her food and took time to masticate it. She did not encourage conversation. At the end of the meal she rose and, followed by her three daughters, walked out of the room. When the door had closed on this sedate procession Henry resumed his seat, and Jefferson came forward with the port decanter and cigars. He then retired from the room. Charles watched Henry light his cigar with great deliberation. They smoked in silence for a few minutes.

"You seem very comfortable here," said Charles, unable to endure the silence any longer.

"Comfortable and dead," answered Henry, laconically.

"Dead?" echoed Charles, startled somewhat.

Henry peered at him through his glasses. The light from the red-shaded candles seemed to emphasize the natural melancholy of his face.

"Dead but not buried," said Henry, bitterly. "Well, now you've seen us, what do you think of us?"

Unprepared, and somewhat embarrassed by this candour, Charles made no answer; and, as though none was expected, his cousin continued:

"I suppose a dutiful son should not make a remark like that to a newly arrived guest. I really can't think why you've come, unless you are making a study of still life."

He peered at Charles, and his expressionless face had now taken on a malicious smile.

"Oh, I have looked forward to this visit—I've always heard so much about you," commented Charles, weakly.

"About Mother—never about us," said Henry, firmly. "We've never been allowed to exist. You're surprised to hear me talk like this—very odd in a dutiful son, eh, and not quite natural. Do you know you are the only man who's been allowed to stay in this house for the last fifteen years? We've not been away from this place, not once, in ten whole years. It is a prison, not an orange grove!"

He picked up the decanter and filled his glass again. Had Charles not known it was only the second helping he would have wondered if Cousin Henry were drunk.

"You're young and alive—I can see that—and you've had the strength to break away from home ties," said Henry, raising his glass and regarding it. "I never had the courage. She kept me here, and now I'm no use to anybody, and would just starve if I got out of here. She knows that. It's the same with all of us—look at poor Grace. She could have married anybody with a face and figure like hers. Emily, too. She's still pretty, with some life in her—and young enough, unlike the rest of us. But that terrible old woman——"

"Oh, come now!" protested Charles, growing more and more uncomfortable at this sudden outburst, astonishing from one who had seemed so docile. "Do you think we should join the ladies?"

Henry stood up, and stumped out his cigar.

"No smoking in the drawing-room," he said, and then looking at Charles, his weak eyes magnified behind the strong lenses of his spectacles, "I've made you uncomfortable with what I've said? I'm sorry. But, Cousin Charles—you don't know—you don't know!" He approached and took hold of the lapel of Charles's coat. His hand shook, and his thin voice had a tremor of passion in it. "I hate this place. I can't think why you want to come here. It's sucked our blood. I'd like to see it burnt up!"

"Oh, but that's ridiculous!" expostulated Charles. "It can't be as bad as that. You shouldn't say such things."

The man in front of him seemed rebuffed at once. His hand fell weakly. He became abject with the vanishing of a temporary passion from his face.

"No—I suppose I shouldn't. I'm sorry—but oh, you don't

know what I suffer here," he said, weakly. "If only I could get away—but I never shall, never!"

He looked at Charles with his weak eyes, and it was impossible not to speculate how the son of a woman of such forceful spirit could be so weak a creature. It was very embarrassing to hear this confession, and yet a degree of compassion was evoked in Charles's heart by the pitiable ineptitude of the man. He was not actually as old as he had at first appeared; probably he was a man in his early forties, but the lines around his eyes, and his greying hair, together with the slight stoop of his meagre figure, created an impression of approaching decrepitude.

"Perhaps we had better go in," said Henry, lifting the shades and blowing out the candles. His hand shook, and again Charles wondered if he were a secret drinker. He began to fight a feeling of contempt for this downtrodden creature. It was obvious that Great-Aunt Woodfall was a tyrant, a highly capable tyrant, who dominated every aspect of life at Sundown Grove. Her character, repellent in some way, fascinated Charles and compelled his admiration. If she was like this at eighty, what must she have been like in middle age, he wondered?

The ladies were seated in the same chairs when the two men entered the drawing-room. Mrs. Woodfall, in the wing chair by the great fireplace, had a small table in front of her and was playing crystal solitaire. She rattled the coloured marbles over the board in a spirit of complete concentration. Eugenie was sewing. Grace was reading. Emily sat looking at the fire, her gentle face pensive as she watched the lively flames consuming the pine logs, whose pleasant odour pervaded the room.

Mrs. Woodfall with a decisive click completed the game, swept the penultimate marble off the board, and popped the last one into the box at her right hand.

"Now," she said, looking up as Charles came into the room, "do you play backgammon?"

"A little," answered Charles. It was two or three years since he had played with Uncle Wyndham.

"Then we will have a game. Henry, bring the board," commanded the old lady.

Henry brought the board and the box of pieces. His mother dexterously set the game. The pieces were beautifully carved ivory disks, in red and white, of Chinese pattern. Charles wondered for how many generations they had been moved over the marquetry board.

"Shall we play for five dollars a game?" asked Mrs. Woodfall, looking at Charles, with a smile on her old face. There was something puckish about her when she smiled like that. A little astonished at her readiness to gamble, Charles agreed.

It was soon very obvious that Mrs. Woodfall could play backgammon. She threw and doubled the game. She moved the pieces with the same determination as she had shown with the solitaire board. And she was courageous in the chances she took. But were they chances? Charles began to wonder. She took the first game with a masterful final manœuvre, and looked at him with that puckish smile on her face.

They began the second game, with Charles more wary this time. He could not take risks with the old lady. Her moves were superb. The dice favoured her. Henry, sitting by watched the board in complete silence. When Charles, making a bold move, drew an approving "Ah!" from Henry, his mother gave him a swift look and, as if to rebuke his satisfaction, made a triumphant counter-move, and then looked at her son with a smile of derision. After a brief tussle the second game went to Mrs. Woodfall.

"You're too good for me," confessed Charles.

"Nonsense—you'll get into form soon. Another game—for your revenge?" challenged the old lady.

Charles agreed, as his great-aunt marked down the score on a pad. He reset the board.

"Henry, another log on the fire," said Mrs. Woodfall. "Emily, when we've finished the game, we'll have the reading."

"Yes, Mama," answered Emily.

"Now, let's see what you can do this time, Charles," said Mrs. Woodfall. "Perhaps you'll have better luck."

But he knew, both from the manner of her speech and from the look in her eye, that she was out for his scalp. She played with a reckless daring, for such it might seem except for the success with which she emerged from each manœuvre. Sometimes her white bony hand fell like the talons of a preying bird, in her eagerness to make the next move. Try as he would, she drove him into an inextricable position, and then with an arrogant demonstration of invincible skill marched through to her final triumph—a double game.

Mrs. Woodfall sat back in her chair, the puckish smile animated her face, her eyes bright and keen with the joy of battle.

"You play a good game, Charles—when you've played a little more I shall have to look to my laurels," she said, and began packing the pieces into their box. She glanced at the pad on the table. "You owe me twenty dollars."

Although Charles was not a gambler he did not mind losing money. He was a cheerful loser, in a spirit of sportsmanship. But when Mrs. Woodfall announced her winnings there was something in her voice that gave him a jolt. Had she played, not for the pleasure of the game, but for the money she knew she could make out of it? The thought was ungenerous but, despite himself, the ring of triumph in her voice provoked it. He was astonished also by the amount. If the old lady played every night it was not possible she took so large a sum off her children, even if they had it. There was something amusing in the thought of poor Henry being brought to the board and skinned of his weekly pocket-money.

"I haven't my wallet—if you don't mind later?" said Charles, feeling the empty pocket of his dinner-jacket.

Mrs. Woodfall picked up her pencil, wrote on the pad, and then tore off the sheet.

"That will serve to remind you," she said, passing the slip on which she had written the amount, and the date.

"Thank you," said Charles, meekly, folding the slip and putting it in his waistcoat pocket. Then suddenly he felt a surge of resentment sweep through him. This old woman was treating him in the same peremptory fashion as she treated the others. Somehow he must make a stand against her. He was not going to be dominated and nose-led. It was ridiculous, but even thus soon he found himself on the defensive against her dominating spirit.

At her behest Henry had taken away the backgammon board and the table. The clock struck nine.

"Now, Emily," said Mrs. Woodfall, and, turning to Charles, "We are reading Browning's *Ring and the Book*. I hope you like Browning?"

"I'm afraid I haven't read much of Browning," confessed Charles. He was not a poetry reader, and in his slight acquaintance with that poet he had found him rather incomprehensible.

"Then it will be an education for you—as well as a pleasure, I hope. We have reached the third book. Now proceed, Emily."

The blood rose to Charles's face. The arrogant old woman! He was of a mind to get up and say Good-night; but it was only nine o'clock, and he could not make a scene on his first evening at Sundown Grove. He glanced around him angrily and caught the eye of Grace, who smiled at him wanly. Eugenie sewed, sitting stiffly upright.

Emily began to read. Mrs. Woodfall sat back in the wing chair, her features composed. Charles, observing her more closely, begrudgingly admired the clean-cut line of her profile, the firm-set mouth, the imperious droop of the eyelid over her commanding eye. He saw she was easily capable of shooting eight men and driving her son-in-law into the lake. She was all and more than he had ever expected. Hard, alert, unsympathetic, and a tyrant undoubtedly, he could not withhold admiration from this old woman of eighty. She expected him to stay a month. If he stayed that long, on one thing he was determined. He would maintain his independence, he would give her battle, even if Sundown Grove fell in ruins about them.

CHAPTER FOUR

SOMETHING STRANGE

I

IN the light of morning the island was a revelation of luxuriant Nature. After Jefferson had entered his room and pulled up the blinds, Charles got out of bed and went to the large bay window. He gasped with surprise at the landscape before him. Through a break in the live oaks, cut away to present a vista, he looked down a green slope towards the lake, which lay sparkling in the clear, rich sunlight. To his right the long parallel lines of orange trees made a geometrical pattern, innumerable trees laden with white blossoms and golden fruit, with sandy lanes between, down which a youth was driving a truck piled up with crates of oranges. Across the lake, on the far shore, there was a jungle waste of palmetto scrub, and beyond, dense and dark in the bright morning, rose the forest. And as if to emphasize this nearness of untamed Nature, there was a sudden screeching and chattering in the branches of the great magnolia tree at the end of the verandah. Darwin and his wives seemed engaged in vicious argument.

Charles turned from the window. The coloured servant had brought in two great pitchers of water and had filled the tin bath on the floor. Stripping off his pyjamas, Charles stepped into the bath, feeling like a bird in a saucer. There was an enormous sponge on a tray at his side, and, immersing this, he squeezed it over his head. Not since he was bathed in the nursery had he experienced this form of ablution. For some reason he wondered at that moment whether Great-Aunt Woodfall had permitted the intrusion of the telephone. He was astonished to see that an automobile truck was used in the orange groves. Obviously it was used solely on the island, which must be larger than he had imagined.

He was dressing when the servant tapped and entered, carrying a large tray. To his surprise it contained a breakfast service, which the negro proceeded to lay out on a table near the window. Evidently he was expected to breakfast in his room, an indulgence he had not anticipated in this rigorous household. It proved to be an elaborate breakfast consisting of fruit, toast, coffee, and, under a large silver cover, bacon and eggs. The pot of marmalade completed the English character of this breakfast. Had the butler entered bearing a copy of the London *Times* it would not have seemed incongruous.

Charles glanced at his wrist-watch. It was half-past eight.

"Am I late or early?" he asked the negro.

"Ah would say, sah, you was anyhow," replied the old man, smiling.

"Mrs. Woodfall—is she——"

"Oh, Mrs. Woodfall, sah, she's early. She's gitting around in the groves by seven, sah. She's allus mighty early, sah."

"Not out in the groves?" queried Charles.

"Yessir—she's out and a-riding everywhere right now, sah," answered the negro, smiling.

"Riding?"

"Sure, sah—riding, she be—every morning the mistress be there—her eye on everything among them thar groves."

"Your name is——" asked Charles, recovering from his astonishment.

"Lincoln Robinson, sah. Ah fetched you in the chariot from the station, yesterday."

So it was the same old negro. He stood now, smiling, as Charles poured out the coffee.

"You've been here a long time?" asked Charles.

"All my life. Ah was born here, sah, and I hope I'll die here," answered Lincoln Robinson. "Ah's been through trouble and happiness, through rejoicing and mourning, through the freezes an' all the ruin they brings, but the Mistress she be a mighty powerful person, she hold everything in her hands."

"Yes—yes," said Charles, a little impatiently.

"There be anything you's wantin', sah?" asked the old negro.

"No, thanks. Is Mr. Henry around?"

"Oh, yessir—he be ridin' in the groves with the Mistress. Ah've a horse for you when you be ready, sah. Mr. Henry, he thought you be glad to see the dusting."

"Dusting?"

"The plane's come for dusting the grove," said Lincoln Robinson. Then, seeing the bewilderment on the Englishman's face: "They dust the groves with sulphur 'gin the insects. They fly over the groves in an aryplane and sprinkle them."

"Gracious! That's being up-to-date!" exclaimed Charles.

"We've everythin' up-to-date. Every invenshin there be. Mrs. Woodfall, she be best grower in these parts," asserted Lincoln Robinson. "She sure do know all the up-to-date invenshins!"

The proud retainer withdrew. Again Charles marvelled at the astonishing incongruities presented by his great-aunt. She would not have a motor-car for personal use but used them in the orange groves, of all places. There was no electricity in the house, no sign of anything contributed by science to the comfort of living since the last century, and yet here was the astonishing fact that the orange groves were dusted by an aeroplane. And the old lady herself was out riding through the groves! He would not be surprised to learn she was flying the plane herself.

His toilet and breakfast finished, Charles descended to the hall. Outside in the garden Emily was trimming a hedge of scarlet hibiscus. Charles crossed the lawn to join her, and for the first time saw the loveliness of this old place set amid the live oaks. Down by the lake a single row of royal palms struck the tropical note, with their slender trunks and tufted heads silhouetted against the blazing azure sky. Nearer, there was a clump of coco-nut palms. A thick-leaved banana tree, its bright fan leaves in vivid contrast to the darker green of the woodland, competed vainly with a coral vine that was aflame in the sunlight as it covered a pergola backed with a hedge of blue thunbergia. Bougainvillaea, azaleas, hibiscus, the garden blazed in the clear January sunshine. Last night this place had seemed the approach to a Dantesque *Inferno*, to-day it was the gateway to Paradise. Had he been misled by his environment into imagining something sinister about the Woodfall household?

Emily greeted him with a smile. Beneath an enormous Mexican straw hat she looked even younger this morning, and with her soft complexion, rosy cheeks, and smiling blue eyes, Charles felt that in her youth she must have been a beautiful girl. Why had she never escaped from this stern though lovely prison house? Surely some youth or young man had thrilled to her beauty. He wondered, then, concerning the rebellious Harriet. Had she been as lovely but with a stronger spirit, defying the jailer?

She told him the names of all the trees and plants as they examined this exotic garden walled in by the forest of live oaks. Red cardinal birds flitted about from branch to branch. Then Darwin gibbered in a giant banyan tree that spread, snake-like, in one corner of the garden.

"Mama's expecting you in the groves. Lincoln will get you a mount. You can ride?" asked Emily.

"Oh, yes—but I'm astonished at Aunt Josephine. Is it safe at her age?"

"Never refer to her age, Mama's defeated Time," answered Emily, with a laugh.

She led him to the stables behind the house, where Lincoln saddled a horse. The negro directed him to the groves. As Charles rode over the sandy loam, warmed by the sun, with the aromatic scents of the morning wafted about him, he burst, spontaneously, into song. This place was a little heaven, even though its presiding deity was a grim old lady who, overnight, had taken twenty dollars off him at backgammon.

Charles found his hostess, accompanied by Henry, also on horseback, down one of the groves in which the pickers were working. Mrs. Woodfall rode side-saddle, and wore Mexican riding boots with large silver spurs. She was a splendid horse-woman, obviously. This morning she wore a flat-brimmed black felt hat with a chin strap, and a white blouse. She looked slimmer than she had appeared last night, and no one, seeing her thus seated on a light grey mare, would have credited her with more than sixty years.

The pickers were mostly coloured men brought in on day labour. They placed ladders against the fruit-laden branches and carried a deep, rubber-rimmed bag, hung from a strap slung across the shoulder. The rubber rim was to prevent bruising of the fruit as the picker dexterously clipped the oranges and shot them into the canvas bag. One picker, Charles learned, could average ten thousand oranges a day. The picked oranges were poured into boxes and collected by a motor-lorry mounted on six wheels that ran easily over the sandy loam. Six crews of thirty men each were picking the grove this morning.

While they were talking the aeroplane went overhead.

"Follow me!" said Mrs. Woodfall, giving spur to her horse. They galloped through the long avenues of trees to a small knoll from which they surveyed the long panorama of groves below them. They ran for mile on mile in green orderly rows, lit with the golden glow of the oranges and the white, scented blossoms. The island was much larger than Charles had imagined, crescent-shaped, with a small sandy bay fringed with pine trees.

They watched the plane working over one section of the groves. Up and down it went, a powder fanned out at the tail. The pilot flew so low that his undercarriage almost brushed the tops of the trees. He wore an asbestos suit. Pilots had been known to crash and be burned alive.

At noon they returned to the house. Letters, brought from the mainland, lay on the hall table. There were three from England for Charles. Great-Aunt Woodfall, after opening hers, turned to Charles and said:

"I'm glad you will see Laura. She is coming next week, for

a short visit. Laura will supply all the gaiety which you must be missing here."

Surprised at her recognition of the restrained atmosphere at Sundown Grove, Charles, nevertheless, politely demurred.

"I'm enjoying every moment," he asserted, "but, of course, I shall be delighted to see the beautiful Laura—is she like her pictures?"

"The films?"

"Yes."

"I've never seen her act. I am told she is very good. Laura is a clever child—but I do not approve of public exposure of one's emotions," said the old lady, tartly.

The gong sounded for lunch.

II

A week passed, a week that slipped by on wings. He began to understand how Time lost its significance on this citrus-island. More and more, certain curious facts were impressed upon Charles's mind. There were strange, unsolvable problems that began to assert themselves in his consciousness. He had always understood that Great-Aunt Woodfall had a severe struggle to keep the establishment going at Sundown Grove. Charles was certain that Uncle Wyndham had said the place was heavily mortgaged. This struggle seemed borne out by the antiquarian atmosphere, by the worn, old-fashioned furniture, the complete absence of modern amenities. Even eccentricity could hardly explain the lamps, the absence of electricity, the shabby creaking carriage, the general air of faded gentility.

And yet, incongruously, the groves seemed to want nothing in the nature of scientific equipment. The sheds were all splendidly equipped, three motor-trucks ran about the island, there was an office with a manager, and two clerks. It transpired that Great-Aunt Woodfall owned other groves on the mainland, some fifteen hundred acres. But the manager, in a talk with Charles, had told him that the groves did not pay.

One bad "freeze" killed all profits for three or four years. When crops were heavy, prices were low, when prices were high the crops were scanty. There was the growing competition of California. Only growers with canning sheds, who could thus utilize the surplus fruit, could make headway. All around them bankrupt groves were for sale. It was a fight for existence, affirmed the manager.

Then how and why did Great-Aunt Woodfall maintain such a lavish table? There was a domestic staff, Charles discovered, of at least a dozen indoor servants. Despite the antique note pervading the place there was a Victorian lavishness. Dinner was never less than six courses, always with wine. Lunch was almost as elaborate. Did Great-Aunt Woodfall pinch herself in other ways in order to keep an excellent table, an adequate staff? Two gardeners were not a sign of poverty, neither were a butler, two men-servants, a cook, and three maids, although coloured. Apart from the under-servants no one lived on the island. All the workers came from the mainland each day.

There could be only one explanation, Charles decided. The old lady had money, but kept alive the legend of impoverishment in order to gratify her thrifty nature. Neither she nor her daughters ever left the island. Through the intense heat of summer, when all who could went North, they remained at Sundown Grove. Eugenie, Grace, and Emily had never seen New York.

There were a hundred questions Charles wanted to ask, but loyalty to his hostess prevented him from seeking the answers outside Sundown Grove, even had that been possible. Actually, he was somewhat of a prisoner on the island. To get into Witterwittee meant crossing the lake and a seven-mile drive. None of the family ever seemed to make that trip. He might have been on a Pacific island for all the contact he had with the outside world.

At the end of the first week Charles found that he had lost some fifty dollars playing backgammon with his great-aunt. Every night after dinner the board was set out, and she had made it clear that it was his duty to play. No one else was invited to have a game. Once, when Charles had suggested taking on Henry, after playing with the old lady, she folded up the board with a slam, and said, "We will have our reading now." There was no challenging the finality of that announcement. Every night they went from backgammon to Browning. Great-Aunt Woodfall in her winged chair by the fireplace, Eugenie on the opposite side, Grace sewing, steel spectacles perched on the end of her nose, and, bolt upright in her chair, Emily reading in her quiet voice. Across the room, in the shadow, sat Henry. Charles suspected that he dozed. Promptly at ten o'clock Mrs. Woodfall stopped the reading and they all went to bed.

On the tenth day of his visit Henry was missing at lunch, and all that day he was not in the groves as usual. At dinner he was also absent.

"Where's Henry? I haven't seen him all day," asked Charles, as they sat at table.

"He is keeping to his room. Henry has very bad attacks of indigestion periodically," said Mrs. Woodfall. "I hope he will be down to-morrow."

As she spoke Charles intercepted her glance across the table at Eugenie. Instinctively Charles was certain that, for some reason, the old lady had lied to him, and that Eugenie knew she was lying. There was a secret between them. Grace and Emily, lower down the table, had apparently not heard his question, or if they had, showed no interest.

Charles looked at Eugenie in the conscious moment of silence that followed her mother's answer. Eugenie looked back at him, and he was aware that she knew he did not believe her mother's explanation. He thought there was something besides resentment at having detected Mrs. Woodfall in a lie, there was hostility towards him. It provoked a conclusion that had long been running in his mind—that the family was divided for some reason. Emily and Grace were outside the understanding that united his great-aunt and Eugenie.

Henry's position, he could not define. He was completely dominated by his mother, but whether he shared the confidence that existed between mother and daughter Charles could not tell. Possibly, thought Charles, his own imagination was running away with him. There was no evidence, no single fact whatsoever, that entitled him to weave a mystery about the household at Sundown Grove. And yet, despite himself, he began to feel uneasy, to be listening and looking for something he could not define. At moments he could swear there was tension in the atmosphere despite the carefully ordered existence, the tranquillity of each day. Even Jefferson, suave, composed, had an air of mystery. He had a habit of always being just behind the door, and was too instantly aware of one's needs, as if he spent his whole time listening and watching.

Annoyed with himself because of these flights of imagination, Charles repressed many questions he wanted to ask. Even in this thinly populated country people visited each other; but Mrs. Woodfall seemed scornful, even hostile, to all social contacts. No one ever called. The island itself made calling a difficulty. With no telephone and no transport, except that which Mrs. Woodfall controlled, they were cut off from the outside world. It explained the spinsterhood of the daughters. Did Henry never venture abroad?

The conviction grew, sustained by his great-aunt's explanation, that Henry had drinking bouts. Perhaps it was to hide the shame of this fact that he was lied to. There was an unhealthy look in Henry's eyes. They were clouded and heavy. He had fits of brooding, when he showed a dislike of any conversation, and yet, Emily apart, Charles liked him best of all in the Woodfall household. He was victimized, and induced compassion. There were moments when Henry seemed on the verge of becoming confidential, and then the cloud of brooding rolled back over him and he became furtive. It would not surprise Charles to learn that, despite Mrs. Woodfall's vigilance, Henry led a life of his own, that he escaped from the cage occasionally. Perhaps he went into Witterwittee and caroused.

That night, after the household had retired, Charles felt restless. Moreover, he was the prey of curiosity. He did not undress at once but sat in his room and attempted to read. It was useless, his mind wandered. He raised the blind and looked out, down the avenue between the live oaks to where the lake lay sparkling in the moonlight beyond its guardian palms. Somewhere in the woods a bird screeched fearfully, the only sound in the night. One ray of light lay across the lawn. It came from the window of his great-aunt's room. Did the old lady read in bed, he wondered?

And then something caused him to catch his breath. A figure crossed the white shaft of light, coming from the wood, momentarily illumined. Brief though the vision was, Charles identified the man. It was Jefferson, the butler. He passed quickly out of view, coming towards the house. Charles listened intently for the sound of a door opening and closing below. No sound came. The ray of light suddenly vanished, but the light from his own room, with his own shadow blocking it, made Charles aware that he must have been seen by Jefferson as he stood at the window. He drew down the blind, and then laughed at himself. His nerves were playing on him. He began to feel like a conspirator in a crime story. Why shouldn't Jefferson cross the lawn? He might have taken a stroll before going to bed, or have remembered something that had been left out of doors.

Impatient with himself, Charles began to undress. He was in his pyjamas when unsatisfied curiosity filled him with a desire to know the truth about Henry. Was he drunk in his room or really the victim of indigestion? He slept in the third room down the corridor.

Charles opened his bedroom door stealthily. The corridor was in darkness. Jefferson had put out all the lamps. The moonlight came through the window at the end and offered a faint illumination. Charles walked noiselessly along until he was opposite Henry's door. He decided not to tap. He tried the door, turning the knob. It opened. He peered inside.

The floor was flooded in moonlight. The swaying branches of a large royal poinciana tree outside flung a restless pattern of shadows across the polished floor. The room was a large one. A big four-poster bed with cretonne curtains almost touched the ceiling with its barrel-canopy. In one glance Charles satisfied his curiosity. His great-aunt had lied to him. Henry was neither sick nor drunk. He was missing. His bed had not been occupied, the blinds had not been drawn.

For a few moments he stared into the room. Then, quietly closing the door, he retraced his steps. He felt elated by his discovery, not because he had confirmed a suspicion that the old lady had not told him the truth, and that Eugenie knew it, but by this evidence that Henry was not so docile as he appeared. He had spirit enough, it seemed, to defy his mother. He was, to put it bluntly, a bit of a lad.

Charles turned out the lamp, got into bed, and lay wondering just when Master Henry would recover from his attack of indigestion and make an appearance. It would be amusing to ask him a few questions concerning his adventures abroad. On the morrow Laura Lanier was arriving. Life at Sundown Grove began to offer new interests.

III

Henry made no appearance the next morning, and when Charles inquired about him Jefferson replied that Master Henry was a little better but would probably keep to his bed until evening. When Charles suggested that perhaps Henry would like a visit from him, Jefferson was most emphatic that whenever Master Henry suffered from one of these periodic attacks he wished to be left absolutely alone.

At lunch Mrs. Woodfall announced that Henry might get up that evening. Charles looked at her keenly as she spoke, but her glance never wavered. Charles had now arrived at a satisfactory solution of the mystery. Henry was probably a secret drinker and went off to Witterwittee for his debauch. The old lady was too proud to admit defeat in this matter, hence her fiction about Henry's indigestion.

He had expected that his great-aunt would wish him to accompany her when she went into Witterwittee that afternoon to meet Laura Lanier. To his surprise she informed them all that she expected to be back at six o'clock, with Laura, and made no suggestion that he should go with her. He had not been off the island for more than a week.

"I think I'd like to come with you, Aunt Josephine. There are one or two things I want to buy in Witterwittee," he said, as they sat at table.

He was conscious of having administered a shock to the company. It seemed no one ever suggested going into Witterwittee without the approval of the old lady.

"Another time, Charles," replied the old lady, graciously. "The carriage is so small and Laura is sure to have a lot of luggage, and it would be most uncomfortable for all of us."

"Oh—well—if——" replied Charles, lamely.

"If you require anything you have only to tell Jefferson and he will have it brought in for you," said Mrs. Woodfall.

It was clear now beyond all doubt. She did not want him to go to Witterwittee. Like the family, he was virtually a prisoner on the island. Probably she was afraid he might learn something about the habits of Cousin Henry. His mind was now made up. He would remain a little longer to have a look at the glamorous Laura, and then he would leave for New York, *en route* for home. He had a new play simmering in his mind. He was afraid it was going to have a monstrous old woman for one of its chief characters.

So when Mrs. Woodfall had departed with Lincoln Robinson in the motor-launch, he went, as usual, with Eugenie, Grace, and Emily into the sun-porch where they had coffee. This porch, screened in against the flies and mosquitoes, commanded a westerly view of the lake, and of a plantation of some sixty varieties of azaleas, of which the great-aunt was particularly fond. The conversation was languid and polite, but after three or four days of life at Sundown Grove Charles found they had exhausted the limited number of subjects on which it was possible to converse. For these poor, flattened-down cousins of his had been nowhere, seen nothing, and had ceased to desire to go afield. They had asked him a few questions about Hollywood. As might be expected, they had the customary opinion of this place as the home of incredibly vulgar, hard-drinking, and licentious actors and actresses, who earned fabulous sums of money under the direction of illiterate Jews. They were astonished to learn that the only Hollywood that he had seen was one in which extremely hard-working actors and actresses, who kept themselves in training like boxers, were on the studio sets at seven o'clock in the morning, and laboured with incredible patience, repeating over and over again minute actions until the director felt fairly safe in 'shooting' the scene.

His own experience had no glamour about it. There had been no South Sea love, no midnight orgies. For weeks on end he had sat in a small room, one of twenty in a row, in a building that might have been a factory in any manufacturing town. His secretary-stenographer arrived on the lot promptly at nine o'clock each morning, having motored forty miles from a ranch in the San Fernando valley, where a consumptive young husband raised British bulldogs, then a fashion among the film colony.

From nine till twelve, and two till five, he was commissioned to dictate romance to this fashionably attired young woman, who warned him that illegitimacy was taboo as a film theme, and that the word 'bastard,' almost a term of affection in some intimate circles, was on the film censor's Codex Expurgatorius. When, in his youthful exuberance, assisted by a fertile imagination, he dictated twenty sheets a day, he was solemnly warned that he was jeopardizing the scenario writer's profession, the standard rate of a good day's work being not more than four pages a day, of which only a few mutilated lines finally reached the set.

"But you must have heard all this from Laura," said Charles, balancing in his rocking-chair.

"Mother doesn't encourage Laura to talk about her life in Hollywood," observed Eugenie.

"She talks to me a lot—it's not an easy life, but most exciting. I should love it!" exclaimed Emily.

Her two sisters looked at her in pained surprise.

"Laura's not married by any chance?" asked Charles, in pure mischief. As he had hoped, the two elder sisters were shocked by the thought.

"Married—why, Cousin Charles, Laura's only a child! She's only twenty-two!" cried Grace.

"Some girls are mothers at that age," declared Charles, recklessly, "or divorced."

Somewhere in the garden the monkeys screeched as if in ribald endorsement of this opinion.

Emily smiled at Charles, her hands busy, as ever, with knitting.

"I'm in favour of early marriages—look at us. It is then or never!"

She said it artlessly, and with an impishness which she revealed occasionally, but only in the absence of her mother.

"Emily!" exclaimed Eugenie, severely. "What an awful thing to say!"

"But is it an awful thing for a woman to obey her instinct?" asked Charles, enjoying the embarrassment shown by Eugenie and Grace. They had blushed at their sister's statement. "I agree with Emily—the younger you are, the easier the jump."

"One should not regard marriage as a jump," said Eugenie, stiffly. "And instinct must be properly controlled. I'm glad to say there's nothing light about Laura. We have been rewarded for all the care we expended on her."

"You mean she survived us," said Emily, quietly.

"Survived? Emily, what do you mean?" asked Eugenie, reproof in every line of her stiff figure.

"The darling remained herself, quick and living and warm, despite us all," said Emily, her cheeks now burning with self-consciousness. "She's Harriet all over——"

"I hope not!" said Grace. "That was always our fear."

"Well—say what you will, Harriet was worth the whole bunch of us. She had guts!" declared Emily, now quite reckless under Charles's encouraging smile, her cheeks glowing.

"Emily! Need you be so vulgar!" protested Eugenie.

"Yes. There are times when a good strong dose of it would do us good. Sometimes I think we've ceased to be human, drying up in this beastly backwash!" cried Emily. Then, rising to her feet, she turned to Charles. "Oh, I'm sorry—forgive me," she added, tears hovering in her eyes, and before he could recover from his surprise, or make any response, she had hurried from the porch into the house.

There was a strained silence. Eugenie stabbed viciously at her sewing. Grace kept swallowing, her eyes staring into space.

"I must apologize for Emily," said Eugenie, after a long pause. "She's inclined to say rash things."

"Rash?" asked Charles. "I wouldn't call it rash. I rather agree with her. You can behave so beautifully that you miss a lot of fun."

"Fun!" echoed Eugenie, her voice loaded with reproof.

Charles looked her squarely in the face. He had some admiration for Great-Aunt Woodfall—she was a forceful old woman, of original character; but Eugenie was aspiring to tyranny with no equipment but her inhibitions. Poor little Emily had not yet admitted complete defeat. He was not going to desert her.

"Fun," he repeated firmly. "In this sense—sex, if you'll pardon my brutal frankness, Eugenie. And now I think I'll go and bathe," he added, smiling at the two scandalized women.

"I think you had better," rejoined Eugenie, in a voice that implied he was an unclean thing.

He went indoors, took his towel and costume, and set off for the lake. Perhaps he had been a little outrageous, but he felt quite unrepentant as he thought of poor, scared little Emily making her stand for freedom. He had long wanted to drop a stone in that pool of primness, and, now he had done it, he enjoyed the splash he had made. As for Laura, he began to fear she was the model niece instead of a slip of sin from the garden of Goldwyn.

CHAPTER FIVE

BRIEF IDYLL

I

THROUGH all the experiences of the years that were to follow, the first occasion when he saw Laura Lanier lost nothing of its sharp delight, its vivid outline. He knew it was love, the magic, overwritten, oversung thing that underlay all the motives so complexly woven through the warp and woof of life. A note quivered, as if in him a harp-string had been plucked; all that lay in the silence of a starry night, the bright wonder of the dawn, the splendour of the sunset, everything that in the symphony of life contributed its note of ecstasy or sorrow, was welded in that incandescent moment of his first consciousness of her.

He had entered the drawing-room, early, and ahead of the others, on the evening of Great-Aunt Woodfall's return from Witterwittee. He knew they had returned, for as he went up to his room to dress, on coming in from the groves, a pair of lavender gloves, a sunshade, and a camera-case lay on the hall table. In his curiosity he had picked up one of the gloves, scenting it, a soft, delicate thing, symbol of exquisite femininity, and faintly perfumed. She had arrived, and somewhere in a room upstairs the child of poor rebellious Harriet, the young Laura, who had so early won a career of fame, was robing herself for dinner.

He was prepared for a disappointment, he told himself as he stared into the newly lit fire in the drawing-room. The loveliness of the cinema screen was a rehearsed and fortified loveliness. Men could lie with lighting and angles as they could lie with words and figures. He had seen in those Hollywood studios the most commonplace of faces achieve a transcendent beauty. Would he not be foolish to expect, therefore, that Laura in the flesh might rival Laura on the screen? And the screen version had not greatly stirred him. He had a youthful sophistication to protect him against stage and screen glamour. Such interest as he now felt was directed more to the great-aunt's granddaughter than to the film actress, to the child of Harriet, the rebel, and not to the glamour girl of transient screen fame. It was possible, it was indeed probable, that she was just an ordinary little girl whom Nature had made photogenic.

Jefferson entered the room with two more lamps as Charles stood by the fireplace. He placed them on the tables and proceeded to lower the blinds. A crimson sunset had just faded out of the upper sky, giving place to the cool green and orange afterlight in which a solitary star scintillated. Charles inquired if Master Henry was likely to appear at dinner and learned that he was not yet sufficiently recovered, but he hoped to rise on the morrow.

"Has he had the doctor?" Charles could not forbear to ask.

"Oh, no, sir. It is not necessary. Master Henry knows exactly what to do when he has these attacks. It is a matter of diet and rest," replied Jefferson, now placing another log on the fire.

If the fellow was lying he was a very calm liar.

"Is my cousin in his own room?" asked Charles, boldly, watching the butler intently as he asked this question.

Jefferson slowly put down the tongs with which he had placed the log, and turned to Charles, without a sign of embarrassment.

"Yes, sir. Master Henry is still in bed—he sleeps a lot," he answered. And then, straightening himself, "It's been a wonderful sunset again, sir."

"Yes, wonderful!" replied Charles.

The butler withdrew. Nothing had been gained by questioning him. There was not a sign of surprise or resentment. Was he mistaken after all? Had he gone to the wrong room last night? It did not seem possible. He was certain that Henry slept in the third room down the corridor.

The opening of a door and the sound of footsteps on the polished floor caused Charles to turn from the fireplace where he mused over the mystery of Henry. In the dim soft light of the lamps he could see a slim figure in white coming towards him, but the head and shoulders were obscure in the shadow. Then a voice fell upon his ears, and the music of it gave him a thrill of pleasure.

"You must be Charles—I'm Laura Lanier. How nice to see you here!"

She came forward then, and the utter loveliness of her stood revealed as she came into the pool of light thrown by the lamp on the central table.

She had put out her hand, delicate and white, for him to take, and he felt a slight bewilderment such as he had never known before. Although she resembled the girl he had seen in the film she was quite different from what he had expected. He had imagined her to be self-assured, and somewhat regal in the consciousness of her importance. She had fought in the fiercest of arenas, the glare of publicity had invaded whatever private life she had known. She was an asset to be produced and marketed. It was scarcely possible, with such a background, for her to evade the hardening process of success. And yet she had nothing of that professional air, that artificially assumed simplicity so evident in those who never forget that an impression must be made.

"Yes—I am Charles," he said, taking her hand and holding it. "So you are our famous Laura—it's very strange to see you in the flesh at last!"

"Am I a bit like what you expected?" she asked, with a flash of small white teeth, and cheeks that dimpled as she smiled.

He regarded her steadily for a few moments.

"No," he said, at length.

"No?"

Her eyebrows arched slightly as she looked at him, his thin fine face so serious before her.

"You are——"

He paused. He was about to use the word 'spiritual' and then thought it would sound affected. Again, he felt aware of her utter delicacy, of a loveliness as yet undefinable.

"I am——" she pressed, and then laughed, seating herself on a chair. Her white dress flounced out about her. Two feet in gold slippers escaped from the white waves of organdie spread over the floor. She was fair, with soft hair shading her brow and bound with a simple white ribbon. The design of her dress had lost no point of emphasis in displaying the superbly moulded throat, the poised white shoulders, the taut virginal curves of her bosom, held like a sheathed lily in the slim corsage. The mouth, warm-lipped and full, so red with youth that it scorned all artificial aid, was sensitive and yet expressive of character. He learned, later, that her eyes, so dark with the intensity of her glance, were actually blue, but now they took a lustre from the lamplight.

There were a few moments of silence, each conscious of mutual appraisal. For her part she found immediate pleasure in his young, well-groomed body. His face was sensitive, such as one might look for in one who analysed the human emotions, and there was a flame in his eyes as he spoke with a voice that was oddly grave in contrast with the warm liveliness of his expression. She liked the set of his head, neat, black-haired, on his trim shoulders. It was a clever head, long, with a wide brow and rather deep-set eyes. He had the air of a young aristocrat, not the odd kind she had met, endorsed by Debrett, but the kind created by the magazine illustrators. Her grandmother, on the way from the station, had described him as "a very pleasant young man with a lot hidden under the surface." She understood that description. He suggested a reserve of character.

They began to talk of Hollywood, and all the time she saw how closely his eyes were watching her. They discussed mutual acquaintances they had met in the studios. They agreed it was a place for hard work rather than the riotous pleasures of public fancy.

"And Florida—here? Do you like it better?" he asked.

"It has its own kind of loveliness," she answered, quietly, but something in her voice caused him to look at her sharply. There was no note of enthusiasm such as one might expect in reference to the home-place. "Do you like it?" she asked, adjusting the orchids on her bosom.

"I find it very interesting," he answered and, feeling he was a little lukewarm, added, "The groves are very beautiful."

He watched her hands, fascinated. Long and white, they expressed her intense vitality. Then, their eyes meeting, they each knew they had not made a candid confession. He had a feeling that she had not been happy here, was never happy here, and wondered why she came back to a place which must have unpleasant memories. Her mother had fled it, her father had been driven from it.

"What have you been doing here?" she asked, to break a silence so full of inference.

"Oh—wandering in the grove, riding and swimming. And quite a lot of sleeping—a beachcomber, in short," he said, with a smile. "And you?"

"Very much the same. I come here to get away from people —and see Aunt Emily, and——"

Her sentence went unfinished. Eugenie had entered the room. She greeted her niece effusively. A few minutes later Emily and Grace came. As the clock struck, Mrs. Woodfall appeared.

"I hope you feel rewarded, Charles, for staying on," she said, with a gleam in her eye. "Laura, dear, it has cost this young man some fifty dollars to await your coming—he loses to me every night at backgammon, and he doesn't think we are nice people."

"My dear Aunt!" protested Charles.

"You needn't apologize, Charles. What possible attraction could any young man find in a place like this—once his curiosity had been satisfied," said Mrs. Woodfall. The door opened and Jefferson appeared, announcing dinner. "Laura, Charles has had no one but an old woman to take in to dinner. Take his arm."

Laura gave Charles a brilliant smile and slipped her hand over his arm. Mrs. Woodfall swept on ahead, straight as a Guardsman.

"Amazing old dragon, she loves breathing fire," whispered Laura.

"And sticking in her claws," added Charles.

They agreed, he felt, on the subject of Mrs. Woodfall. When he knew this radiant creature better he would ask how she had escaped so early from this cage.

— II

Life at Sundown Grove had taken on a tempo of gaiety for Charles with the coming of Laura. They saw much of each other, since there were no duties calling them away; and the pleasure each found in the other's company made them conspirators in planning escape. It happened they both loved horses and riding, and in a few days they knew every sandy track through the groves and the undergrowth. They had found a swimming beach and a hut, or rather Laura had revealed them, a haunt of her girlhood, where a smooth slope of silver sand ran down to the translucent blue water. Here they bathed and lay in the warm sand discussing art, literature, and life until they had thoroughly explored each other's life. She was eager for every detail of England, which she had never seen, and soon she was familiar with life in the doctor's old house at Henley, with the river life, with Auntie Janet and her gay verandah-parties.

He was astonished by her knowledge of the poetry and literature of his homeland. There were times when she could supplement his own knowledge by her quick remembrance of things read, her gift for apt quotation. Her mind raced side by side with his own, they loved the same kind of things, laughed at the same absurdities. At the end of that first week, after long hours of perfect companionship, he knew that she had conquered him utterly. His heart lay in the hollow of her hand. Every glance remembered, word spoken, contributed to the richness of life in this paradise of sunshine and tranquillity. He had become oblivious of the sinister atmosphere which he had felt surrounded the Woodfall house. His great-aunt no longer dominated him, and he began to treat her with the bantering independence that marked all Laura's relations with her grandmother. How Laura had ever achieved such liberty was a mystery, but, as Emily had confided to Charles, "The child always had magic—and Mother was her victim from the day she brought her home from Witterwittee."

How much had Harriet—who had a 'flame on her head,' according to Emily—how much had the drunken ne'er-do-well, James Lanier, contributed to this vivacious, quick-witted young woman? Her education had been excellent. Grandmother Woodfall had not stinted her in that respect. A ladies' school in South Carolina, a university in Pennsylvania, a drama school in New York, had equipped her with grace, intelligence, and technique. She could sit down at the piano and play Beethoven, Mozart, Bach, and also the moderns, Stravinski and Gershwin, with exceptional proficiency. Music was perhaps her first love: "I think it's the perfect language of all our emotions," she declared. For drama she had a passion, but that was something to labour at, something beckoning her ever onwards to an unrealizable perfection. "Réjane, Duse, Bernhardt—that is the divine gift, not achievement!"

"I have never seen you on the stage," said Charles, lying on the sand, and letting its silver grains sift through his fingers.

"Don't—I am unbelievably gauche," she warned, laughing down at him, slim and brown in her white bathing-costume.

"I can see that," mocked Charles, looking up. Her hair, released from its cap, and wind-blown, was an aureole against the sunlight. Every line of her built a lyric of youth. Last night in the orange groves, whither they had gone in the enchantment of the blossom-scented night, in defiance of Great-Aunt Woodfall, who had sounded the tocsin for bed, he had almost lost control and smashed down the barrier of polite reticence that divided them. There had been, just now, a perilous moment when, helping with a difficult fastening on her bathing-cap, the small face so near to his, with its fine curve of the eyebrows, and sweeping lashes, had offered almost irresistible provocation.

The sun, rapidly falling to the wooded horizon, threw long shadows as, clothed and remounted, they rode back towards the house. The crimson evening began to spread in the upper sky. Another perfect day was drawing to its close. As their horses, sure-footed, picked their way across the palmetto scrub, and the lake caught up the crimson fire of the upper clouds, their talk turned to the Woodfall household, and, greatly daring, he told her of his sense of something furtive around him, of business from which he was kept apart, of undercurrents of thought and action that seemed to flow beneath the sustained tranquillity of that well-ordered house.

"Perhaps I shouldn't say this to you. You'll think me an imaginative fool. It's not my business anyhow. I'm a guest here, and a stranger, but——"

He broke off, regretting his words, but she would not let him lapse into silence.

"Go on—I'm interested. What in particular has worried you since you came here? Grandma Woodfall?" she added.

"Oh, no—she's downright and domineering. There's something magnificent about the old bully, but the others——" He broke off again. "Tell me about Henry, I can't fathom him."

In reply to her questions he told her of Henry's feigned illness, of his absence from his bedroom, of Jefferson's lies about him, of Great-Aunt Woodfall's deceit. She listened without interruption, but when he had finished she reined up her horse, and sat for a few moments staring out across the glowing lake over which some birds made their evening flight. Then she turned to him, and he was amazed to see that tears were dimming her eyes.

"I have been very happy and very sad here," she said. "Like you, I felt I was never a part of their lives, that something was proceeding from which I was kept apart. I have never loved Grandma Woodfall. It makes me feel guilty of terrible ingratitude, for she has been very kind to me—and perhaps you know how I came here?" He nodded, and she proceeded: "Aunt Eugenie, I think I always feared, though, to be truthful, I never suffered anything at her hands. Aunt Grace has never quite existed. But Aunt Emily I loved from that first day of my coming. It's because of her I return. I want to take her away, but she will not go."

"Away from what?" pressed Charles, as their horses began to move on.

"Like you, I don't know—it's something, I feel. How strange that you, too, should feel it, and in such a short time here! Often I have told myself I have imagined it all—except for Uncle Henry and his sham illnesses and his absences."

"Then you have noticed it before?"

"Often. Once I asked Aunt Emily what really happened to him and where he went, and she begged me never to speak of it again, it would make Grandma terribly angry."

"Then there is a mystery of some kind?" asked Charles.

"I don't know. I'm puzzled," she answered. "When I go away from here I begin to think it is all in my imagination. When I come back I have the same old feeling of something hidden from me. You are the first person to whom I have ever spoken about it—why, I wonder."

"I began it," said Charles. "I'm sorry—it's impertinent and outrageous of me. But you inspire confidences."

She saw the admiration shining in his dark eyes and smiled at him, gratefully.

"Thank you—and now I wonder if we can face them like a pair of innocents!" she exclaimed, laughing.

They entered the straight path up to the house, now dark in the shadow of the live oaks.

III

Their evenings followed the same pattern. After the elaborate dinner, eaten mostly in silence, with Jefferson hovering in the shadows, and Lincoln Robinson, white-jacketed and white-gloved, waiting at table, they returned to the drawing-room, to leisurely conversation, some talk of work in the groves, then the radio for fifteen minutes of news, and, after that, backgammon and the reading of Browning. They were nearing the end of *The Ring and the Book*. Charles wondered what they would read next. There was a bookcase at one end of the drawing-room, and he examined the titles of the books. There did not appear to be one published later than the death of Queen Victoria—Mrs. Oliphant's works, a set of Thackeray, Longfellow's *Poems*, Prescott's *Conquest of Peru*, Ruskin's *Stones of Venice*. Charles felt chilled by this array of worthies. He would have like to insert the more flippant works of P. G. Wodehouse and Arlen. When, in the presence of Mrs. Woodfall, Laura and he had discussed the work of Proust, Joyce, and Hemingway, the old lady had listened and asked whether they thought she would like their work. Rather bewildered, Charles had said she would find it somewhat experimental. Once a week the London *Times Weekly Edition* and *The Spectator* arrived. Eugenie read extracts from them. This was the extent of their contact with the outside world. Emily confided to Charles that Henry read detective stories in his bedroom.

Mrs. Woodfall insisted on her evening game of backgammon with Charles, who, now familiar with her tactics, sometimes won. She met defeat with an offended spirit. It was obvious she hated losing. He wondered whether she would discontinue the game if he gave signs of becoming her equal. On the evening that Charles and Laura came in from their lake excursion she challenged Laura to a game, and doubled four times. Charles felt disgusted with the avaricious old woman. He knew she was certain she could defeat her granddaughter. In three games she took a hundred and six dollars off her. She crowed with delight. Afterwards Laura told Charles that she knew she was going to be skinned. "She does that on every visit. I can afford it, and it gives her pleasure, so why not?" Charles said he thought it disgusting. "I wish you could win for once." Laura laughed. "Then I shouldn't get a game. Henry's a wizard at it. She's forbidden him to play in the house. We used to play in the harness-room. He and Jefferson have a passion for it and gamble madly."

Henry was absent at dinner again. He had made his re-appearance, but was out in the groves this evening. At six o'clock each day the Weather Bureau's report came in over the radio, and it gave a forecast of the lowest temperature likely to prevail during the night throughout Florida's citrus-growing districts. A frost, with a temperature of 34 degrees Fahrenheit, was fatal to the blossoms, 32 degrees blackened the fruit, 25 degrees was fatal to the trees. Thousands of groves had been bankrupted and put out of business in the old days by a sudden fall in temperature. But to-day they were forewarned by the Weather Bureau. This evening it had announced the possibility of the thermometer falling below 40 in the Lake Witterwittee belt. Henry had gone hurrying off with the foreman to see that the oil smudge-pots were all ready in the groves, and where these were not available, that pine logs were under the trees for lighting the fires that broke the frost.

"I knew it was coming," said Henry, on hearing the weather report. "Darwin's been gibbering all day—he feels it in his bones long before the Weather Bureau." Henry expected to be up all night. You couldn't trust the hands, he said, to watch the smudge-pots and fires. "Niggers'll sleep with the frost nipping their toes," he said. Four o'clock in the morning was the critical time, and the low ground the most susceptible. He expected to be up till dawn. For the next two months all growers lived in dread of the great enemy who could ruin them with one bad freeze.

So even in this earthly paradise man had no security, Charles learned. In addition to the great enemy, Jack Frost, there was aphis on the blossoms, and red scale, for which the trees were sprayed with oil emulsion, and rust mite, for which the groves were dusted with sulphur; and if the groves sur-vived all these threats, as well as bad markets and gluts, there was the ever-present threat of a roaring hurricane, with the sky growing black, the barometer oscillating wildly, a sudden hammering of wind and water, with trees snapping and up-rooted, timber houses pancaked, and an aftermath of ruin and debris that took a year to clear up.

"We've sat in this house while it rocked like a ship, in a blackness you could cut, and we couldn't hear ourselves shouting at each other," said Mrs. Woodfall, as they talked of past hurricanes.

"Are we likely to have one now?" asked Charles, not unwilling to go through the experience.

"No—it's not the season," said Eugenie, looking up from her sewing. "We have a rhyme:

> July—stand by.
> August—look out you must.
> September—remember.
> October—all over.

September's our dangerous month. We've come through five years now without one."

"If we get through without a freeze this year we'll have a profit for the first time in four years," said Great-Aunt Woodfall. "The fruit's heavy on the trees, and the market's strong, if it holds."

A profit in four years. If this were true, then how did they carry on at Sundown Grove, pondered Charles.

"Surely you don't lose three years out of four?" he asked.

Great-Aunt Woodfall looked at him sharply.

"I didn't say we lost—I said we had no profit. We balance out mostly: one year the tangerine crop's good, another the grape-fruit—we scramble along, somehow. My husband lost his fortune here in ten years. That and the quarrelling among the settlers broke his heart. Twice we were for quitting, but we held on. I came here as a young woman, full of health and ambition. I've seen freezes and hurricanes and murderings. But we've held on. This Florida soil'll take my bones, as it took my husband's."

She looked at the bronze clock on the mantelpiece.

"Where's Jefferson and the tray?" she said, looking around the room. "Ring, Charles."

Charles got up and went over to the bell-rope by the fire-place, but as he put his hand on the tasselled cord the door opened and Jefferson entered, bearing the nightly tray with the whisky and soda, the ginger ale, and Coca-Cola.

Charles, like Jefferson, had learned his duties. He smiled inwardly at the manner in which he had fallen under the whip in the Woodfall circus. He went over to the side-table to get his great-aunt her whisky and soda, the prelude to back-gammon.

"Make it a stiff one," she called. "And you'd better make it stiff for yourself. I'm going to trounce you!"

She turned to Laura who was touring America on the radio.

"My dear, must we have that abominable racket?" she called. "After our game we'll not have the reading. You can give us some real music. I heard you playing *The Moonlight Sonata* this morning. You played the second movement very well—but a little slower than I like it."

Laura switched off the radio. She exchanged looks with Charles, as he crossed the room with her grandmother's drink. Eugenie was sewing, as always. Grace sat staring into the fire, with a contemplative air that never produced any noteworthy remark. Emily placed the small table and the backgammon board in front of her mother and then resumed her reading.

Charles sat down opposite the old lady, more angry with himself than with her. Why didn't they all defy the old tyrant? Why didn't he?

Mrs. Woodfall rattled the pieces, setting the board. The game began. She doubled twice. Her old eyes gleamed.

IV

The days passed for Charles like an enchanted dream. There were long hours in the sunny groves, when they rode their horses along the sandy avenues with the white blossoms and the golden fruit shining in the crystal air. They made excursions on the lake in a small canoe, and watched from some backwater, while the saw-grass swayed in the wind, the flight of heron and ibis over the glittering water. They transported their horses by barge over to the mainland and began to explore the wilderness beyond, penetrating deep into the hammock which had not changed since the days when the Seminole Indians had roamed the land. They came to mangrove swamps and heard the slithering of a surprised alligator as it took off into the creek. Strange birds flew up at their approach, and then, in a clearing, civilization sprang forth in a settler's house, with a lawn won from the scrub, with royal palms, magnolias, and eucalyptus trees giving dignity and shade in the blazing noon.

But most of all Charles loved the hours they spent lying on the white sand, basking in the sun, slipping in and out of the clear water where the blue catfish darted away. Their faces shaded by large Mexican straw hats, they lay and discussed the whole wide world and the endless delight it held for them in the days to come. Books, music, drama, travel, and life as they meant to live it, they discussed each in turn, sometimes disagreeing, more often agreeing. She wanted to know why he had given up medicine.

"I wanted to travel—for years I dreamed of coming here. Aunt Woodfall is a legend in the family. I wanted to see her."

"And now?" asked Laura, one slim bare leg rocking on the other as she lay on her back.

"I suppose she's unique," he said, not wishing to commit himself too far. "However did you escape?"

Laura made no reply for a few moments.

"I didn't, not of my own accord," she said, quietly, after a pause. "One day she asked me what I would like to do. I was so surprised I couldn't think what to say. I had a great friend at college whose one ambition was to be a great actress. She had just gone to a dramatic academy in New York. I thought it would be fun to live in a great city and share an apartment with her. So, astonished at myself, I said I wanted to learn acting and go on the stage. I expected a shocked refusal. To my amazement, the old lady said it might be possible. And then she said something that made me unable to believe my own ears. 'That's what I would like to have been,' she said. 'Instead, I've been burnt up in this wilderness. Get away soon enough, or you won't have the courage.' Do you wonder I was surprised?"

"Nothing that she would do or say surprises me. I admire her and detest her—and I believe I'm afraid of her," added Charles. "So I must get away!"

They laughed then and the inquisitive squirrels scurried up the pine-tree trunks at the noise of their merriment.

"The poor aunts!" said Laura, reflectively.

"The poor aunts—that is, two of them. I'll leave Eugenie to her fate gladly," commented Charles.

"Every time I go I wonder if I shall ever see Grandma again—she must die soon, she's eighty. Next Monday when I go——"

"Go—but you're not going away yet?" cried Charles, startled out of the semi-drowsiness that followed their long swim.

"On Monday."

He sat up and looked down at her, so brown and svelte in her white swimming-costume.

"Oh, but you can't go yet! You've only just come. Why—I thought you were here for a month!"

"I begin rehearsing for a New York production next week," she explained. "I'm sorry to go—I've never enjoyed a visit so much before."

He made no answer to what might be a compliment. His world had suddenly been shaken. They had drifted through these idyllic days—it seemed impossible they should end so quickly. And yet why should he be so troubled? She had her work to do, she must go when it needed her.

"I shall go too, very soon," he said, quietly.

"I wonder where we shall meet again?" she asked.

"Again?"

He leapt at the word, and for a moment felt the weight lift from his heart.

"Of course, New York, London, Paris—the world's not very big, really," she said, gaily.

A cloud went over the sun. The shadow it threw seemed to cover the whole earth. A hawk hovered in the fathomless sky. The cloud passed, the dazzling light blinded him again.

"I think we should be dressing—it's lunch-time," he said, sitting up and brushing the sand off his chest.

"When you are old and grey and full of sleep——

You know the lines?" she asked, standing up, a smile lighting her eyes. She took off her cap and fluffed out her hair, with a free artlessness that set his heart racing.

"Why—why—do you quote them?" he asked, gravely.

"Because even then we might remember days like these," she said, laughing a little, as she led the way to the dressing-hut.

V

The frost threatened the groves for the next three nights, and Henry was scarcely visible in the house. He slept during the day, his nights spent with the men lighting the fires in the groves. By constant vigilance they warded off disaster, except for a belt of some fifty acres near Lake Kissimmee, where they owned a grove. There the fruit was utterly ruined, and there was a possibility that some of the trees, fine ten-year-olds, were ruined too. Then the menace passed, the thermometer climbed. For the time being they could relax, though another visitation was possible any time until the end of April.

Laura and Charles had enlisted among the pickers, and now spent some of their time mounted on ladders rocking against the thick-leaved trees. With bags slung from their shoulders they clipped industriously in the sunny groves, the blossom scent around them, the clear blue sky above. Some of the coloured pickers sang at their work. Strange to think that England was in the grip of winter. The mist would lie late over the river at Henley, and Auntie Janet, sewing by her fire, would look out on a feeble sun that scarcely dissolved the hoar-frost whitening the leaf-strewn lawn. The river, swollen with the rains, reflected the leaden skies. Auntie Janet and Whiskey would battle the wind, walking through the deer park. The dog hated the rain. Auntie Janet loved it, and came in glowing and apple-cheeked. Charles thought of his mother throwing out crumbs on the frost-bound ground for the sparrows and robins. He could hear Uncle Wyndham pushing the self-starter, in repeated attempts to start up a cold engine. Ice would form overnight on the small rain puddles, and Miss Whissitt would appear in her blue-felt overshoes and yellow knitted gloves. "*Il fait très froid, n'est-ce pas?*" she would observe to everybody, and they would answer, "Frightful!" Miss Whissitt had once informed him that in winter she always read books about sunny Italy, they helped to keep her warm. How her tourist French and Italian would spill over in ecstasy with this sunlit landscape!

The sulphur-dusting aeroplane had gone. Henry had left to attend a citrus growers' convention at Orlando, some fifty miles away. He had said good-bye to Laura as she was leaving before his return on the following Monday.

The last golden days slipped by, with riding and swimming, with orange picking and lying on the beach, with canoe picnics, and drifting talk on the shady verandah when the garden lay still under the midday sun, and the giant butterflies flitted over the azalea bushes, a bank of vivid colour against the dark background of the woodland. Jays, catbirds, red-winged cardinals, shy chipmunks, and bold squirrels flashed and scampered across the clearing where Aunt Emily, an indefatigable gardener, coaxed the soil and composts and chemicals to nourish her seventy species of azaleas, and her more precious gardenias.

Two days before Laura's departure they planned a whole day's excursion by canoe to the western end of the lake, where the wild life was to be seen at its best. Starting off a little before ten o'clock on a perfect, windless morning, they carried with them a picnic-basket. The lake looked like a sheet of glass, a few white clouds sailed slowly across the blue dome of the sky. After some two hours of steady paddling they came to the dead end of the lake, where it disappeared into a swamp of saw-grass and mangrove-roots rising from the ooze. They took a narrow channel that offered an approach to the hammock whose pine trees and scrub oaks rose above the level of the swamp. Suddenly the silence was broken by a whirr of wings, and between them and the sun, shutting out its light with a great wave of bodies that rose, white-crested, a flock of ibis took flight. A multitudinous crying mass, they hovered and circled and hovered in a great scything movement that filled the morning with beauty and the whirr of wings. Shuttering the light, they went southward and were soon merged with the quivering horizon.

Filled with the wonder and beauty of this wild life, they paddled on. The creek grew narrower, and presently the canoe grounded. They could go no farther.

"The end of the world," said Laura, as they stepped out.

They could see nothing, shut in by a wall of grass, shoulder-high. Charles pulled up the canoe and went forward. He was checked by a sudden cry from Laura, and turned to find the cause. Something slipped through the undergrowth.

"Did you see that—you almost trod on it. A coral snake—it's deadly," she said, catching her breath.

"Heavens! Ought we to go on?" he asked.

"We must go carefully—there might be rattlers too—we ought to have boots and leggings."

They were both bare-legged, in canvas shoes. He wore nothing but an open shirt and blue linen shorts. She wore a chequered blouse, and American sailor's white pants that gave her a boyish air, setting off the slimness of her figure.

"Look—why, there's a path! It must lead somewhere," he exclaimed. The thick grass had been beaten down, and the tangle of undergrowth chopped away by some pioneer. It was strange to find this path cut through the wilderness.

"Someone's been hunting here," said Laura. "I thought no one ever came to this end of the lake."

They followed the path, shut in by the menacing saw-grass. Charles had heard grim stories of men being lost in these swamps, and cut to death in their frenzy by the imprisoning razor edge of this giant grass.

"Shall we go on?" he asked, after a quarter of an hour's walking. It was hot under the high noonday sun, with the air shut off. The smell of wilting undergrowth assailed them, fetid and swampy.

"It must lead somewhere—perhaps to a clearing in a hammock—let's go on a little," answered Laura.

They pressed on for a time. Then, abruptly, Charles stopped and picked up something in the path.

"Look!" he said, holding it out for Laura's inspection.

It was an electric pocket torch, its metal container thickly rusted.

"That means someone uses this track in the darkness. Clue number one. This is exciting!" he cried.

They moved forward along the track. A little farther on it took a sudden turn, coming to solider ground. Next, rising before them, where the saw-grass fell away, stood the hammock, a thick forest of hickories, live oaks, dwarf cypress, magnolias and sweet gums. Some of the pines and oaks had barren branches, or gaunt trunks, broken off and splintered, witness to the violence of old hurricanes. The path ran straight across the thick palmetto scrub, into the dark heart of the forest jungle. The wild life stirred and screeched as they approached, protesting against this intrusion of their domain. Two buzzards flew up and wheeled in the blue, the bitterns called a warning from the swamp, there was a whirr of quail rising. Men seldom came here. This beaten path seemed a contradiction. It led on into the heart of the forest. Charles halted. The place was eerie in the half-light, the day shut out by the bearded moss hanging heavily from the trees.

"Shall we go on?" he asked.

"It may lead us through the hammock. Let's go a little farther," answered Laura.

And, presently, they found the reason of this track through the swamp and hammock. They halted, wholly surprised by what they saw ahead. In a clearing among the trees there was a low hut, made of roughly hewn logs. They came upon it, end on. The path continued around one side. They followed it and at the opposite end found two wide doors fastened by a padlocked bar.

"Whatever is it for?" asked Laura.

"Look!" exclaimed Charles, trying the doors.

He pointed down at the ground. Two parallel tracks ran away from the opening. Stooping, Charles examined one of the sandy ruts made by wheels. It carried the impression of a rubber tyre.

"My heavens, it's a garage! There's been a car here!" he cried. There was a space between the bottom of the rough doors and the ground. He went down on his knees and peered under. His surmise was confirmed. There was a car inside.

"But who would want to garage an automobile here?" asked Laura. "It could only be someone going down the creek, someone who must be using the lake!"

"And therefore going to the island?"

"Yes."

"How many boats have you?" asked Charles.

"The launch, the horse float, the crate barge, and the sailing dinghy."

"And the canoe—and the canoe's the only one that could get up the creek?"

"Yes."

They looked at each other, baffled.

"There must be some explanation—no one ever comes to this end of the lake. It leads nowhere," said Laura.

"Nowhere—but this track?"

"It must run for miles through the hammock. The nearest settlement's ten miles away at least—on the edge of the prairie, north-west of Lake Okeechobee. No one could want to go there."

"But someone goes there, or comes here in a car. The tyre marks have been made since it rained last."

"That was over a week ago—the evening I arrived," said Laura. "I can't think who would come here."

She followed Charles. He walked along the track, but it went on interminably.

"Well, we'd better go back," he said. "Who uses the canoe?"

"Hardly anyone ever uses it, or did when I was here."

"No one stays on the island after dark, except people in the house?"

"No."

"Then it's someone in the house who comes here," said Charles. "It's someone who comes in the dark, who uses a torch—someone who doesn't want to be seen, and who for some reason wants to go somewhere in a roundabout and secretive way."

Laura laughed, as they came out of the forest into the clear sunlight.

"Charles, your imagination's running away with you. It can't be so mysterious—why should it?"

"I don't know—it's all very strange."

"Ask Uncle Henry—it's his canoe, though I've seldom seen him use it."

He was about to say it would be better not to ask Uncle Henry but checked himself. He was certain this track, the garage, the canoe, the empty bedroom, and the feigned indigestion had some kind of unity. But his suspicion was so lacking in corroboration that he felt unjustified in stating it. He would say nothing. He would wait and watch. Laura would be gone before Henry's return.

"I'm ravenous!" cried Laura. "How awful if the canoe was missing! You've put frightful ideas into my head."

The alarm was vain. As they regained the creek the canoe lay there, safely beached on the white sand. In a few minutes they had opened the basket and began eating hungrily. The sun at its zenith reigned in the azure heaven. There was not a breeze, the only sounds that invaded this land of the world's end were the cries of the wild fowl, the rustling of small things busy in the undergrowth.

VI

The last day of Laura's visit arrived. Charles rose with a heavy heart. The place would not be the same when she had gone. He began to feel oppressed by Great-Aunt Woodfall, he felt himself being drawn near to a violent collision of their wills. His detestation of Eugenie grew. The knowledge of it was tacit between them. They were polite to each other, their eyes saying more than their mouths. As for Emily, shy, smiling, and gentle, he felt sorry and protective towards her. All the spirit had been beaten out of her, not in the manner of Grace, who was a nonentity anyhow, and scarcely existed in the house, but by inference. Eugenie had an air of superiority towards her, the old lady treated her like a servant, to fetch and carry without thanks, to accept the burden of all the odd jobs without a murmur. All this did nothing to destroy the innate loveliness of Emily's character; like a saint she took grace from her domestic martyrdom.

"Where did you get those flowers—they're awful!" Eugenie would snap, after her sister had spent an industrious hour decorating the rooms.

"Why do you drop your voice like that?" her mother would complain, as she read something from a book or paper, under command.

For most of the day she escaped into the garden, where she worked hard. The wilderness blossomed under her care, but it was a victory won, inch by inch, in the teeth of insects, birds, animals, the merciless sun, the long weeks of drought, and, at times, the torrential rains that swept away the light subsoil.

"Has there ever been anybody?" asked Charles, as he and Laura set off for the swimming beach, their last visit to that delectable spot where the cypress grove ran down to the jade-green water.

"Yes—a doctor from Witterwittee. I remember him. He was called in when I had mumps, and he kept on calling until one day Grandma refused to send the launch across for him, when they signalled from the jetty. Poor Aunt Emily rushed up to her room, and I followed her, and found her standing at the window with field-glasses trained on the far shore, which she couldn't see for tears in her eyes."

"But why? Why shouldn't she have had a lover?" asked Charles.

"Grandma always hated anyone who threatened her sovereignty. My mother fled the place, you know. Grandma will tell you she wrecked her life, running off with a rapscallion. I've heard her say it, and it's been hard to forgive her. It is a lie, too. I'm sure my mother was happy, despite the hard life she led. My daddy adored her. I can hear him talking about her now, and see his face bright with his love of her—although he died when I was eight."

"Do you hate this place very much?" asked Charles, as they threaded their way through the cypress grove. The lake glistened beyond, sun-burnished. Laura paused ahead of him and turned.

"Oh, but I don't hate it—I love it! You know what they say—once you get Florida sand in your shoes you always return! Grandma Woodfall has been kind to me. You see, she is an autocrat, she enjoys power, and as I never threatened her rule, being a child, there was no conflict between us. My leaving spared us anything like that. Aunt Eugenie is another Grandma Woodfall—she likes power. She dominates Uncle Henry and Grace and Emily."

They came to the bathing-hut and undressed. They were both tanned with the sun. They swam out vigorously into the lake and lay on their backs, floating. The surface water was warm, but a foot below it was chilly. They were both good swimmers and teased each other, gambolling like a pair of dolphins.

They were tired when they reached the shore again and flung themselves on the hot, white sand. The heat baked them. Charles had plucked a frond from a palmetto growing near, and held it over his head, to shade his eyes from the sun. Presently, seeing Laura flat on her stomach, head buried between her arms, he let it brush her back, pricking her slightly with its sharp leaf tips. She sat up with a cry and wrenched the frond from him. He caught her wrists and they rolled over each other. She was strong and he was only just able to hold down her arms. They lay face to face, her breath coming quickly, her bosom rising and falling, her teeth shining as she wrestled and laughed in his grip. Then she ceased fighting, and mocked him with her eyes.

"Strong boy, aren't you?" she said, derisively.

He looked into her vivacious sea-blue eyes. It was like diving into deep water. He went down and down, dizzily, the blood drumming in his ears. He made no answer to her. Her parted lips, moist and red, her mouth dimpled at the corners with her smile, the sweep of her neck from ear to slim shoulder, hypnotized him in a trance of inexpressible beauty; she was the song of youth, desire, wordless adventure. For a moment all life hung suspended above a world of unreal thought. The silence that held him, as their eyes looked beyond sight, checked her laughter in a sudden awareness. His smooth face bent towards her and his mouth met hers, with gentle insistence. Thus stilled, unbreathing, their lives seemed full as a tidal pool that awaits the turn. Then, averting her face, she broke the spell. Her hand pressing against his throat fended his ardour from her.

"No, Charles—no, please!" she whispered.

"But, Laura—Laura," he urged, gazing down upon her, suppliant, intense.

She forced a laugh, born half in fear and half in pleasure. Then, sitting up, she feigned reproof.

"You mustn't misbehave!" she said, softly.

His eyes held hers, the protest ignored, his solemn face level with her shoulder as he rested on one elbow.

"Laura—you know, you must know! I can't let you go, Laura!" he cried. "You've changed the world for me."

"Charles, dear—you mustn't, please, please! You are spoiling everything."

"Spoiling—spoiling?" he repeated. "Laura——"

He saw her mouth tremble, a shadow had fallen between them.

"Charles—don't you know? Hasn't anyone told you about Paul?"

"Paul—Paul who?" he cried, the cold finger of fear touching his heart.

"My fiancé, Paul Korwienski. Oh, Charles, I'm sorry—forgive me!" she pleaded, seeing his pained face staring at her, all his brightness and ardour wilted.

"No—I didn't know. If I had known——"

He stopped speaking, and looked away. She saw the muscles of his cheek quiver. Then he turned to her, kindness lighting the hurt in his eyes.

"You must forgive me," he said, slowly, his hand finding hers and holding it. "I didn't know, Laura. Forgive me—and forget it."

She could not answer him for a few moments, only the pressure of her hand could speak for her. The lake glittered in front of them, a jay-bird chattered somewhere in the cypress grove, an errant wind drew a finger across the water, furring it in a dull track. They lay in silence. The beauty of the Florida morning was cruelly indifferent.

The sun had reached its zenith. It was time to return to the house.

"Shall we go?" he asked, standing up. He held out his hand and pulled her to her feet.

She stood before him, and they looked at each other, too baffled for words. Finding this silence unbearable, he forced a smile to his face and spoke.

"I'm an ill-mannered clown. I've not congratulated you. Tell me about him," he said, slipping his arm through hers as they began to walk towards the dressing-hut. "He's Polish? Is he in this country?"

"Yes—he's a professional pianist. I met him first in New York, two years ago—he was playing with the Philharmonic Orchestra at the Carnegie Hall. Someone had given my friend, Carol Bower, two tickets for the Friday afternoon performance. He played the Rachmaninov *Concerto*—he had studied with him—he was magnificent. Carol knew him, and we went behind afterwards. Then we went out to tea. I liked him. He was very gay and——"

"Handsome," interpolated Charles, fighting his bitterness. A Pole, one of those suave, hand-kissing foreigners. Odd that he hadn't a title, as ever.

"No—on the contrary, very plain, but with something."

"Something?" he echoed.

"In the eyes, the voice—the way he talked. A genius, Charles—don't laugh," she said.

"I'm not laughing—I'm hating a little bit."

"You're too nice for that, Charles."

"Why shouldn't I hate him, damn the lucky fellow!"

"You'd like him, Charles—everybody does. And when he plays——"

"But you're not marrying a pianist, I hope?" commented Charles.

"That's bitter!"

"I'm sorry, Laura," he said, repentant at once.

"I'm marrying the man."

"Go on. I'll behave—tell me about him. How old?"

"Twenty-eight—medium height, pale complexion, black hair——"

"A lot of it," Charles could not help saying.

"No—quite neat. He's delicate, talks English, French, and German fluently. His people have an estate in Poland, somewhere near Kraków. It's an enormous family, grandmothers, grandfathers, aunts, uncles, cousins, two sisters, three brothers —I think I've got it right. His father's dead. They all live in an enormous house."

"And are very poor. I suppose he's a prince at least?"

The words slipped out. He could have bitten his tongue.

She flushed, a hurt look was in her eyes.

"Yes. You think that's very clever of you?" she cried. "Let's not talk about it."

He had hurt her with his cynicism. She walked on ahead, slipping her arm from his.

"Laura—forgive me," he called, catching her arm. "I'm a worm, I can't take it. You see—you see—it's hit me very hard."

The pain in his eyes as he spoke to her melted her anger. He detained her with his hand, his voice sincere with regret. She was conscious, as she had been conscious from that first moment of their meeting, that here, for her acceptance, was a devotion, a flame that burned intensely, to which no woman could be insensible. His fine, grave face stirred her, and the touch of him had a communicable quality of strength and ardour. There was in him something that encompassed her with a sense of security. Whatever demands she might make on his loyalty, he would not fail.

She made no answer to his apology except to smile at him and take his arm. Without a word spoken, they reached the dressing-hut; and there, with an impulse of compassion, like one who has scolded a small boy and felt contrition, she suddenly held his face in her hands, and kissed him.

Even as he wondered at this swift assault, she turned and ran into her dressing-cabin.

VII

Laura departed soon after breakfast the next morning. Charles came down after a restless night to find her already in the hall, cool and lovely in a white costume, with a scarlet felt hat and a feather, stuck jauntily on one side of her head. They all breakfasted together, Grandma Woodfall having descended earlier than her custom, in order to accompany Laura to the station. Overnight Charles had made it unmistakably clear that he would go to Witterwittee with them.

Shortly before nine the launch took them across to the

mainland, the three sisters receding from view as they waved farewell from the jetty. Lincoln Robinson was waiting with the carriage. They began the long drive to Witterwittee through a landscape of orderly orange and grape-fruit groves. The morning was intoxicating. There was a tonic sharpness in the air, which was crystal clear. From a slight eminence the landscape of groves and scrub woodland spread in a great plain to the far, flat horizon. They passed groups picking in the groves. Mrs. Woodfall looked with a disapproving eye at a large canning factory springing up at the roadside. Its owner was eating up the surrounding groves by his efficiency and enterprise. A vast signboard depicted a lightly clad girl voluptuously reclining on a bed of oranges.

"Vulgar and impractical," asserted Mrs. Woodfall, as they drove past. She had had many a price-duel with the owner of the factory when he had come to buy her fruit.

The station came in sight at last. Farther north, Laura would join up with the New York express. They waited about ten minutes for the local train to come in. Charles had announced his own departure for England a week ahead.

"When you come through New York, you'll come and see me?—I shall be rehearsing at the Elysium," said Laura, "and I'm staying at the St. Regis."

He made no direct reply. It would be better not to see her, the wound would heal better. They said Time healed all things. At the moment he had no faith in that dictum. A dull ache was in the core of his heart.

The last moment had come. The coloured porter stood impatiently by the coach, waiting to pick up his yellow footstool. Laura kissed Grandma Woodfall. She turned to Charles, and took his hand. Tall, slender, grave, she thought he had never looked more attractive than at that moment, his sleek head shining in the vivid morning, his eyes contradicting the smile he gave her.

"Good-bye, Charles."

"Good-bye, Laura."

The little red hat, the pert feather, the clear sweet line of her chin, the trim figure, small feet high-arched on scarlet shoes, the image was clear beyond forgetting.

She climbed into the coach. The iron platform fell. The train ambled out noisily. Forgetting the old lady at his side, Charles watched it diminish down the line, drawing the heart out of him. When, finally, he turned to Great-Aunt Woodfall, he knew he had betrayed himself. She saved any comment until they were back in the carriage; then, as Robinson whipped up the horses, she spoke.

"That's the girl you should marry, Charles. She's throwing herself away on a trumpery Pole," she said, grimly, her eyes on his face. "Aren't you in love with her?"

He laughed awkwardly, embarrassed by her blunt attack.

"That's a thing already settled by Laura," he said.

"A pianist—a Pole and a pianist!" she cried, contemptuously. "Well, I suppose, like her mother, she's determined to make a mess of it."

"The tradition is impressive—Chopin, Paderewski," retorted Charles, annoyed by her disparagement. "Laura doesn't seem to have made a mess of anything, so far."

"So far is so short—there's time yet," said Mrs. Woodfall.

She leaned forward and poked the coachman in the small of his back with her parasol. "Faster!" she commanded.

With a clatter they rode down Main Street, through Witterwittee and out into the country. The miles of groves stretched before them, but it was not orange trees he saw as they rode on, raising the dust. It was Laura's face, wistful under the jaunty red hat. He never expected to see her again, but he would never forget that moment of farewell.

CHAPTER SIX

NOCTURNAL ADVENTURE

I

HENRY returned that evening from the orange-growers' conference at Orlando. He looked pale and seemed very anxious. Dinner proved a trying meal. Mrs. Woodfall was not talkative. Eugenie had that businesslike air which she assumed when things were not proceeding smoothly. Charles, depressed by Laura's departure, made a vain attempt to appear cheerful, but his effort collapsed early. The meal went on in moody silence. Charles tried to believe that the heavily charged atmosphere was due to the change in the weather. A hot wind straight off the Mexican Gulf had sent the temperature up into the seventies. The air was heavy and moist.

After dinner, they moved into the drawing-room, where the fire had not been lit, so that the cheerfulness of its blaze was absent. Charles played backgammon with Great-Aunt Woodfall, and to her annoyance won eighteen dollars. He was beginning to know the technique of her game and was no longer such easy prey. At the close of play she commanded Emily to read. They had finished *The Ring and the Book* and had now embarked on Wordsworth's *Excursion*. The pedestrian verse seemed suitable to one who had been a great walker, thought Charles. Even the old lady nodded and brought herself back to consciousness with a jerk. When the clock struck eleven she arose and dismissed them all to bed.

Charles was not tired, and he was in no mood for sleep. He moved the lamp on to a small table at the side of a chaise-longue and, lighting his pipe, a thing he had never dared to do in the drawing-room, tried to settle down to reading. Cousin Emily had given him a novel produced by a local writer which dealt with the Florida countryside. To his surprise it was excellent, and he was already half-way through the story of the early settlers in the scrublands. He had just settled down with his book when a hideous racket broke the silence of the night. He recognized the sound at once. It was the screeching of Darwin and his entourage, who generally slept in the magnolia trees at the end of the garden. Something must have disturbed them.

Going to the window Charles raised the blind and, shading his eyes from the interior light, peered out. The waning moon, high in the sky, was riding swiftly through a billowy sea of white clouds. The silver light came and went on the lake-water at the end of the avenue of live oaks. There had been a lurid sunset, the upper sky pale green, the horizon glowing with crimson and orange against which the woodland stood dense and black. It seemed to promise a storm coming up rapidly, but after a short blow the evening had again become breathless. Charles listened. An intense silence enwrapped the garden and the woods. The monkeys had ceased their uproar as suddenly as they had begun it.

Charles drew down the blind and returned to the chair and his book. He must have been reading about an hour when a faint pulsing sound made him listen intently. There was no doubt about it. Outside in the night, very faint, there was something which sounded like the rhythmic beat of an engine. It grew and faded, but slowly came nearer, with an undulating pulsation as though a door were being opened and closed between him and the sound.

Charles rose and again went to the window, but, before going, turned down the lamp on the table so that the room was almost in darkness. Then he moved to the window, and raised the blind to look out. He had forgotten that the window, like all the windows and doors in the house, was screened against insects, but only the lower half. He lowered the top half, and had an unobstructed view of the sky. The sound came nearer, and he knew now what it was. An aeroplane was flying through the night, in the direction of the island. He listened intently.

Except for the plane which had visited the groves for the dusting, not one had flown over Lake Witterwittee during the whole of his visit. They were right off the track of modern civilization. The nearest aerodrome, Charles had learned, was thirty miles away, at Lake Wales. This plane, therefore, was a singular nocturnal visitor. To his surprise it drew nearer and nearer. He waited and watched the sky, for the thing could not be very far away now; the pulsations grew louder and louder, and developed into the steady hum of a machine almost overhead. A sudden silence told him the engine had been switched off. It came on again with spasmodic reverberations, much nearer and lower. Without any doubt the machine was now over the island, and it seemed to be landing.

Charles listened, excited and mystified. Had the pilot lost his course? Perhaps it was a hydroplane and was landing on the lake, which would be visible in the moonlight. Even as he speculated, with a chortling of its engine, the plane swept between him and the moonlit sky, a greyish object, not very high above the tree-tops. It could not be going to make a lake landing, for it came inwards, over the cypress grove. It must be landing somewhere towards the orange groves.

The sound receded. He listened intently. It had filled the night with dramatic suspense. Was the pilot going to crash? It was dangerous landing among these groves. There was only one place, about a mile away, a long sandy fairway used by the dusting plane. It might be landing there, but a strange pilot, flying in the night, would not be likely to attempt such a landing, for the fairway was unmarked.

Whoever he was, whatever the risk, he had attempted it. The engine had suddenly died out. Not a sound broke the stillness of the night. Charles waited by the window. The silence was absolute. He drew the blind, went back to his chair, and turned up the lamp. But he could not read; his mind wandered from the page, speculating upon the cause of this nocturnal visitor. He might have thought that it was the pilot who had come again to dust the groves, but in answer to one of his inquiries the grove foreman had told him the dusting was finished. Moreover, it was extremely unlikely that the pilot would arrive in the dead of night, risking such a landing.

For a time, he puzzled over the mysterious visitor. Then, aware that his curiosity would keep him awake, he put on the shoes he had removed, found the pocket torch he kept in a drawer, and turning down the lamp, went to the door and stepped into the dim corridor. There was no lamp burning. Stealthily, picking his way on tiptoe, he passed Henry's bedroom door, and then Eugenie's. The stairs creaked abominably as he descended to the dark well of the hall. He paused several times, afraid that the creaking would awaken some of the household. He considered briefly how he could explain this nocturnal excursion if someone suddenly confronted him. Well, he could plead insomnia and a desire to walk in the night air.

The main door was reached safely. With the aid of the torch and, feeling like a burglar, he manipulated the three bolts, and the main and subsidiary locks on the heavy old door. He turned the handle and it swung back soundlessly. Then he stepped out on to the wide verandah, and closed the door behind him, having taken the precaution to fasten back the slip latch. He stood, watchful on the verandah, hearing, in the heavy, still night, his own breathing quickened by this adventure.

The passage of the lawn, towards the small gate that opened on to a path through the woods, had one peril. The monkeys, hearing him, might make a sudden alarm, for he had to cross right in front of the magnolia tree where they slept. As he feared, the moment he came by the tree there was a sudden outburst of screeching and gibbering that seemed to fill the night. He hurried on, leaving the uproar behind him. Thank goodness, Darwin and his associates did not attempt to follow. He hurried through the wood, eerie in the half-light of the moon, which at times was covered by the scudding clouds. The heavy trees with their falling curtains of moss seemed like watchful giants. He heard a scurrying of live things in the undergrowth and was comforted by past assurances that all snakes had been killed on the island.

In five minutes he had come to the edge of the grove, and the clearing, leading to the orange groves on the east side of the island, came into view. The lake glistened on his left, its shore-line dramatically fringed with palm trees. He hurried on and came to the first orange grove, an old one. This was the most unpleasant part of the journey. The path led into the heart of the grove, and it was here, where the old trees were so thickly branched and overgrown that even in the noonday there was gloom, that the early settlers, killed in their feuds, had been buried. Only a few of the crude inscriptions on the small tombstones still remained. Who was Ebenezer Obadiah Walker, dead in 1888, wondered Charles, as he read one inscription. In a more pretentious grave, marked by a kerb and a well-kept headstone, slept Captain Arthur Woodfall, consort of Josephine Woodfall, aged thirty-two. With a shock Charles, on reading that inscription, learned how young his great-uncle had been when he met his violent end.

Past the tombstone, lighting his way through the blackness with the aid of his torch, Charles walked on. He came next to the newer graves. It was easier going now down the avenues between the trees. The orange blossom pervaded the warm night with its scent. Another half-mile through the groves, and he began to ascend the only eminence on the island. From it there was a view of the house and the lake. It also commanded a view of the clearing used as a fairway for the dusting-plane.

Charles was half-way up the slope when he was startled by the sudden noise of an engine being started up. There was no longer any question whether the plane had alighted on the island. The engine spluttered, and began to 'rev' up. It seemed to roar in the night, now that he drew closer. He wondered why the engine had been started up again, and, even as he wondered, the answer came, leaving him standing dumbfounded. With a roar the plane seemed to charge in his direction. Suddenly up above the top of the trees a grey mass passed. It was the plane in flight again. With a roar it took off into the night, and soon the reverberations in the upper air had faded away. The machine was going northwards. It had a single propeller, but the light was too bad and its passage too quick for him to gather any details of its make. It might or might not be the plane with which the groves were dusted.

Charles stood still in the shadow of the long line of orange trees. The moon came out of a cloud and lit the green avenue. The runway lay vacant. It was then that he saw two smudge-pots burning. They might be pilot lights. Why should the plane make a landing for such a brief stay? Obviously the place was well known to the pilot. He had descended, not because he must, but because he wished to. That being so, argued Charles, as he stood there, he had a mission of some kind. Either he had got out of the plane to deliver or collect something, or if he had not got out, then, most probably, there was someone in the grove awaiting the machine, some-one who might even have gone off in it as a passenger.

It was very mysterious. The perspiration broke out on his brow. The night was warm. If someone had got out of or into the plane there would be footmarks in the sand. He decided to go and inspect the landing-place more closely.

Charles soon picked up the track made by the undercarriage of the plane where it had first touched the sand. He could not help admiring the quality of the landing. It had been skilful. Presently he came to the end of the track where the machine had finally stopped; but he saw at a glance that all clues had been obliterated in the ruts made by the turning of the plane for its take-off.

He played his torch over the ground. His search was unre-warding, the surface was too churned up by the wheels and the tail-prop for footprints. But in turning away he chanced to notice a path that led off from the runway, in between the lines of the grove. The sand was trodden down into a beaten path by passing feet. He began to follow it, and after a hundred yards it suddenly ran clear of the groves, coming to a young plantation. Beyond, to his surprise, there were some outbuildings, a projection of the main sheds in which the crates and the tractors were stored.

Charles was about to cross the plantation when he was startled by the opening of a door in the shed. A light wavered in the darkness, from a torch that was held by someone. Quickly Charles drew back into the cover of an orange tree. Two men came out of the shed, and the one with the torch, which he now put out, led the way along the path across the plantation. They were coming towards the orange grove, and, afraid of detection, Charles hurriedly withdrew into the deeper cover of the trees. From this vantage-point he watched the men approach.

Neither of them spoke. They walked slowly up the path, but before they reached the grove they turned aside. One of the men was carrying a bag. Evidently there was another path running down the side of the plantation, and Charles remembered, then, that it cut across one end of the grove and, skirting a cypress wood, led down to the boathouse and landing-stage on the lake. It was possible, if his surmise were correct, to intercept these mysterious visitors, by cutting across the orange grove. By waiting in the wood near the landing-stage, to which he was now certain they were proceeding, he could get a near view of the men without revealing himself.

Charles almost ran through the orange grove and reached the open wood so much in advance of the two men that, after waiting a time and seeing no one, he began to wonder if he had miscalculated. There might be some other path of which he did not know. His misgiving was soon dispelled by a wavering pool of light coming through the wood. Darting behind the trunk of an old cypress tree, within sight of the landing-stage and the moonlit lake, Charles waited. Presently they passed him, so close that he could identify the man with the torch. Without any doubt it was Cousin Henry.

They passed unaware that they were being watched. When they gained the landing-stage Henry said something to his companion and disappeared into the boathouse. The stranger put down the portmanteau he was carrying, and, removing his Homburg hat, proceeded to wipe his brow with a pocket handkerchief. The night was warm, and the walk from the shed had made him perspire.

Slipping from trunk to trunk Charles got so near to the landing-stage that he could clearly see the face of the stranger, who looked up at the sky as he fanned himself with the handkerchief. He was a middle-aged man of medium height, dressed in a well-cut, double-breasted suit. On his left arm he carried an overcoat. The face, now lit by brilliant moonlight, for the moon had come out of the racing clouds, was that of a man of about fifty, clean-shaven, with a long, thin nose. The mouth, compressed and turned down at the corners, together with the long nose gave the face a Dantesque air. It was finely modelled and saturnine, but the most noticeable features were the hair and the eyebrows. The darkish hair was so thick, brushed back from the brow without any parting, that it gave him a leonine appearance. He had very bushy eyebrows, bushy almost to a point of caricature, and his eyes, sunk deeply, peered out from underneath them.

Presently as he stood there, Henry appeared in view, paddling the canoe from the boathouse. The stranger put on his hat, picked up his bag and advanced to the edge of the stage. Here, Henry, now alongside, took on board the portmanteau and the overcoat. Then, while he held the canoe firmly to the stage, the stranger got in, not an easy operation, for he was heavily built and somewhat clumsy in his movements.

When he was safely seated in front of Henry, the canoe pushed off. It took a course straight down the lake, going northwards, exactly as Charles had expected. For in that direction, in a wilderness of saw-grass and mangrove roots, ran the narrow creek leading to the hammock on which he and Laura had discovered the garage.

Charles watched the canoe slowly ride out into the lake, diminishing from view, a black object silhouetted against the glistening moon-flecked water. The owner of the car in that hidden garage was now revealed. But for what purpose, in the dead of night, in circumstances of so much mystery, was Cousin Henry conveying up the lake a man who had reached the island by plane?

Here was a mystery indeed. The sense of something elusive in the atmosphere of Sundown Grove had not been the result of his imagination. Behind the tranquil façade he had been aware of a life hidden from his sight. Just what that life was he had no idea, but the events of this night had given reality to his surmise that some strange business, masked by the exaggerated conventionality of the Woodfall household, lay under the direction of Great-Aunt Woodfall. He had no doubt that, whatever was afoot and whatever part Henry played in it, Mrs. Woodfall was the directing force.

When the canoe had faded from sight, Charles, on his way back to the house, had a sudden curiosity concerning the shed from which the conspirators had emerged. He went back on the track and approached the building where he had first seen the light held by Henry. The door was unlocked, and he entered, flashing his torch around. It was a small room evidently used as a kind of office. It had a high ledger-desk, three chairs, and a ledger-rack; but what held his astonished sight was a large tray on a table. It contained a dirty plate and a drinking-glass. Someone had been having a meal. Charles examined the plate: it was marked with smears of crab meat. That night at dinner they had had crab meat, a speciality, so Mrs. Woodfall had informed him, that came over from Tampa, on the Gulf. This meal, therefore, had been sent from the house. It suggested that the visitor had ended a journey whose distance created hunger. Then Charles laughed at himself for being so fanciful. Some clerk or workman might have been eating there. On the best house china? His nostrils caught an odour in the air. It was stale tobacco smoke.

Closing the door Charles took the direct path that led back to the house, on the kitchen side. It would be easy to carry the tray across to the shed, the whole way by the high hibiscus hedge. Who had carried the meal there—Jefferson?

Charles looked up at the windows, a little apprehensively, as if fearful that the ubiquitous butler might be watching him. He made his way around the house, across Cousin Emily's garden, until the magnolia tree was in view. The moon was clouded over again, and he had to pick his way cautiously until he struck the path leading up from the lake. Again he was afraid of arousing the monkeys, but he got past the tree safely. He looked up at the house. Not a light showed.

He opened the great door, closed it, and stood for a moment in the dark hall. The grandfather clock at the foot of the stairs spaced the silence with its beat. He began the ascent of the staircase, treading as lightly as he could. He had almost gained the landing when the sudden opening of a door flooded it with light. Startled, he looked up at the apparition of Great-Aunt Woodfall. She stood above him, holding a porcelain-shaded lamp in her hand. She wore on her head a white mob-cap, and was wrapped in a heavy, brown dressing-gown. But it was her face that brought him to a standstill on the stairs. Pale in the lamplight, her eyes glowed with anger, the whole of her face expressing undisguised malignancy. She was a frightening spectacle of hate. Poise and dignity had fallen from her, and the withered repugnancy of extreme age showed itself in her quivering face.

"What are you doing—prowling about the house at this time of night?" she demanded, in a voice vibrant with passion.

"I've been out for a walk. I'm sorry if I've disturbed you," said Charles, calmly.

"Disturbed me! I don't expect to have my guests wandering about in the early hours of the morning! You woke me up —where have you been?"

"Out for a short walk," he said. He would not mention what he had seen. He would keep a close watch.

She looked at him with her hard, bright eyes, surveying him from head to foot.

"Haven't you been to bed at all?" she asked, seeing he was fully dressed.

"No—I began reading. I suppose I dozed off. Then the

night seemed so lovely I was tempted to go out. I'm sorry if I've frightened you."

He knew he had not frightened her; she was not the kind of woman anything could frighten. She must be an extremely light sleeper to have heard him, for he had moved catlike up the creaking stairs. And then he saw something that told him she had lied. She had not been awakened by him. She had not been to bed. Her dressing-gown, hitched up by the arm holding the lamp, revealed her black evening dress below. She was wearing not slippers but leather shoes, and at a glance he saw where the dust on them, the dust of the sand from the groves, as on his own, had been swept off by the trailing gown.

"Please don't walk about the place at night, if you can't sleep. It's most unpleasant to feel people are prowling around. The slightest thing disturbs me. Good night, Charles," she said, standing aside for him to pass. Her face had regained its set expression.

"Good night, Aunt Josephine," he answered.

She waited while he went down the corridor to his room, then she entered hers.

For a few moments he stood still inside his dimly lit bedroom. His heart was thudding, his brain racing. Step by step he was advancing into this maze of deceit. What would he find at the centre of it, if ever he reached the centre? Two participants in this strange affair had been uncovered: first, Cousin Henry, and now Great-Aunt Woodfall, for he could not doubt that she had played a part in the reception of the nocturnal visitor. Those dusty shoes and her dress proved she, too, had been out of the house. Her anger had betrayed her also. She had made an error in challenging him on the stairs. Henceforth they would be curiously watching each other, their visors down.

II

The next morning, as soon as he had breakfasted, Charles went out into the garden and made his way down to the boat-house. The canoe was there. Presumably Henry had returned. He seldom was present at breakfast, so his absence was not significant. Charles wandered across to the stables to saddle a horse for his morning ride. He never went out without thinking of his companion on other rides. The thought of her still obsessed him day and night. He heard her voice, saw the light in her eyes when he came to spots where they had spent such happy hours together. The bathing beach was almost unbearable now.

He rode down to it, bathed, and left again. The silence depressed him, the ache in his heart grew heavier. He wondered how long she had known this Paul Korwienski, for he had forgotten to ask her any details when she mentioned his name. Her engagement, he learned from Aunt Emily, was quite recent. He had never visited the house. They knew nothing about him. "My mother dislikes the engagement, I know," said Emily, "but she is too fond of Laura to interfere. And I don't suppose Laura would let her," she added, with her quiet smile.

Charles turned his horse in the direction of the upper groves, on the ridge of ground that commanded a view of the islands. When he had gained this vantage-point he found what he sought. The men were picking in the tangerine grove. He could not see Henry, but he hoped he might find him there.

In a few minutes, galloping through the sunny air, he came to the grove. Henry was standing beside a tractor, dressed as usual in khaki shirt, gaberdine riding-breeches, and laced leather top-boots. Charles dismounted and greeted him.

"Try one," said Henry, offering him a tangerine. It was Henry's characteristic gesture. Laura and he had often made fun of Henry. "Try one!" they would shout at each other, thrusting out a hand. They had both tasted oranges and drunk orange juice until they had no desire to see another.

This time Charles accepted the proffered fruit.

"I hope we shall finish this grove to-day," said Henry. "It's been a good tangerine year—but unfortunately there's not much demand for them."

He surveyed the boxes, each filled with fruit and bearing the picker's ticket number. The truck was collecting the boxes as it came along each avenue.

"Good, isn't it?" asked Henry, skinning a tangerine for himself. He was more genial than usual. He talked about the groves they had still to pick. He gave no sign of being suspicious, yet it was almost certain his mother had told him about last night's incident. For a person who had probably not been to bed all night he looked remarkably fresh. Charles resisted a desire to ask him about the aeroplane and the canoe trip. He would only be told lies. He might yet find a clue to the mystery.

But throughout the remainder of his visit there was no clue. Life flowed on quietly at Sundown Grove. Great-Aunt Woodfall never referred to his nocturnal adventure. Dinner was as elaborate as usual, and after dinner there were the backgammon and the reading. Charles lost heavily at backgammon these evenings. His mind wandered. He had, in fact, become bored with life at the Grove. There was a monotony in these unchanging sunny days, the quick lurid sunsets of orange and crimson, the dragging formal evenings in the heavy drawing-room. The sparkle had gone out of everything with the departure of Laura. He found he could not concentrate on anything. He had ridden all over the island several times, and began to feel like a prisoner. And all the time he was conscious that he was watched, by the old lady, by Henry, Eugenie and, he was sure, by Jefferson, the butler. There had been no further visitation by plane. Cousin Henry had had no attacks of dyspepsia, confining him to his bedroom. When, one evening, Charles suggested cutting short his visit by several days he thought the old lady seemed relieved.

"We can't be very amusing for you here in this backwater—we lead very simple lives. It's been very delightful to have you here—I hope you'll come again," she said.

"Oh, please don't go yet—I was hoping you'd stay through February," cried Emily, looking up from her sewing.

"I am sure Charles has had more than enough of us," said Eugenie, directing the remark to her sister.

"Oh, no—really, I've had a splendid time," asserted Charles.

So it was settled that he would leave on the coming Thursday, for New York, *en route* for England. He was homesick now, or thought it was homesickness. Laura was in New York, but he would not go to see her. Why probe that wound?

The day before his departure he made a proposal to Cousin Emily. She talked so much of England. It was the land of her dreams. She knew its history, she had travelled in fancy to all the famous haunts.

"I've a little model relief map of Great Britain up in my bedroom, and oh, Charles, I can almost believe I'm there! I touch the map and I am on the mountains, the Lake District, with Helvellyn where Wordsworth went walking with his sister Dorothy. And then I follow the valleys, and the rivers —the Avon at Stratford, and Henley, where you live, and the Thames. And I go north into Scotland, to Melrose and Loch Lomond. I go everywhere, Charles. I shut my eyes and let my finger wander, and I see England!"

"Then you must visit us," he said.

"Oh, that would be wonderful—but I never shall," she sighed, as they sat together on the bench in front of the garden pool, where she fought a losing battle for her goldfish against the household cats.

"Why not? Look! You come away with me now. We'll go straight back to England. You'll be in time for the spring, you'll see Henley Regatta. We'll tour the Lakes and Scotland and go to the summer Shakespeare Festival at Stratford——"

He stopped. There were tears filling her eyes.

"Oh, if I could—if I could!" she murmured.

"Of course you can! You'll come with me, and stay with Mother and Uncle Wyndham—there's nothing to stop you," he cried, catching hold of her arm. He felt her tremble with excitement.

She looked at his eager young face beside hers. All the joy

and strength of youth filled him, in a world full of adventure. The presence of this handsome young cousin, with his alert mind, his quick response to everything about him, had been like a cool fresh breeze in the stagnation of her life at Sundown Grove.

"Charles dear—I couldn't. You see, Mother would not like me to leave her. She——"

"Oh, Mother be damned!" he exclaimed, impetuously. "I'll deal with her. She's trampled on you long enough."

"Charles, please—you mustn't say such things! Ever since Father died Mother has disliked being left. We're a united family—and now that she's so old and needs attention——"

"Rubbish, Emily!" he cried, interrupting her again. "Why, she's as strong as a horse and will outlive all of you. Have you never been away?"

"We've been to Jacksonville, to Savannah—and once, some years ago, we visited New Orleans," she answered. "But there were difficulties, leaving the groves, and the cost of it."

"Do you mean to say you have to stick here year after year, being fried alive, through all the summer? Doesn't it get frightful?" he asked, appalled at her revelation.

"Yes—it does get very trying."

"That settles it, you're coming with me. She can spare one of you—it's nonsense! We're leaving on Thursday. Leave it to me—and you're my guest, you're going to England for six months, and if you like it we'll keep you longer!"

She looked at him, his face lit with excitement at the idea. She liked to see him happy again. She had not missed the cloud that had settled upon him after Laura's departure, and her sympathetic nature knew the cause of his wretchedness. Young love was for ever beyond her, but it still called to her blood.

"Charles dear—it's wonderful of you," she said, quietly, "but please don't ask Mother. It will upset her, and my sisters, too. We have never been separated."

"Upset her—it's time she was upset! I'll deal with it, leave it to me," he repeated.

She threw him a startled look, and he felt her tremble again.

"Oh, Charles—don't speak of Mother like that. She's very wonderful, you know—we owe everything to her," she pleaded.

"Wonderful! My heavens! She's an old tyrant—she's sucked all your blood. It's time——"

He broke off, seeing the colour on her face.

"I'm sorry, Emily. I'll be diplomatic," he said, rising with her from the bench. "We'll have a few days in New York, and then Southampton, London, Henley—oh, you'll love it!"

She smiled at him, but with no relief in her heart.

"Perhaps you'll see Laura in New York," she said, greatly daring.

"Laura!" he repeated, and stood still, his eyes gazing across the garden. "No—I'll not see Laura."

"Charles—I'm so grieved for you," she said, quietly, after a pause.

He made no answer, but his arm pressed hers. They walked towards the house. Then he spoke.

"I'll get over it, I suppose. I must," he said. "But it's—it's hit me hard."

He tried to smile at her, but a trembling lip betrayed him.

"Oh, Charles!" was all she could say, finding no adequate words to comfort this boy in the misery of his love.

III

He chose his moment carefully. Just before tea-time he found Great-Aunt Woodfall sitting on the screened verandah, amid the shrill singing of her five cages of canaries. She was reading the London *Times*. The death of King George had turned all eyes upon England. Then one morning, soon after breakfast, they heard over the radio the burial service for the King, in far-away St. George's Chapel, Windsor. It had been a strangely moving experience to sit there in the golden sunshine of a Florida morning, amid the tufted palms, the great live oaks and cypresses, with the lake glistening in the distance, and hear the solemn words of the service, the military tread of the pall-bearers, the trumpets, the soul-stirring voices of the choristers. And about them, as they listened, the morning was alive with bird-song. Scarlet cardinals called and flashed their wings as they dipped to the pond, the canaries had to be silenced, the jays screeched irreverently. Great-Aunt Woodfall had promptly gone into mourning, Henry had put on a black band.

She was reading about the ceremonies now, in the copy of *The Times* which had just reached her.

"Dear Mr. Baldwin made a beautiful speech in the House of Commons," observed the old lady, as Charles came on to the verandah.

"Mr. Baldwin does make beautiful speeches—he's hypnotized them, and himself too. If only he'd govern the country!" commented Charles, acidly.

"Whatever do you mean?"

"I mustn't ride my hobby-horse. They call me Cassandra at home," said Charles, smiling grimly. "There they all sit in a day-dream, while Germany sharpens a knife with which to slit our throats."

"I think you exaggerate. The Germans have learnt their lesson," said Mrs. Woodfall.

"They have—but we haven't learnt ours. I've spent three holidays in Germany; I know!" declared Charles.

"That is the common prerogative of youth," retorted the old lady. "I am sure Mr. Baldwin knows what he is doing."

"He does indeed. What alarms me is that the rest of my countrymen don't know what he's doing—or isn't doing."

"You should tell them, if you think they would listen to you, Charles," retorted Mrs. Woodfall, sarcastically. "I expect they prefer Mr. Baldwin, with all his experience."

His blood mounted. He longed to do battle with the old dragon, but he had come on a diplomatic mission. He ignored her challenge.

"I was talking to Emily yesterday about England. She tells

me she has a relief map—and it fills her with longing to go there," he said, quietly.

"We all have that longing—it never dies in us."

"When were you last in England?" he asked.

"Fifty years ago. My husband and I had always hoped to get home for a holiday, but he died before our wish was fulfilled. I've never left the States. I've always had to look after the groves."

"Why don't you visit us—Henry can take charge?"

"Henry?" she asked, her voice rising. "Henry has no idea how to run anything—none of my children has any business instinct. Eugenie is the most capable. You have no idea, Charles, what a bitter struggle I have had to keep this roof over our heads."

"I wonder if you could spare Emily? She dreams so of going to England. I've asked her to be my guest for the trip," said Charles.

Mrs. Woodfall dropped the paper to her lap. She took off her steel-rimmed spectacles and put them into their black case with a snap.

"It is very kind of you—but that is quite impossible," she said.

"Why impossible? As I am going, she could——"

"It is for me to decide. I have said it is impossible," interrupted Mrs. Woodfall.

"But, Aunt Josephine—it won't cost anything, she's dying to go—we'd all be delighted. We'd show her——"

"My daughters are not free to run about."

"Run about! Heavens, why, Emily tells me——"

"If Emily is disloyal enough to complain, I don't expect you to encourage her disobedience. I see it is a conspiracy."

"Oh, rubbish!" exclaimed Charles, hastily, and then, seeing the stare that met him, knew he had blundered. "Oh, I'm sorry. But why can't Emily come with me?"

"Because I do not wish it. We'll say no more about it," replied Mrs. Woodfall. "And please do not disturb the tranquillity of my home by these inconsiderate invitations."

"Inconsiderate!" exclaimed Charles. "I think it is you who are inconsiderate! They aren't children. They want to see the world, they ought to see it. They can't go on living here like caged canaries—really, Aunt Josephine, I think you should give them a little liberty."

The old lady stood up. In her anger he was reminded of a cobra about to strike.

"I shall be much obliged if, after your insulting attack on your hostess, you'll make it convenient to leave here as soon as possible," she said, her voice cold with hate.

"Certainly—I see you can't take it," he retorted, angrily.

"I think I understand your vulgarism. How dare you, you insolent boy!" flared Mrs. Woodfall. "You thrust yourself upon me, spy about my house, talk disloyally to my children——"

"A moment, Aunt Josephine. You aren't going to treat me in the way you treat what you call your 'children,'" said Charles, firmly. "It is a lie to say I have thrust myself upon you. I came as a result of repeated invitations. You say I spy on you. Some things here have aroused my curiosity, I'll admit. There's something odd going on, I couldn't ignore that——'

"Ignore what—why not specify your charges?" said the old lady, her face hard in repressed anger.

"Must I? Very well. What is going on here? Why does an aeroplane come here in the dead of night, dropping its passenger? Why these lies about Henry's indigestion and headaches, when he's not in his room? Why does he take a mysterious stranger, dropped out of the plane, two hours' journey by night in a canoe to a creek where he's got a car in hiding?"

"You are contemptible and crazy! So this is how you abuse my hospitality. I won't attempt to answer your ridiculous fancies!"

"Fancies?"

They looked at each other. Never had Charles seen such hate in a human face. The shrunken flesh scarcely shrouded the skeleton beneath, and Death stood there, held in leash by the intense vitality of those glowing eyes. The spirit, corrupt though it seemed to him then, mastered the body and endowed her with forbidding power. He saw her sway slightly, but the fire in her eyes never diminished. She met his challenge with a courage that conceded no inch in the stand she made. She was the first to speak, breaking that terrible silence.

"You will leave my house at once. You cannot expect me to harbour you a minute longer after your vile slanders. I shall tell Jefferson to pack your bags. You can catch the Express, which connects with Witterwittee. Please be ready to leave in one hour," she said, in a cool, level voice.

"Very well," answered Charles.

With her head high, indignation expressed in every line of her body, registering her contempt of him, she passed into the house. The canaries sang on, shrilly. Charles took out a handkerchief and mopped his face. Then he went out into the garden.

He found Emily working as hard as ever among her azaleas. She was on her knees, pressing in the earth around a new plant which she had just bedded. As he came towards her she got up, clapping her hands to shake off the soil. She looked very frail under her enormous straw hat, but he knew from the amount of work she did in the garden that she was wiry. No one else seemed to bother with the garden.

"Something's happened?" she said, apprehensively, on seeing his grave face.

"I'm sorry, I've bungled it. I'm afraid I lost my temper with Aunt Josephine. I'm ordered out of the house—at once."

"Charles! And I'm the cause! Oh, Charles, I'm so distressed," she cried, rubbing her dress in nervous agitation.

"It's not because of you at all. It's——" He paused, knowing he could not give her the true reason. "I couldn't help telling her she was selfish. Emily, I've made an awful mess of it, forgive me."

She removed the big straw hat that hid her face and smiled up at him.

"I shall never forget your kindness, your wish for me to visit England. It was too much to hope. I knew that. I was born here, and I suppose I'm not ever likely to get anywhere else."

They looked at each other, and there was nothing he could say. She was the prisoner of an inexorably selfish old woman.

"Well—it's been lovely seeing you, Emily. There'll always be a welcome for you—you know that," he said, lamely.

"Yes—thank you, Charles. I hope you'll be happy."

There was another pause. Darwin went swinging from a bough, and called to his wives. They followed gibbering. Then all was quiet in the garden. The shadows were lengthening, the falling sun began to light up the under branches of the live oaks, and strike through the cypress wood.

"I'll be gone in about half an hour. Don't come into the house," he said. Then he put his arms around her and kissed her on each cheek. Tears had wetted them.

"Good-bye, Charles," she whispered, chokingly.

"Good-bye, Emily."

He held her for a few moments, and then, releasing her, he walked rapidly across the garden into the house.

Jefferson was in his room, packing, when he got upstairs. He did not know how much the butler knew, but he said nothing to enlighten him. Soon his bags were packed and carried down into the hall. Through the open door Charles could see the launch at the jetty. Lincoln Robinson came up the path to fetch the bags. To Charles's astonishment Great-Aunt Woodfall stood in the hall, dressed for going out.

"We have good time," she said, calmly, as his bags went out to the launch. She drew on her lavender gloves, and picked up a parasol.

"You——" he began, dumbfounded.

"We will keep up appearances," she said, quietly, as Jefferson carried out his coat and sticks.

"Eugenie and Grace——" he said, as she walked towards the door.

"They are resting upstairs," she answered.

He followed her down the path, and along the jetty to the launch. Jefferson waited until they were seated, then the boat began the crossing. The sun had reached the woods. The orange and crimson glow was reflected in the water. Smaller and smaller grew the island until it was a low, black line floating on a silver mirror.

The carriage awaited them. They made the journey into Witterwittee in silence. They were just on time. When Charles said "Good-bye" to his great-aunt she ignored his hand. "Good-bye," she repeated. Not another word escaped her.

IV

Charles had business in New York. He went straight to the Gotham Hotel, and rang up his literary agent. His play had been running for three months. He had another play in his bag, one he had begun in Hollywood and finished at Sundown Grove. There would be no difficulty in placing it. He was a first-class risk, his agent assured him. When he learned what his play was earning for him he tried not to feel dizzy. He began to feel the freedom and power of money, the many things he had dreamed of doing became possibilities. "Wait till they've finished taxing you," cautioned his agent. Charles was a little dismayed to discover that with agent's commission, income-tax in America, income-tax and surtax in England, he would receive about one-third of his earnings for himself. Happily the third seemed substantial.

He had booked his return passage on the *Aquitania* due to sail in five days' time. A celebrity of new vintage, he was flooded with invitations. He lunched and dined up and down Park Avenue, chiefly, he found, among the widowed and superannuated. In the scramble for diversion that afflicts the affluent unemployed, he found a few choice souls. And all the time, his vanity flattered as he basked in the warmth of exaggerated celebrity worship, he felt an undercurrent unhappiness. Laura was here in this city. He carefully avoided the Hôtel St. Regis, and fought a desire to telephone. Once, coming from a lunch at the Century Club, he found himself passing the Elysium Theatre, whose boards announced the forthcoming play, starring her name. Five days hence, he would be away from all possibility of self-torture.

There was almost a disaster on his last day in New York. On his arrival and departure from this hospitable city he had enjoyed the freedom of Mrs. Beverley Lipvander's stone palace on Fifth Avenue, a nineteenth-century fortress holding out against the engulfing sky-scrapers of twentieth-century business. Here in the galleried hall with its massive green malachite vase and tapestries, in the library, in the art gallery, the ballroom, the long *Régence* dining-room, the more intimate small dining-room with its exquisite French *boiserie*, the exclusive ghosts of the old Four Hundred retreated before the onrush of the vociferous Ten Thousand.

Yet something remained. He admired the deft grace with which his hostess dominated a dinner-table with forty-six guests, or kept the conversation flowing proportionately from behind the silver urn at tea-time in the library. And if, from tables laden with autographed photos of Royalty, there rose an Edwardian odour of a day for ever gone, he was glad to scent this backwater, strewn with old galleons of Fashion and Fame left by the outrunning tide.

It was in the library of this hospitable house, where some twenty guests were gathered for cocktails, preliminary to lunch, that Charles was suddenly startled out of his pleasant *tête-à-tête* with a Greek countess, of American endowment, by overhearing his hostess enumerating her guests to the Polish Ambassador.

"—and Laura Lanier with M'sieur Korwienski—you know him? He's engaged to her. I heard him last night with the New York Symphony—magnificent! Why is it you Poles are such wonderful pianists? I always go to——"

The butler announcing more guests broke the sentence. Charles desperately kept himself attentive to the Countess. He was trapped without any possibility of escape. The hum of conversation, mounting, American-fashion, to a strident competition of voices, deafened him beyond all hope of making any coherent response to his companion, and his mind deserted her reminiscent excursion down the Adriatic on the

Lipvander yacht. Panic seized him. To meet Laura here, to meet her with her fiancé, the ill-fortune of it overwhelmed him. His imagination leapt to the possibility that he might be placed at Laura's side for lunch.

His eyes watched the door, where guests still entered, and his hostess, her hair bound in a green bandeau, extended a glittering hand, and presented them to His Excellency. And then, solitary, flushed, a young man, conscious of his tardiness, hurried forward almost before the butler could announce, "Mr. Korwienski!" He kissed the hand of his hostess, and began an apologetic explanation. Straining, Charles caught the gist of it. Miss Lanier was much distressed, but she was held at the theatre by a rehearsal and, alas, would not be able to come. The young man bowed to his Ambassador. Charles lost him then in the crowd between them. The company began to move in to lunch.

At table, in the long *Régence* dining-room, he found himself seated between an Italian Marchesa, and the American wife of a tired Frenchman who expressed aloof decay. A Polish count, with a name like an eye-test, was opposite, and he heard him discussing the concert at which Korwienski had played the previous evening. Charles's eye surveyed the table. A visiting British battleship had contributed an admiral with a face like the rising sun, who sat on Mrs. Lipvander's left. He surrendered his hostess to the Ambassador, and was enjoying himself enormously with a pretty young woman, expensively and simply dressed. Next to her he found Paul Korwienski. He examined him critically, and found him agreeable. He was by no means good-looking, but he had an alertness that relieved his thin, pale face. The mouth was too large, and he gesticulated a little too much with his hands, which, despite his reputation as a pianist of genius, were stubby. Medium in height, with black hair, well-groomed, his eyes were the most striking feature about him. They were large and very alert, with an almost feverish brightness. He seemed to be amusing his companion greatly with something he was telling her.

Conscious that he had made several inconsequential replies,

his attention drawn to Korwienski, Charles devoted himself to the Marchesa for the rest of the lunch. She was musical. From her he obtained a brief outline of the Polish pianist's career. He was twenty-eight, had visited the States twice, and had made a conquest whenever he had appeared. He played as Mr. Korwienski. Actually he was Prince Korwienski, the eldest son of an old Polish family living near Kraków. He had just become engaged to Miss Laura Lanier, the actress.

"Just?" repeated Charles.

"Well—three or four months ago. I think she's fascinating. Have you met her?" asked the Marchesa. "Not a bit actressy —charming! And she's delightful. I'm having an afternoon party in my apartment at the St. Regis—she's staying there. He's coming; I'm getting him to play duets with Miss Arburton, who's a wonderful amateur. I'd like you to meet them, won't you come? You'd like them, I know. To-morrow at four."

"Thank you—but unfortunately I can't. I'm sailing to-night," he replied.

"For England—you're English! I didn't get your name."

He pushed his place-card forward for her to read.

"Woodfall. You've been visiting the States?" she asked, with engaging curiosity. A woman around fifty, she had lost none of the zest for life.

"Yes—I've been to Hollywood and——"

"Then you act—you look as if you act—you're decorative. I like decorative men," she said, with laughing frankness.

"No—I write," he replied. "I'm a dramatist."

"How interesting!" Then, dropping her hand to the table —"You didn't write *Good Morning, Children*?"

"Yes—that's mine."

"Oh!" she exclaimed, in discovery.

He knew that 'Oh!' and the halo of fame was freshly enjoyable. It made him like her still more.

"Then before you go you must meet Paul Korwienski. Who knows, one day his fiancée might act in one of your plays!" she said. "They're a charming pair."

To his surprise he assented, and, as the guests were crossing the great hall, after lunch, she found her opportunity to introduce them to each other. Charles's first pleasant impression was endorsed by their few words together. It became clear that Korwienski was highly strung. His thin face, lit with those brilliant eyes, had a nervous excitability. He was neurotic, judged Charles, but undeniably stamped with the mark of genius. It was not difficult to understand why Laura had felt his attraction.

Charles took leave of his hostess. This was his last engagement in New York. Nine hours later, the *Aquitania* slipped from the Cunard pier, slowly passed the window-lit panorama of Manhattan's sky-scrapers, as viewed off the Battery, and speeded for the open sea. He remained on deck while Long Island's line of coastal lights sparkled over the dark flood, and then, America dim on the horizon, he went below, sadly. He knew he had left there behind him something he could never recover, his singleness of heart.

In his cabin there were books, papers, and flowers, some last letters, and telegrams from friends, hospitable to the end. He opened the telegrams first. The third one set his heart pounding. Transfixed with astonishment and pleasure, even though it increased his burden of despair, he stood reading the three words over and over. "Bon voyage. Laura," it ran.

CHAPTER SEVEN

HENLEY ROYAL REGATTA

I

THE doctor being the first down, sorted out the letters the maid had placed on the hall table. Among them was one with an Italian stamp, marked Venezia. It was for his sister-in-law, from Charles in Venice. He put it aside, and with half a dozen letters in his hand went into the study. A few minutes later he heard young Peter come bounding in with the dogs, after his bathe in the river.

" 'Morning, Uncle!" called Peter, rosy from his swim, seeing Dr. Woodfall through the open study door.

"Oh, good morning, my boy," exclaimed the doctor, and, rising, put out his hand as his nephew came in. "My very best wishes, Peter, my dear boy. Twenty-one to-day! I confess I don't like this leap into manhood, for I've lost the nicest boy alive—but bless you!"

The old doctor put his arm around his nephew and kissed him, then held him off and looked at the young giant proudly. Tall, broad, his muscular chest was set firm under the clinging polo sweater. The doctor often wondered how Mary and his brother, both so meagre in build, had produced such a bounding young giant.

"I hope it's going to be a double event to-day," said the doctor, alluding to the final race, for which Peter's boat had qualified at the Regatta yesterday.

"I jolly well hope so, sir!" cried Peter, who was rowing number two. "Letters?" he asked, seeing the doctor's correspondence.

"Yes—there's one from Charles, for your mother, on the hall table."

"Any for me?"

"No—I fear not," said the doctor. "I must say I thought there would be. I think Charles might have written—he's only one brother—and you're only twenty-one once."

"Oh, don't worry, sir. Charles was always a rotten letter-writer. I don't bother him much!" replied Peter, cheerfully. "He'll write some time—perhaps there's a note in Mother's. I'll take hers up."

He bounded out of the room, picked up the letter on the hall table and raced up the stairs, two at a time.

That brother in Venice should have written, mused the doctor, filling his pouch for the day from the tobacco-jar, the very one Charles had given him for his sixtieth birthday. Something had happened to the lad, he had changed. Ever since that trip to the United States he had been restless and moody. Success seemed to have had on him the reverse effect from that on most men. It wasn't vanity that made Charles so grave, there wasn't a spark of vanity in the lad, he was sure of that. Would he be the old Charles when he came home again? And when was he coming home again? These last two years he had been a ceaseless wanderer. Within two months of his return from Florida he had gone off again, immediately after his second play had opened in London, another bumping success. Paris, Milan, Berlin, Vienna, four months abroad, then home for a month, then off again, and a whole year of running about the Continent. It had produced a third play.

His last visit home, last September, had been almost disastrous. He had grown irritable, and had lost all his characteristic buoyancy. A symptom, utterly surprising in one so level-headed as Charles, had revealed itself. It had shocked and filled him with misgivings. The lad had been too ready to pick up the whisky decanter. There had been one evening when he had returned home late from some engagement in London suspiciously talkative, a surprising change from his now customary taciturnity. Happily his mother was in bed. It was long after midnight before he could induce the exuberant young man to retire.

Dr. Woodfall sighed as he replaced the stopper of the jar. Success had changed Charles. He stayed away from his home, he neglected to write. Even when the much delayed letters came they told them nothing. Now he had settled in Venice apparently, a kind of beachcomber's paradise, and he had failed, not only to come home for young Peter's twenty-first birthday, and to see him row in his college boat at the Regatta, but also to send any word that he knew it was the boy's birthday. It was the more singular because he had hitherto always shown such affection for his brother. He had paid all his fees for Oxford, and had done it lavishly.

Dr. Woodfall went to the window and looked out over the garden, beyond the lawn and the sun-dial, down to the river shining in the morning sun. It was the last day of the Regatta, a perfect Regatta this year, unmarred by any rain, and with record crowds. Sitting in the Umpires' launch he had proudly worn his pink cap. He had dressed himself again this morning in white flannel trousers and gay pink socks. The Stewards' Enclosure pass hung from the lapel of his blue reefer jacket. The pink cap, symbol of ancient prowess, was perched on the hall-stand. He would wear it to-day. It would be a day of days if young Peter's boat was stroked to victory. Forty years ago he had known that dizzy moment when, almost blind and all out, his own boat had passed the Judges' box, only a canvas ahead. Yes, Charles should have come home for such a day.

Dr. Woodfall went into the dining-room. Breakfast was an individual affair in his household. He had to hurry out to make his morning round earlier because of the Regatta festivities. Happily there was usually a lessening of calls during Regatta week, perhaps owing to the increased tempo of life that quickened the blood of all natives of Henley on this notable occasion. The doctor was just finishing breakfast when his sister-in-law and Peter came in.

"Good morning, Mary," he said. "I see you've had a letter from Charles—any news?"

"Well, he doesn't tell us much—as usual," answered Mrs.

Woodfall. "He's not coming home for some time, he's working on a novel."

"A novel—that's a new line!" observed the doctor. "I hope he isn't going to do what that beefy-looking woman did who came down here last year with three dachshunds and a tired husband—put us all into her book, grossly caricatured."

"May Filton Webb was quite kind to you, Wyndham—you were a 'charming old gentleman'!"

"So I am! But not 'portly' and not a 'veterinary surgeon beloved of all animals.' What tosh—as if any animal ever loved a veterinary surgeon!" exclaimed Dr. Woodfall.

"Why do women novelists always have triplicate names? There's a fellow on my staircase, his mother's Ann Capel Moon. We call him Waney, he always looks like the last quarter," said Peter, coming from the sideboard with two sausages. He sat down, his big fist seized the coffee-pot. This was a second breakfast. He was not living at home but with his crew lodging in a near-by farm-house, and under the strict eye of a coach. He had dashed in for birthday greetings. "Please don't say anything about this!" he cried, a sausage in his mouth.

"I feel I should report you," said the doctor, with mock severity. "I shall, if you lose to-day."

Mrs. Woodfall opened her handbag, and took out her son's letter. "Would you like to read it?" she said, passing it to the doctor, who put on his pince-nez. "I think he'd have made an excellent doctor—his handwriting's quite illegible!"

"That's a bad outlook for me—mine's very good," exclaimed Peter, munching.

"Yours has the pot-hook clarity of all semi-illiterates, my boy!" observed the doctor, peering over his glasses.

"Crushed!" cried Peter. "Read the letter, Uncle. I haven't heard it."

The doctor propped the letter up against the marmalade-pot, and read:

> "c/o COOK'S WAGONS-LITS,
> "VENICE,
> "*July* 26, 1938.

"DARLING MUMS,

"There's nothing to report except that it gets very hot here, and I spend quite a lot of time under the pergola, dressed in a minimum, with a grand view of the lagoon and Venice shimmering in the heat haze."

The doctor looked up and addressed Mrs. Woodfall.

"By the way, where does Charles stay? He talks here of looking at Venice—I thought he was in it?"

"Oh, I think he wanders around—he always gives Cook's address," answered his sister-in-law.

"He never settles anywhere—he's a swivel-bottom," commented Peter. "The lucky devil!"

The doctor continued reading:

"I began writing a novel last week, for a change. I wonder what you'll think of it? I find I am drawing heavily on local characters at home——"

"There you are!" exclaimed Peter. "I know I shall be the local bonehead! If he calls me a 'blond Apollo,' like that dog-woman, I'll sue him!"

"I wonder if I'm in it?" asked Mrs. Woodfall. "How exciting!"

"You'll be a sweet old lady living in a Georgian house with white hair, my dear!" commented Dr. Woodfall.

"Bad literary style, Uncle," said Peter. "You've never seen a Georgian house with white hair."

Again the doctor peered over his glasses, but, withholding comment, read on:

"——local characters at home. I suppose I should be writing another play, but I pine for new worlds to conquer. Somehow the time slips by. We do——"

"We?" repeated the doctor.

"Aha! Lord Byron's at it again!" exclaimed Peter.

"We do nothing much all day except bathe, sail, dream and eat. I can never satisfy a passion for *scampi* which we get fresh out of the lagoon. Like you we've got a Regatta ahead which I'm looking forward to. It seems less of a regatta than a carnival. They have a *galleggiante*—an enormous barge, decorated with small coloured lamps, that carries a complete orchestra. It floats down the canal from the station to the Doges' Palace, while they play an opera, and a tenor makes the air reverberate with Verdi. It should be very good fun. One has to book a gondola weeks ahead. I don't like being away from Henley for the Regatta, this is the third I have missed. I long to sit with the crowd on Auntie Janet's verandah and 'look down on the damn people,' as a proud peer once said. I had a letter from her last week, she seems in great form, and says her visitors grow. One day that verandah will crash. I feel I should have come home for Peter's twenty-first and to hear Uncle Wyndham's oration at the dinner-party. My spirit will sit at the table. I haven't forgotten the child. My present will arrive on wheels——"

"What's that?" cried Peter, at once.

"I can't think what he means," said Mrs. Woodfall. "Charles can be so irritating in that way. You remember he said he was sending me a pheasant for my birthday, and when it came it was in diamonds!"

"Something on wheels," murmured Peter.

"A bassinet probably," commented the doctor.

Peter flung up his arms in sudden ecstasy.

"Holy smoke! It's a car!" he shouted, with shining eyes. "He knows I've worn his old one out! Oh, boy!"

"Are you sure?" asked Mrs. Woodfall, quietly. "Charles is very generous but——"

"I'm his beloved little brother. Joseph and Esau, and all

that," he cried. His great paw reached out for a banana and skinned it. "I shall sit on the steps all day listening for a crunch on the gravel."

"I don't advise that, young man," said the doctor. "The thing on wheels, I suspect, is Harrod's delivery van. Esau, by the way, was very hairy. Charles isn't. After that interruption, I'll proceed."

"I'll bet anything it's a car! He's what they call in the land of gasolene 'a swell guy.' Sure!" said Peter, his face radiant.

The doctor repropped the letter before him, having turned over the sheet.

"I hope he will like it, and not pull it to pieces like most little boys. I expect to stay on here for some time. Life is agreeable. Europe seems to be in a state of increasing turmoil. The serenity of this place is occasionally marred by black-shirted hobbledehoys bawling *Giovanezza*, and last week the Balilla gathered here in force, a tadpole swarm of urchins in grey shorts, with daggers. One drew his, and with mock ferocity made a pass at me growling, 'Inglese!' Which shows how the young are being bent from the tradition of British prestige, so laboriously celebrated by Elizabeth Barrett Browning in the good old days of the solid gold sovereign. They are even being taught to lose their reverence for the dollar, which shows how Mussolini's head ignores his pocket. He hopes for bigger game. It looks to me as if he'll end up on a diet of *sauerkraut*, which the Italians will hate. But enough of politics. The rumble of the storm is shut out here. I never even listen to the radio. That's my news. Love to Uncle and the New Man.

> "Affectionately,
> "CHARLES."

The doctor took off his pince-nez, turned the sheets over, scrutinizing them, and passed the letter back to his sister-in-law.

"Well, he doesn't tell us very much about himself, does he?

He talks about the house. What house; surely he's not taken one?"

"Or bought one, or married a widow, or is living in sin with a black-eyed Santuzza!" cried Peter.

"Peter!" remonstrated his mother.

"You never know, Mums—those literary blokes! Remember Byron, who ran off with the old Count's wife, and then went to live with her family. Sublime audacity!" exclaimed Peter, rising with the doctor. "Now where is that something on wheels? I must get back to the fellows. Telephone me when it comes. If it's what I hope I'll desert the boat. Bye-bye, darling."

Peter stooped and kissed his mother.

"Good luck, Peter—I'll be watching," said Mrs. Woodfall.

"And praying—by the Bald Pate of Bingo," he added.

"By the Bald Pate of Bingo," answered Mrs. Woodfall solemnly. Since infancy the solemnest vows had been taken on this nursery deity, a coal-black negro figure, *sans* hair, who still sat huddled on the mantelpiece of the deserted room upstairs.

With a word to his uncle, Peter strode out, the floor shaking under him.

"I must be off on my round. I'll fetch you at twelve," said the doctor to his sister-in-law. He paused a moment, then added: "I'm glad he remembered Peter—but I wish he'd stay home a little more. We've seen almost nothing of him since he came back from Florida."

Mrs. Woodfall made no answer for a few moments; then quietly, looking up at the doctor:

"We can't interfere, Wyndham. I feel Charles wants to forget something—someone," she corrected, "he met in America."

"That girl Laura Lanier?"

"I believe so. He talked so little about her—I noticed I couldn't get him to talk about her."

"But she married some Pole—didn't she?" asked the doctor.

"That, I think, is the trouble," answered Mrs. Woodfall.

"Heavens—I hope there's going to be no mess of that kind. There're plenty of nice girls in the world. Charles is a sensible fellow, or was, till things went wrong."

"Wrong?" repeated Mrs. Woodfall.

"Perhaps 'wrong' is not the word. Well, it'll come out all right. He's young enough," said the doctor, cheerfully. "Good-bye, my dear."

He left the room, and went out to the garage. His mind was still on Charles as he drove through Hart Street, gay with bunting, flags hanging from hotels and houses where crews were staying, and red geraniums and white marguerites in wire baskets suspended from the lamp-posts. A change had come over Charles. It was plain from his appearance and his moods that running about the Continent was not doing him any good. A steady life, that was the thing. If only the boy had settled down to the practice!

He sighed, and was so preoccupied that for once he ignored the salute of the town's policeman standing at the cross-roads.

When he returned, soon after twelve o'clock, Charles's present had arrived, a large, low sports car, with twin seats, raked wind-screen and preposterously long body. "Suicidal," commented the doctor, as he and Mrs. Woodfall examined it. It spoke of speed in every line. The doctor was firm against informing Peter about its arrival. He could be told after the great race.

They went to lunch at the Farnsworths', who lived in a twin bow-windowed Georgian house set back against a copse above the Thames. It had been for years the Mecca of all rowing men. Their host's past prowess was denoted by the oars lining the staircase walls. The lunch was served out on the colonnaded terrace. Old Blues and young Blues, Leander Club notabilities in pink socks and metal-buttoned blue flannel jackets, shy youngsters from Oxford, Cambridge, and Eton, a couple of Harvard lads, a bevy of pretty girls, Mrs. Farnsworth manœuvred them all into easy acquaintance and flitted from table to table. The day was gloriously sunny, there was a record crowd on the course, the racing so far had been good. One or two 'surprises' had lent spice to the events. An afternoon of exciting finals was in view. As ever, the old boys in pink socks began giving the dates of records.

"No, sir—1892, not '91," said an old gentleman, lighting a cigar. "I was married that year—spent the honeymoon on a houseboat, so I remember the date!"

" '91—so it was, you're quite right, General!" agreed the first speaker.

Dr. Woodfall looked across the meadow towards the river.

"There's a crew going down to the starting-post," he said. The eight went smoothly by on the silver water. He examined the colours on their sweaters and blades. "Magdalen!" he proclaimed.

Their host looked at his watch.

"Gracious! We must go!" he exclaimed.

There were hurried thanks and farewells, and a general scurrying to the cars parked on the gravel drive.

"We've plenty of time. Peter's race is three-thirty. I'll put you in the grandstand—I'm going up in the Umpires' launch," said the doctor to Mrs. Woodfall.

The Royal Regatta. It was well named, thought Mrs. Woodfall, as she looked around her from her seat in the grandstand. Across the river, under the awning, there was a long line of spectators seated above the rose-covered embankment wall of Phyllis Court. A military band played under a copper beech on the great lawn, alternating its spirited airs with those of another military band on this side of the river. Behind the booms there was a multitude of punts, rowing boats, canoes. Upstream, the graceful old bridge carried a human frieze along its balustrade. The boathouses opposite were gay with flower-boxes and striped awnings, their verandahs filled with guests. Partisans applauded crews paddling downstream to the starting-post. A fair breeze upstream assisted good times for the racing. Away down the course, in mid-river, arose the white classical temple on Temple Island, dramatically set against a background of graceful trees. The vista was closed in by an amphitheatre of the Chiltern Hills, clothed in beech-woods, with fallow fields like a coloured counterpane sloping to the Thames valley. Earth had not anything to show more fair, thought Mrs. Woodfall, borrowing from Wordsworth. It was a glorious festival of youth in its prime matched by an English summer scene in all its glory.

The names of two crews were on the announcement boards, framed just above the boom opposite. By sliding one board over the other the relative positions of the racing crews would be indicated. Mrs. Woodfall had seen the doctor go down-stream in the crowded Umpires' launch, its flag gaily flutter-ing. She had seen Peter's boat go by, with him at No. 2. How young and godlike they looked, with their neat heads, broad shoulders, and long brown legs! She looked at her wrist-watch. It was three-thirty now. Soon—the sound of the starting-gun came to her ears. Away down there, out of sight, sixteen young men, in superb physical condition, matched their strength and skill.

Dr. Woodfall, sitting in the launch following, watched the backs of two coxes, the water furrow of two rudders, the rhythmical swing, poise, and dip of the oars. A quarter down the course they were level, at Fawley they were level. Both crews were rowing well. The doctor could see Peter, as his head and body came forward. They had the Berkshire side. He looked at his stop-watch and timed the stroke. It should be put up now. Canvas by canvas they raced. Their coming, seen by the concourse ahead, provoked an outburst of cheer-ing. Cyclists and runners on the towpath bellowed through megaphones.

On they went, ding-dong. Yes, stroke had put it up, but the rival crew took up the challenge. The last quarter now. The uproar increased. Peter's boat began to creep forwards, a can-vas, half a length. Spectators in boats and punts leapt to their feet, cheering, applause swept across the water from the en-closure, the grandstand, the towing-path crowd. Half a length still. Dr. Woodfall, on his feet now, prayed. It was anybody's race yet. He was dimly aware of young bodies and heads swaying before him, of people shouting madly on either side of the course, of the rose-covered wall of Phyllis Court, of the old bridge and church ahead, of figures crowded on Auntie Janet's verandah, of sun-flecked water, of frenzy vociferous under the blue sky, and then a flag falling at the winning-post.

It was over. The shouting changed to applause. The crews slumped in their boats. The military band broke into a lively tune. Dr. Woodfall removed his pink cap and mopped his brow.

"A grand race! Half a length!" said someone.

Charles should have been here, thought the doctor. He looked ahead at the crews, resting midstream up near the bridge. Then the victors began to paddle in, amid applause from friends on the landing-stage.

The doctor was first out of the launch. Forgetting his sister-in-law in the grandstand, he pushed his way through the crowd, and hurried to the dressing-tents. He was just in time to see them bring in their boat, hefty young lads, flushed, sweating. He waited while the cox steered the long shell in past guide ropes, tent flaps. A few moments later the crew emerged, to fetch their oars.

"Peter!" cried Dr. Woodfall.

"Uncle!" exclaimed Peter, grinning, wet chestnut hair plastered on his brow.

"Oh, grand, my boy! Grand!" cried the doctor. "Peter, it's come—a sports Fiat."

Peter stood still, wide-eyed, open-mouthed, the sweat trickling down his strong brown throat. Then, with one bear-hug his arms went around his uncle, oblivious of the smiling crowd.

"Oh, boy! Oh, boy!" he murmured, ecstatically.

II

At the tea interval the doctor, Mrs. Woodfall, and Peter punted across the river to Willow View. As they drew near they saw the verandah was crammed with Auntie Janet's relatives, friends and friends' friends.

"Hello! Come up, come up!" shouted Auntie Janet, seeing them.

She met them at the head of the staircase, despite the circus of human beings revolving around her.

"Oh, my dears, what a day, what a Regatta!" she exclaimed, kissing Mrs. Woodfall and greeting the doctor. The next moment she was in Peter's arms.

"Hold me tight and kiss me publicly, and make me the most envied woman in Henley!" she cried, laughing up into his face.

Peter picked her up in his arms and soundly kissed her, to general applause.

"You've not shamed me, Peter. Oh, you were grand! Come along, there's tea going," she said.

There was a mob in the big room. Everybody was there, standing or weaving in and out to get to the table.

"Peter darling, do go out and have a word with Captain Grenfell on the verandah. He was in the Cambridge boat ages ago. The poor soul's been paralysed since the Battle of Mons. I told him you were coming over. He'd love to talk shop with you. Here, take him this cup of tea, and a cake."

Peter found the captain sitting at a point of vantage in his invalid's chair. They were friends at once. The river below them was alive with boats, a band played blithely. The grandstand in the Stewards' Enclosure was empty, they were all in the tea tent. There were only two more races on the programme, then the prize distribution followed.

"Who's giving 'em away?" asked someone.

"Oh—some politician's wife—time we had a Royalty again, it's ages since we had one—after all, it's a Royal Regatta."

"The Wimbledon tennis championship's taking the limelight these days. Why, I remember this river so thick with boats you could walk across!"

"And the houseboats that used to line the river—now there's not one!" moaned a dowager.

They had clustered around the captain. Peter slipped away

from the Jeremiahs. There was an hour yet before the prize distribution.

He ran over the bridge, covered with spectators and traffic, and arrived, breathless, at the house. A turn in the drive, and there it was.

He paused, his eyes worshipping the beautiful thing—its long low lines, its exaggerated bonnet, the raked wind-screen, the twin bucket seats, its tail like a wasp's bottom, the big driving-wheel, and the glorious dashboard crammed with gadgets. Reverently, he opened the low door and slipped into the red leather seat, turning the ignition key. The engine moved into life, the throaty chortle of the exhaust was music in his ears. He let in the clutch. Proud Beauty glided forward, down the drive, out of the gate and into the main road. She slipped like a destroyer through tugboats in that stream of traffic. In a halt at the cross-roads, he let the exhaust splutter like an angry dragon. Small boys stood and worshipped. The gorgeous creature moved on again, tiger-strong and smooth. He turned down New Street, towards the river.

Janet Cherwell, still sending out tea-cups with the deftness of a conjurer, was suddenly aware of a blond giant with shining eyes leaning over her.

"Auntie Janet—come outside! I've something to show you," he whispered.

"Peter, my lamb, I can't, I——" she began.

"Please," he urged, and his big hands, closing on her, impelled her from the table. She succumbed. He piloted her down the stairs, outside into the driveway.

"Look!" he said, holding her from behind, his young face over her shoulder.

Auntie Janet looked.

"Oh, my God!" she cried, not irreverently.

"Charles's present. Get in!"

"But, Peter, I can't——"

He propelled her into the seat and slammed the door on her.

"You're the first to ride in her," he said, seated before the wheel. "Charles'll like that."

The car moved forward. At the end of New Street it turned into the Oxford road. Presently they came to a long straight avenue flanked with tall elms. It was the Fairmile. She knew his intention. She sank herself down into the seat, she was Fate's plaything.

III

The coming-of-age dinner was given at Phyllis Court Club. Forty people sat down to it. Somehow Peter got through his speech. The champagne flowed. Then the dusk having fallen, they all crossed the lawn to the embankment. The moment it was dark the fireworks would begin in the meadow across the river, and after the fireworks the annual ball would open. Boats were already massed for the spectacle, with paper lanterns at their prows. The organs of the Fair roundabouts blared in the summer night. The moon rose over the dark woods. Phee-e-whooo! went a rocket, soaring into space. The crowd cheered. The fireworks had begun. The dark, silver face of the water reflected the colour-smitten heavens while the hills echoed back successive cannonades of explosives.

Loud applause greeted the grand finale, with pyrotechnic portraits, somewhat wobbly, of the King and Queen. Then, the last spluttering 'Good Night' flamed and died into darkness. The drift of lanterned boats went homewards, the raucous Fair made merry in the meadow. Across the cool, dark lawn of Phyllis Court flowed the music of the ball.

Young Peter Woodfall, dancing with Marjorie Ungar, who plied him with questions about his mother, told her of his wonderful plan. He and his friend, Tony Farnham, were going to motor across Europe to Venice, surprise Charles, and give him sight of his own marvellous gift.

"Take him my love," said Marjorie Ungar.

"Oh, of course," responded Peter, lightly, but Marjorie's eyes, meeting his, told him it was not a casual request. He remembered that early affair with Charles. Everyone thought her marriage to the Austrian had been a failure, then there had been her father's suicide. She had a baby now, and lived in a cottage with her mother. Folks said they were dreadfully poor. What rotten luck some people had! Everybody should be happy, deliriously happy as he was

The orchestra was playing a Strauss waltz. Its rhythm ran through his veins. His arm tightened around the delicious burden of frail femininity. With a smile on his lips he swept her onwards.

CHAPTER EIGHT

NIGHT IN VERONA

ON the surface a more ill-assorted pair than Anthony Farnham and Peter Woodfall could not be imagined. People wondered why they were such friends, and what they could find in common. Tony was short, delicate in appearance, and highly strung. His interests were music, art, literature, and criminology. Almost a small boy in appearance, he had been the cox in Peter's boat. For some reason Peter treated him with mingled awe and affection. It was Tony says this, and Tony says that, until it became almost a joke. "The Big Dane and the Peke," someone called them jokingly, and it stuck. It was Tony who planned the trip and had suggested it the moment Peter had shown him his present. It would all fit in nicely. Tony had an invitation to spend a week with Austrian friends at the Salzburg Festival. While Peter visited his brother in Venice, he would make the side trip to Salzburg.

In a week of glorious motoring they had reached Vienna, coming through Switzerland from France, along the Rhône valley and over the Simplon Pass. At Verona they were parting. Here Tony was to take his train to Salzburg.

They spent a night together in Verona, where Tony was thrilled to find a company from La Scala performing *Turandot* in the old Roman amphitheatre, under the stars. They bought tickets and cushions, and clambered up the tiers, looking down on the arena. The Emperor Diocletian's amphitheatre, designed centuries ago for the entertainment of the inhabitants of a military outpost set against the Goths threatening the fertile plain, was now thronged with spectators applauding, not gladiators combating lions, but singers interpreting Puccini.

The opera somewhat bored Peter, but he found interest in an Italian girl, young and ripe for mischief, whose wandering eyes had met his early in the performance. Unhappily, a fat and swarthy father, with tiers of chins, who perspired profusely in the hot Italian night, often obstructed the view. But an opportunity, seized by both, occurred during an interval, when the audience wandered in the vast ill-lit galleries. The girl gave her father the slip by one of the arches, and Peter was quickly at her side. A great pillar of masonry provided shelter from watchful eyes. She looked at him as he came up to her, eyelids fluttering, half fearful, half smiling. She was even younger than he had thought, deliciously young, an exotic flower in the warm dark night.

"*Buona sera, bellissima, Signorina!*" he said, boldly, drawing on his extremely limited vocabulary.

She raised melting eyes to his, wordless before the handsome stranger. Then, "*Inglese?*" she almost whispered. The next moment she was in his arms, his mouth crushing hers. There was a long breathless moment of heady intoxication, and then, with a swift movement of panic, she fought free of him and fled. Peter stood against the pillar quivering, exultant. It was a mad thing to do, but, the girl apart, the setting, the music, the warm Italian night had all conspired. And she had wanted it, as much as he. The warmth and softness of that mouth, the stir of her in his arms, palpitating like a captured bird! He gave a great sigh, then brought himself back to earth. Tony, gone for a drink, would be hunting for him.

"Well—how was she?" asked Tony, coolly, holding a beer bottle.

Peter looked startled. Tony laughed.

"I saw you stalking her—and I kept an eye on Papa for you," he said. "Well?"

"She was—gorgeous!" confessed Peter.

"I expect many a hot-blooded Roman made use of these arches long before you. But for Heaven's sake stop eyeing the girl. If that Papa catches you he'll knife you!"

The bell rang. The crowd went back to their seats.

Tony left, northwards, the next morning. Peter began the journey to Venice. They were harvesting in the Venetian plain.

The landscape had an air of lazy content. The only discordant note was struck by Il Duce's pugnacious visage stencilled on the walls of public buildings and houses. He ought not to glower like that at tourists who brought him money.

Peter lunched at Padua. The car had run superbly as ever. They had soared over the Swiss Alps like an eagle. On a long straight road, between tall poplars, he overtook a peasant girl, carrying a heavy basket of maize on her head. She was bare-legged, proud-breasted. Gallantry and adventure made him pull up, after he had passed. He offered her a lift—as she came by. She shook her head, but laughed.

"*Prego! Prego!*" he cried. It perhaps wasn't the right word, but he tried it. She burst out laughing again, loudly this time. It was music. Her teeth were pearls. His eyes pleaded and won. She let him take the basket, and got in, shyly.

They started. To his amazement her hair was red, not black. Why, of course—Titian-red. Titian had found them like that, centuries ago. She was eighteen, nineteen, not more. They matured young out here. He put on a burst of speed to thrill her. The back draught fluttered her skirt. She tried to hold it down, but the flimsy stuff flapped gaily, revealing still more of her smooth, sun-browned legs. There were dimples at the knees, and though the ankles were strong the lines were seductive with youth and vigour. She smiled in the excitement of the moment, her lips parted, her hair blown back over the small ears. He leaned towards her laughing, and her face almost met his, eyes shining. The next moment romance was dead, beyond resurrection. He drew back dismayed. The pity of it—garlic!

For the next two miles he enjoyed her, at a distance. Then at the beginning of a village she asked to be put down. He handed her the basket.

"*Tante grazie, signore! Tante grazie,*" she said, all smiles. "*Buon giorno!*"

The words were almost sung. He left her, radiantly smiling. Lovely, lovely, but——

In another hour he was in a flat, desolate landscape. Then

across a long low viaduct he saw Venice. His heart fell: it looked a wretched place of untidy buildings, swamp marsh-land, and multitudes of poles carrying cables and telephone wires. Could this be the City of Love, endlessly sung, end-lessly painted? It was a rabbit warren, he thought as, leaving the long bridge, he was directed to the garage, a great modern block, wholly utilitarian.

He garaged his car. A porter took his two bags across the square, and all at once the Venice of fable came alive. There could be no doubt about it. On the canal before him was a gondola, the real thing, long and black, with a bloused fellow, soft-slippered, on a little platform at the rear. There was a shining steel plate, toothed, on the curved prow.

A disreputable old man with hooked pole pretended to assist him into the gondola. The porter stood mumbling, his hand still out. It seemed he had not paid him enough. Peter gave him some more.

"Hôtel Luna!" cried Peter, sinking back on the black leather cushions. A friend had recommended the hotel. He tried to give the gondolier the impression he had been there for years.

"Sì, sì, signore!" came the answer.

But the gondola did not move. The miserable old man with the pole still hooking the gondola was whining, hat in hand. Peter turned and looked at the gondolier, who smiled and pointed to the old man as if he had conjured him out of the ground, and the appearance must be rewarded. Obviously it was a conspiracy. Peter dropped a two-lire piece into the filthy hat.

"Canale Grande?" asked the gondolier, smiling.

"Sì, sì," answered Peter, ready with that obliging word.

He did not know that he had chosen the slowest, most ex-pensive route, that he would be taken the whole length of that S-shaped canal. And this being his first time in Venice, he had no reason to care, soon thrilled by the traffic of the famous highway bordered with palace on palace, with churches and bridges and marts. A balcony, a marble façade, a line of Gothic windows, mysterious water entrances, narrow side-canals, the sudden, noble sweep of the Rialto Bridge, familiar as a friend, the thronged quays, the gay cafés at the water's edge, the luxurious hotel terraces, with marble landings and red druggets, they all glided by, mile on mile of a marvellous panorama. And finally, ere the gondola turned deftly into a side-canal, the sky was filled with a building of incredible splendour. Steps and columns, belfries and flying buttresses of shining marble, rose from the water, and, surmounting all, a vast noble dome, immense and cool against a glowing, western sky.

"*Santa Maria della Salute!*" explained the guide.

They halted at the water steps of the Hôtel Luna.

When he had washed and changed, Peter descended. It was half-past six. There was a chance that Cook's might still be open. They would know Charles's address. If he were in luck he might surprise him that very evening. He asked the concierge the way. The office was just across the Piazza, in a corner by San Marco. A few yards, through the arch on the right, and he would be in the Piazza.

Peter stepped out into a narrow stream of people, found the arch, went through, and then stood still, paralysed with wonder. At first it was unreal, like the drop scene of a theatre. His eye wandered from point to point, across the vast Piazza, over the people crowded at small tables set out in the open, along the colonnades flanking each side of the Piazza, until they rested on the gleaming, multi-coloured domed and terraced façade of the church of San Marco, its upper pinnacles and mosaics taking the fire of the setting sun. Next, with a catching of his breath, he saw the great Campanile, followed it up and up until, in the glory of the upper sky, he beheld the winged angel on the summit, serene above the ebbing tide of day.

As in a dream he crossed the Piazza, through eddies of music from the orchestras of the cafés. Now another vista opened before him, down the Piazzetta towards the lagoon, but he repelled temptation and asked his way to Cook's. Arrived there, he was just in time, for a man was pulling down a roller shutter. He ducked and entered. The clerk at the letter counter could not help him. They could not give the addresses of customers. Oh, yes, they knew Mr. Woodfall. He came at intervals for letters. The best thing he could do was to write a note and leave it. They were sorry, but that was all they could suggest.

Dismayed and baffled, Peter stepped out into the Piazza. He had not foreseen such a check to his plan. It was maddening to think that here he was, in the same city as his brother, and unable to find him. He might even be seated at one of these cafés.

Peter took a seat and ordered a *gelato*. He would ask the concierge at the hotel. There must be some means of tracing Charles without communicating via Cook's.

CHAPTER NINE

VILLA SOSPIRI

I

THE Villa Sospiri, built by Palladio for a noble of Venice, stood impressively in the flat plain served by the Brenta Canal. It was reached by a small waterway, an offshoot of the canal, and had, thereby, direct water communication with Venice, fifteen miles distant. It had been built in the era of Venice's decadent magnificence, when the patrician families, like the city of their origin, were living on accumulated wealth. The Moscarini family, having built a vast palace in Venice, also built themselves a magnificent villa in the country, for hot summer days when the sirocco lay heavy over the lagoon city. Wishing to match with size and splendour their rivals, they called in the most famous architect of the day, Andrea Palladio, who raised for them, on classical lines, a villa that ranked among his *chefs-d'œuvre*.

It was here that one, Andrea Moscarini, rich, arrogant, and jealous, brought his beautiful girl wife, Lucia, and kept her almost a prisoner. Lucia fretted and sighed for the festivities of Venice, to which her husband would not permit her return, and thus it came about that the Villa Moscarini became known as the Villa Sospiri—the Villa of Sighs.

But all that was centuries ago. Time had dealt heavily with the villa. The impoverished line of the Moscarinis still owned the place, but could afford neither to live in it nor to keep it in repair. The magnificent gardens were weed-grown, the stone terraces and arbours, the grottoes and basins were cracked and crumbling. For a period a glassworks had been established in the villa, then tenant farmers had occupied it, using its salons for barns and store-rooms. The tessellated floors had been broken, the fine doors mutilated. A swarm of children had made of it a slum. The great villa, with broken windows, and a roof whose pantiles let in the rain, stood deserted in the flat monotonous land where no one came any more.

It was in this condition when a miracle happened. An Amsterdam Jew, a rich man and an authority on the work of Tintoretto, was led to it in the course of his investigations. He discovered, under the whitewashed walls and ceilings, the frescoes of the Master. Rich enough to indulge his enthusiasm, he took a lease of the villa and began to restore it. In ten years it had regained something of its former splendour. The great frescoes were restored, the roofs and walls repaired, and modern domestic conveniences added. The gardens immediately around the villa were replanned. The connoisseur died then, the lease ran out, and once more the villa was closed. The gardens began to go back to the wilderness. The peasants came and plundered the lead piping, the fittings. Finally a caretaker was put in by the Moscarini family. The place was to be let, cheap.

But no one wanted a palace of twenty rooms, five of them vast and unheatable, fifteen miles from Venice, six from a station, and situated in the desolate Brenta marshlands. Various tenants tried it, lured by the loveliness of the house and its fine frescoes. No one stayed more than a summer. It was too distant from life, the sad monument of a splendid past. For two years it stood empty, except for the caretaker who installed himself in the smaller rooms on the mezzanine floor; then, in the early spring of 1938, it was inhabited again.

It had taken Peter Woodfall three hours to reach it, coming by the steam ferry to Fusina, then by a rattling light railway that skirted a canal on one side and flat maize fields on the other. The rail car deposited him in a poverty-stricken village, and from there he had walked two miles to the Villa Sospiri. The size and magnificence of it, standing there in the solitude of the plain, astonished him. Charles was living like a lord, obviously. There was a boathouse at the side of the canal whose green waters were tidal. A motor-launch was tethered beside some steps. It was a villa with ten columns and a double flight of steps to the colonnaded terrace, the priest in the village had said. Undoubtedly he had found the Villa Sospiri.

He had tracked down Charles through a faint clue. He remembered, the morning after his arrival in Venice, that his brother had sent home to his mother a copy of Marion Crawford's *Gleanings from Venetian History*, saying he had had it specially bound in Venice by a local bookbinder whose work so delighted him, with its coloured endpapers, that he was having a set of Tauchnitz editions bound also. The name of the bookbinder had been neatly inserted at the bottom of the binding, and Peter had remembered it because the name had filled him with mirth at the time—Dante Blotto. "Dante drunk or Dante sober, the fellow's an artist," had commented Uncle Wyndham. That name, and a search in the telephone directory, had sent Peter speeding to the bookbinder's in the Merceria. Oh, yes, the Signor Woodfall came in frequently. They were binding some books for him now. The Signore lived out of Venice, at the Villa Sospiri, beyond Fusina.

So here he was, to give old Charles a great surprise. He hoped he had not yet been seen from the house. He crossed the small bridge over the canal and presently mounted the wide stone steps to the high portico. From the terrace, between the great Corinthian columns supporting the massive pediment, he looked out across the plain. He rang the bell, pulling a chain that hung by the open door. It made a distant jingle. Through the door he saw a large circular hall, lit from a cupola. The glass door across the hall gave a view to a balustraded terrace on the south side of the house. Somewhere a dog barked, and footsteps sounded. Peter watched a vessel sail by, gliding down a canal. A man came across the hall. He looked Italian, and had a striped apron over his linen trousers, on which he was wiping his hands.

"*Signore?*" he asked, standing in the doorway.

"The Villa Sospiri—Signor Woodfall?"

"*Sì!*"

"*Sono il suo fratello, Pietro,*" said Peter, slowly, nervously proud of his newly acquired Italian. "*Vuole, per piacere——*"

"I speak Engleesh, mister," said the servant.

"Oh—then will you tell my brother I'm here—his brother Peter?"

"Signor Woodfall is out. He's gone to Venice thees morning. He come-a back thees afternoon."

"Oh!" exclaimed Peter. The irony of it.

There was a pause. A tawny bull-mastiff, still a puppy, rushed out and wagged his tail. It seemed more friendly than this scrubby servant. It was noon. He began to feel hungry, and he was a long way from anywhere that he could eat.

"Could I wait—and perhaps you could give me something to eat? It's a long journey here, and I want to see my brother," said Peter.

The response was not enthusiastic. The servant hesitated.

"I will go and ask-a," he replied.

Peter was left standing on the terrace. A large green curtain had been suspended between two of the columns, to give shade to a wicker chaise-longue. He sat down on it. He was hot and thirsty after his walk. It was a brilliant August day, and humid with a wind from the lagoons. On a table lay magazines—*Vogue, Country Life, L'Illustration.*

Who had that fellow gone to ask, he wondered. Perhaps the cook ruled the place. He was anxious to see the house. There might be guests, of course. Charles was certainly doing it well. He wondered how long he had had this house, and why he should have said nothing about it. Charles had been odd and secretive lately. He had noticed it on his last visit home.

The servant seemed a long time away. He looked through the magazines. Then, at last, he heard the fellow crossing the hall. He rose expectantly. The next moment a woman stepped on to the terrace. They looked at each other in silence for a while.

"I'm Peter Woodfall—Charles Woodfall's brother," he said, breaking the silence.

A smile broke over her face. She was young, about twenty-eight, he thought, and very pretty.

"Oh—of course! How awful, you've just missed Charles! He'll be back this afternoon. You'll stay to lunch? So you're Peter. Do come in!" she said.

He followed her into the hall, and had a glimpse of a large salon, with flowers on tables, a piano, rugs, as they went through out on to the terrace. Like the rest of the house, it was raised up, on the second floor, long and wide, with a stone balustrade and two flights of steps leading round a dolphin fountain to a formal garden of parterres and cypresses.

On the terrace there were easy chairs, coloured sunshades, and a swing couch with a striped awning. Everything was vivid in sunshine, gay colours everywhere.

"Do sit down," she said, looking at him now with growing appreciation. He was extremely handsome. She sat opposite him. "We'll have a cocktail in a few minutes—or would you like a long drink?"

"A very long one," he answered, laughing.

She tinkled a little hand-bell, and, as if he had been listening, the servant immediately appeared at the door.

"Whisky and soda, gin and tonic, beer, lemonade——" she asked, addressing Peter.

"Lemonade, I think," he answered.

She gave the order for them both. "And two places for lunch, Angelo."

"*Va bene, signora*," said the man, retiring.

"Now tell me: how did you get here—why didn't you let us know? We'd have sent the launch," she asked. She wore green linen trousers, with sandals, and swung one leg over the arm of the chair. Her ankle and foot were neat, the toe-nails were stained scarlet, like her finger-nails. She had a mass of dark brown hair, with a glint of gold, that hung, cropped and bushy, about her neck and shoulders. She was slim and well proportioned.

"Well—I wanted to surprise Charles. You see, he gave me a new car for my twenty-first. So we came out in it and——"

"We—you're not alone?" she queried.

"No—I came with a friend—but he's gone off to Salzburg.

When I got here yesterday I went to Cook's—you see, I didn't know Charles's address."

He went on explaining his detective work, while she listened and examined him more closely. He was like Charles and unlike him—the same shaped head, and voice. But Charles was dark and slender. This boy was a strong young giant, with very broad shoulders, and tall. His chestnut hair, close-cropped on the small head, was in the tradition of the Greek god. He grew more attractive every moment in his boyish eagerness.

"What a glorious spot he's got here!" exclaimed Peter, his narration finished. "I wonder how he found it?"

"I found it—or rather I was told of it, by a friend."

"You—oh, I'm frightfully sorry, I'd got the idea it was Charles's house. He's staying here?"

"We're both staying here—we've taken it for the summer and autumn."

He looked at her, bewildered. Her eyes were inexpressibly beautiful, grey, long-lashed. Her face was round, full-lipped, with rather high cheek-bones; the teeth were perfect.

"I say—you'll excuse me—but may I know your name?" he asked, laughing. "I've barged in here and——"

She laughed with him, freely.

"How ridiculous! Of course! I'm Stefanie Kazinczy," she said. "Please call me Stefanie—I shall call you Peter."

"Thank you," he said, politely.

It was clear the name meant nothing to him. The servant appeared with the drinks.

"Tell me, you live in that darling little place, Henley—how is it?" she asked.

"You know it?" he cried, his face lighting up.

"Yes—I was there three years ago. I met Charles there—at a lunch given by a jolly lady—I've forgotten her name. There was a verandah——"

"Overlooking the Thames, lots of people—Auntie Janet Cherwell's?" he asked.

"That's it!" she cried, her eyes sparkling.

"Oh, how wonderful! You've been to Auntie Janet's!" he exclaimed.

"My brother was rowing at Henley, in the Hungarian crew. I'm Hungarian. Did you see them?"

"No—I was at school."

"And now?"

"I'm at Oxford. Did you meet Mother and my uncle?"

"No—you see, I only went down to lunch there, with my friends."

He wanted to ask her how she came to meet Charles again. He could not get the thing straight. She had said, "We've taken it . . ." Perhaps there was a husband or other friends, and they had joined. It was an enormous place. He finished his drink.

"Shall we walk in the garden, or is it too hot?" she asked.

"Oh, no, I'd like it," he answered, eagerly, springing up.

"Come on, Busto!" she called. The dog, who had been lying in the shade, came bounding forwards. "Isn't he lovely! I gave him to Charles in Vienna, a year ago—he'd just been born. Our manager's dog had a litter, and I begged Busto."

"Manager?" repeated Peter. So they were in Vienna together last year.

"Yes—you know I'm in the Russian Ballet?"

"No—oh, how wonderful! I'm afraid Charles has never mentioned you—— I say, does that sound awfully rude?" he added, hastily, catching the fleeting surprise in her eyes. "You know, he's a rotten writer. He never tells you anything."

"Not even his address!" she added, with a laugh.

They came to a long shady pergola with great clusters of grapes hanging, then a small pool, with floating lilies presided over by bronze *amorini* who blew water through their pursed lips. A bell sounded.

"That's lunch," she said, and they walked back to the house.

Lunch was laid on a long refectory table in a room with a high painted ceiling. The walls were covered with frescoes. Nude and robust women, miraculous in their levitation and faded in colour, seemed to be dropping fruit and flowers on a soldier in heavy armour. It was a 'Triumph' he learned, of a Moscarini who had gained a victory, fighting in Candia.

After lunch, during which she threw bones at Busto, with complete disregard of the mess made on the stone floor, she showed him the villa. There was a very large salon, also with faded frescoes, and a ceiling so cleverly painted that it seemed to ascend into a starry heaven, although it was perfectly flat. On the grand piano, and the desk in a window recess, there were large photographs of Stefanie Kazinczy in her various ballet roles—in *Les Sylphides*, in *Carnaval*, in *The Good-Humoured Ladies*, all surpassingly beautiful. There were autographed portraits of a Crown Prince, two Grand Dukes, an Admiral, all admirers, from the inscriptions.

"I suppose you love dancing?" asked Peter, as they passed into the library—a small room, littered with papers, and smelling of tobacco."

"I adore it. I'm grieved to give it up," she answered, and her eyes, so quickly expressive of every mood, were filled with sadness.

"Have you given it up?"

"Yes, after being dragged all round Europe with me last year, Charles insisted. He wanted to settle and write—so here we are."

The surmise that had been growing in his mind took definite shape now.

"Is he writing—he said something about a novel?"

She shrugged her slim shoulders, and indicated the desk.

"He began, but—he is *très méchant*," she answered.

They came back into the hall and mounted the spiral, marble staircase. There was a mezzanine floor, the rooms were decorated with Chinese murals.

"You know Marco Polo's return to Venice established the fashion, it lingered on to the *settecento*," she explained.

They ascended to the next floor, with the main bedrooms, all large, with splendid views across the great plain, toward the lagoon. Like the salons downstairs they were well fur-

nished with period Italian furniture. She opened doors and
closed them, the Primavera Room, so call from the flower
frescoes, the Cardinal's Room, in crimson, named after Cardinal Barbarigo, who had slept in it, a guest suite with bath,
another—— "You can have either!" she said, laughing. And
then, opening another door: "Ours!"

It was the largest room of all, with four Gothic-Romanesque
windows opening on to a balcony. It had a beautiful cipolin
floor and, again, frescoed walls. Their legend, faded with age,
was so lascivious that Peter wanted to examine it slowly but
was too embarrassed. She must have detected the interest it
provoked, for she said, lightly: "It's not Tintoretto. One of
the Moscarini must have been an amorist. I wouldn't choose
it, but you soon don't notice it after a time. It's wonderful in
its way."

Peter agreed. The bed drew his attention. It was like a
throne. The mosquito-net had been drawn back, suspended
from a rococo, gilt canopy. The high head-board was of white
damask, wonderfully embroidered with nymphs, animals, and
flowers, under a flamboyant heraldic design.

"They say it's one of two designs worked for the wedding
of Bianca Capelli—lovely, isn't it?" asked Stefanie Kazinczy.

He stared, but the embroidery had only a transient attraction. The great bed had two pillows, side by side. On a small
table, by the head, there was a book, and a man's wrist-watch.
Then on the dressing-table he saw a leather stud-box, with
C. W. embossed on it.

She smiled at him, noticing his prepossession.

"Nice room, isn't it?" she asked, leaving.

"Very nice," he answered.

He had no further doubt. She must have intended him to
know, or why show him the room? Charles might have married her, but if so, why the secrecy, why this hide-out?

He followed her down, his mind in turmoil. He recalled
how he had joked about Byron in Venice that day Charles's
letter had come. Charles might be angry, but he had come
with no intention of prying. It was done now, all he could do

was to keep his mouth shut. It explained so much about Charles. His first impulse was to get away from the place, but that would not do. Charles would know he had been here, would want to talk to him. In a way he could understand it. She was lovely, and charming to talk to. More than that, she was—he could not find the word he wanted, but he felt in himself the unnamed quality of her attraction.

They reached the hall, she looked up at him.

"Let's talk on the terrace—you can fall asleep if you want, later we can swim, or sail. I want to ask you lots of things— about yourself, about your people, and England. I love it so!" she cried, vivaciously. "You see, Charles didn't tell me he had such an attractive brother. He called you 'a bright kid'!"

"Oh, did he! Will Charles be late? I'll have to get back," he said, awkwardly.

She looked at him, wide-eyed, a little chidingly.

"But why? Of course you'll stay. He'd never forgive me if I let you go! Where are you staying?"

"At the Luna."

"Alone?"

"Yes."

"You must come here—it's ridiculous! Charles'll insist, I know."

"Oh, I don't think I——"

"Come!" she cried, putting out her hand to lead him.

He took her hand, the thrill of her touch ran through him. They went out on to the sun-drenched terrace. The afternoon was filled with the shrilling of the cicadas in the olive trees. She settled herself on the chaise-longue, piling the gay cushions behind her head, and made him sit facing her on a low stool. She noticed the strong square wrists as he locked his hands over his knees, and the firm biceps moulding the white shirt-sleeves. He was Charles's brother, yet so different from Charles, larger, with more body and less mind, and more tractable.

"Now—I know you're just twenty-one and at Oxford.

You've arrived in a wonderful new car—Charles's birthday present. But there's such a lot more I want to know!" she began.

At five o'clock Charles had not come back, and Peter began to worry about returning to Venice.

"You can't go without seeing him," said Stefanie, as they came in from a short sail. "We'll send you home in the launch —it only takes an hour."

They were on the terrace when Busto suddenly rushed in and began barking joyously.

"That's Charles," she said, rising.

Footsteps came across the hall, then on to the terrace came Charles. He stood still the moment he saw his brother.

"Good God! Where've you sprung from?" he exclaimed. He was hatless, clad in a white linen suit.

"Hello, Charles. I came to give you a surprise. I've motored out from England—got to Venice last night—had quite a job finding you here!"

The brothers looked at each other. There was an awkward moment.

"Peter's been here since noon. I wouldn't let him go without seeing you, darling," said Stefanie, going to him and linking her arm in his.

"Of course. Glad to see you, Peter—you'll stay to dinner? A good trip?"

"Oh, grand!" replied Peter.

"I'm going to change," said Stefanie. "I'll leave you to talk. Charles, see about cocktails, won't you?"

With a smile she left them.

"What a glorious place this is!" exclaimed Peter, conscious of the strained atmosphere. Charles looked gaunt and in bad health. His appearance shocked Peter. He was bronzed, but there were heavy lines under his eyes, which were dull. "You're all right—quite well?" he added.

"Naturally," answered Charles, abruptly.

"I say, I hope you're not angry at my barging in like this?

I wanted to give you a surprise. I've brought the car to show you. It's simply marvellous, Charles, I——"

"Come into the library," said his brother, leading the way.

Peter followed. As soon as they were in Charles closed the door and stood with his back to it.

"Well," he said. "You see?"

Peter forced a smile. "Yes, I think she's charming. I hope you're very happy. I'd no idea, of course, or I wouldn't have blundered in like this. You know I'll keep my mouth shut, old boy."

His remarks seemed to go unobserved. His brother walked across to the writing-desk, picked up a paper-knife and twisted it in his hands.

"Sit down," he said. "I want to talk to you."

Peter sat down. Charles began to pace the room, then he stopped and began to speak, in a level, dry voice.

"You're no fool, Peter. You must have wondered why I'm never at home these days, why I've been roaming about the Continent this past two years. That time I was in Florida, at Great-Aunt Woodfall's, I met someone, someone who—who suddenly meant so much to me that when she told me she was engaged to a fellow, I felt the world had crashed. I went home; I hoped I was going to forget her, though in my heart I knew I never could—perhaps you can't understand, but it was like that—and I began to travel, hoping to shake it off. I had three months of hell—then I came home again. I think you must have seen, I gave you all a pretty bad time. Even Auntie Janet jacketed me—she knows the story, that far. I went off again—you know I was drinking by this time, not badly but steadily, I simply couldn't work."

He stopped talking and turned the paper-knife over and over.

"Charles, don't tell me unless you really want to," said Peter, watching, and unhappy at this spectacle of his brother, all his customary gaiety vanished.

"I want to, Peter. Someone said confession's good for the soul. I've not talked to a living person about this. Well—to go on. I met Stefanie again—in Milan it happened, quite by accident, at a party given by some friend to the ballet corps dancing there. She remembered meeting me at Auntie Janet's the year before. Her brother——"

"She's told me about that," interrupted Peter.

"Oh! Well, she invited me to go with her and the company on their tour. They went to Berlin and Vienna. I had my car with me, so I drove her from place to place. At this time I was rather a mess, jumpy, desperate. She was sympathetic, and jolly—and—it began like that. Very easy, motoring from hotel to hotel. In Vienna next summer I left her, and went home. I got letters from her, frantic letters. She couldn't live without me, she'd shoot herself if I didn't come back. I didn't believe that, of course—Stefanie's always going to shoot herself if she doesn't get her way—but I was wretchedly lonely and restless. So I joined her again. For a time it was quite amusing to be moving around with those Bohemians—you've no idea how they live, good-hearted, but absolutely reckless. Then I tired of always moving. I wanted to do some work. Stefanie heard about this place, and—well, you see. Here I am!"

He rose from the desk on which he had been sitting, and paced the room.

"You're still in love with the other woman—you don't hear from her?" asked Peter, quietly.

"Insanely, nothing drowns it, nothing, though I've never seen her, heard from her—I know she's married, she's left the stage."

"An actress?"

"Don't say it like that," retorted Charles, irritably. "You might as well know—it's Laura Lanier. She's married a Pole named Korwienski, the pianist."

"Oh!" said Peter. The lovely Laura. It confirmed the rumour. "And Stefanie—she's content you won't marry her?"

"I couldn't and wouldn't!" answered Charles, bitterly. "She's got a husband, who won't divorce her, a jealous sponger. I've no illusions about Stefanie, or myself. She's gay, she loves life, and means to have it. She likes good food, clothes, jewels, money. She must have attention, adorers around. She'll insist on leaving here soon, already she's bored."

"Are you working—you said something about a novel?"

"I began one—but there it is—thirty pages, on that desk three months. It's gone, here, here!"

He tapped his forehead, angrily. He paced the floor again.

"If you're not happy, why don't you break it—you're not in love with her?" asked Peter.

Charles shrugged his shoulders with a gesture of despair.

"It's not easy, and I don't know that I want to. Sometimes I feel I behave badly to Stefanie, and sometimes I hate her for the leech she is. Oh, I don't know, I've gone to pieces, I suppose. I'm terrified of being alone."

"Then come home—I'll drive you home," urged Peter.

"No—that solves nothing. It's myself I can't get away from, I know that. And Henley would kill me, it's too small now, one's too watched. No, that's no good, Peter," he exclaimed, passing a hand through his hair.

"You're still so in love with Laura?" asked Peter.

Charles halted in his pacing and stood in front of him, as he sat there.

"I shall always be in love with Laura," he said, and the quietness of his answer could not hide the passion in it. "Always, Peter, always," he added, a flame in his eyes.

He flung down the paper-knife.

"Well—here's your brilliant brother Charles! Come along. We'll have a cocktail on the terrace. You'll stay to dinner, in fact you'll stay the night."

He put his arm across Peter's shoulder as they went to the door, and he brushed aside all protests against staying. A little later Stefanie joined them, ravishingly lovely in a white satin gown that showed off her perfect shoulders.

II

Angelo waited upon them at dinner, which was served on the end of the terrace, with the level light of evening golden around them. Stefanie talked, Charles sat moodily at the opposite end of the table. Peter was perturbed to see how often his brother filled his tumbler with whisky, ignoring the excellent Chianti. It confirmed an impression that Charles was drinking too much. With a shock he realized that he had a dissolute look. The old debonair Charles had vanished. He was restless with his hands. When he laughed it was with an ironical note. He derided Peter's enthusiasm for Venice. "Wait until it's got on your stomach," he said. Then, as the evening drew on, he mellowed and talked interestingly about the history of the city, life on the lagoons, cinquecento art, and some details about the Moscarini family. By the time liqueurs and cigars appeared he and Stefanie had decided that Peter must move over to the villa, for a week at least. Then he asked Stefanie to sing something. She went inside, into the salon, whose windows opened on to the terrace, and, seating herself before the piano, sang some *Lieder* of Schumann.

"Good voice?" said Charles, to Peter, as they lay back in the easy chairs. The sky lost its colour, the stars began to shine. Frogs croaked in the pool.

"Very good," agreed Peter, relaxed and happy. It was a perfect night. Stefanie's voice gave it romance, with her slightly melancholy songs. Presently he heard a snore. Charles's head had fallen forwards, he was fast asleep, the half-smoked cigar between his dangling fingers. The sight of him hurt Peter.

The music ceased. Stefanie returned to the terrace. He thanked her as he stood up. She cast a glance at the sleeping figure.

"Shall we walk a little?" she asked Peter, picking up a cigarette.

As he lit a match for her she held his wrist to direct the flame. Her eyes looked into his, grey and lovely.

"Poor Charles, the heat gets him down," she said.

But he knew, and she knew, it wasn't the heat. They went down the steps, across the garden towards a loggia built against a wall decorated with Della Robbia plaques.

"I'm glad you're coming to stay—he needs company," she said. "Sometimes he gets unbearable. I don't think this place is good for him. How unlike you are!" she exclaimed, looking at Peter, as they leaned against a balustrade overlooking the canal. Her hands were long and finely shaped, laden with sparkling rings.

"Unlike—oh, I don't know," he commented. "Of course I haven't Charles's brains."

"He hasn't your looks, Peter."

The remark made him slightly uncomfortable. He laughed awkwardly. "I wouldn't say that—a lot of people find Charles very attractive. What do you do here all day?" he asked, changing the subject.

"You really are sweet and loyal," she said, smiling. "Oh, I swim and read and sleep," she added, answering his question.

She leaned forward. The channel between her breasts drew his eyes. Imagination stirred. She could not be ignored physically. He began to understand Charles's bondage.

"Shall we go back?" he asked, quelling absurd panic.

"Back! Charles won't be awake yet. Look, the moon's coming up."

It rose over the flat plain, golden through the mist. An owl hooted. The frog chorus came steadily from the marsh.

"Sometimes I am very lonely here—when he goes to sleep like that. I come down here and cry," she said, quietly.

"Cry?"

"Yes—I shouldn't have told you that. I'm sorry."

"Oh, that's all right. I think I understand," he said.

Her hand rested on the back of his on the balustrade. With an impulse of sympathy he took it, holding it, soft and warm in his own. They stood thus, as the moon slowly mounted, until it was clear of the mist.

"I think we should go back. And thank you, Peter," she said, her beautiful eyes smiling sadly into his.

Charles was still asleep. She shook him gently, and woke him. He apologized, and poured himself a drink.

"What a lovely night!" he commented, looking up.

III

On the fifth day Peter felt he could not endure it any more. She ran through every vein of his body, and he knew she was Delilah. She was playing him until that moment when, provoked beyond control, he would lose his head. How those five days had changed things! He had begun by feeling sorry for her, now he began to fight for Charles. He came to understand the collapse of his brother. Dreadful quarrels suddenly rose like squalls. He could hear the stormy voices coming from their room. He heard doors slammed, the crashing of glass. Sometimes Charles emerged, wild-eyed, quivering, and he would rush away into the library. Food, the launch not being at the steps, a window one of them wanted closing, her passion for the radio, his teasing habit of setting Busto to leap up on her, some omission of Angelo's, anything was tinder for the conflagration. What had come over Charles to make him so irritable?

Never before had Peter imagined feminine caprice could be so maddening. He had unnerving revelations of the Magyar temper. She would shut herself up and sulk, or suddenly, like the whirlwind, send everything flying within reach. And then, irresistibly lovely, with her arms about Charles, her hand caressing his hair, or her mouth hungrily inviting his, contrite, plaintive, or deliciously playful, she would win him back with laughter, or amorous intention. In this villa so spacious and dignified, there was no settled calm or dignity. How far off seemed Henley, the world of his mother, Uncle Wyndham, Auntie Janet, thought Peter. What would they think of it? But he knew what they would think of it.

It was hard to apportion the blame for this state of affairs.

Sometimes he thought it was Stefanie's fault, sometimes Charles's. How fond of him she was, and how much it was wholly physical, he had no idea. He wondered if they had always been like that together. It was sad to see Charles so lost to self-discipline, worried and restless and irritable. His capacity for work seemed wholly gone. He had lost his companionableness.

Stefanie troubled Peter also. He could not dislike her, though he knew her to be selfish, and physically self-conscious. Her eyes, her voice, the movement of every limb had an alluring quality. When she looked at him he felt her interest in him was as a man, not as a companion. Sometimes she touched him, playfully, or sought his sympathy, and always he had a nervous fear, not of her but of himself. Her body was a flame, he could so easily burn himself. It would be better to go than to stay and have to watch himself like this, and yet he wanted to reach some solution of this problem for Charles's sake.

One morning when he went down to breakfast he was surprised to learn Charles had gone out. When Stefanie came down, and he asked her where Charles had gone, she said she did not know, and did not care. There had been another quarrel.

"Sometimes I think he's mad," she said. "Peter, let's go sailing—I shall scream if I don't do something."

He got the cushions and the tiller, and they set off. It was a still morning with sirocco in the air. In half an hour they reached the lagoon. The heat shimmered over the jade-green water. The big russet sail flapped idly. Stefanie lay on the cushions, a sylph in blue linen trousers, and a sailor's blue and white striped jersey revealing every curve. It was almost noon. She watched Peter sitting by the tiller, clad only in his bathing shorts, the song of youth in this symphony of colour. Presently, he announced his intention of bathing. The boat lay becalmed. He got up, for a moment stood poised and taut on the stern, his brown body sharp against the sunlight. Then he dived.

"Gorgeous!" he spluttered, coming up, and then went off in a fury of threshed water.

She lay back, her eyes half closed against the fierce glare, watched the fair head appearing intermittently as Peter raced with powerful arms through the green water.

After lunch on the terrace Stefanie said she was going to have a siesta. It was the hottest day she could remember.

"That's a jolly good idea. I feel like a shut-eye too. I've eaten too much," he said, following her in.

The telephone rang in the hall as she was half-way up the stairs. Peter picked up the receiver. She waited until he had replaced it.

"It's Charles. He's in Venice. He'll be back for dinner. He hopes we're happy," reported Peter.

She laughed ironically over the balustrade.

"That's a guilty conscience—poor Charles!" she cried.

Peter went into the library to get *Country Life*, in case he didn't sleep. When he got to his room he kicked off his sandals, slipped out of his trousers and vest, and lay naked on the bed. He began to read an article on sea-gulls in the Hebrides.

He was awakened by a tapping on his door.

"Hello?" he cried, sitting up.

"Peter—it's me. There's a bird in my room, and it's frightening me to death," called Stefanie.

"Wait a moment!" cried Peter, springing off the bed. He found his dressing-gown and tied it tight round his waist. When he opened his door Stephanie stood there, in a flowered silk wrap and pink slippers.

"Oh, Peter, there's a bird flying round my room—it scares me. I've rung and nobody comes."

"A bird! Let's have a look!" cried Peter.

He followed her into her room, half dark with the shutters closed. As he entered, something flew around, in wild agitation, and then settled on the Venetian chandelier.

"Let's open the shutters, perhaps it'll go," said Peter.

They flung back the shutters, and he shooed the bird, but instead of going out of the window it flew around the room in panic. They repeated their attempts. Finally it settled on the *palmette* over the curtains.

"Have you a hand towel?" asked Peter. "We'll try bagging it."

She fetched a towel from the bathroom and gave it to him. He mounted a chair, and with a quick movement threw the towel over the bird. There was a great fluttering.

"Got it!" cried Peter, gathering in the corners. He jumped down from the chair. "Let's see if we can get a look at it."

He carefully worked his hands over the live thing in the towel, and then, having secured it, turned back the cloth. A bird's head, bright-eyed, emerged.

"Why, it's a blue jay!" exclaimed Stefanie. "The sweet thing!"

"The Blue Bird of Happiness!" laughed Peter, stroking its head with a finger. "Well, good-bye, Blue Bird!"

He stepped on to the small balcony and released the captive. It flew off into the bright day.

"Thank you, Peter—it quite scared me!" she said, frail beside him.

He looked down at her. The brown hair hung loose over her shoulders. Her throat was bare. The opening of her wrap held his eyes. The particular scent she affected enveloped her. He caught his breath. She leaned towards him like a flame, her face upturned. The next moment she was in his arms, soft, yielding. He kissed her in a delirium of youthful ecstasy, her mouth, her hair, her throat.

"Peter! Peter!" she breathed, one hand on his bare shoulder, his body firm under the silk gown.

He raised his head and looked at her, his eyes wild, his arms crushing her. Then, as if a spring had snapped, his arms fell from her. He stood back, trembling.

"I'm crazy!" he cried, hoarsely.

Her hand stopped him as he moved.

"Stay!" she said, quietly, her eyes pleading.

"No, no! No, Stefanie," he cried, and rushed past her out of the room.

She stood still. Presently she heard his door slam. Then she went to her own door, closed it, and crossed to the mirror on the dressing-table. For a few moments she looked at herself. Picking up a comb, she slowly passed it through her hair.

Peter was on the terrace, trying to read and appear normal, when Charles arrived back about seven o'clock. Stefanie had not appeared out of her room all the afternoon. Peter tried to control his nerves. He was apprehensive, the air seemed charged. Black clouds had obscured the sunset, a storm was brewing, as if Nature were trying to match the atmosphere in the villa.

"Where's Stefanie?" asked Charles, as he came on to the terrace.

"I think she's upstairs—I haven't seen her for some time," replied Peter, hoping his voice sounded normal.

Charles went indoors. A little later he heard voices coming from their bedroom. It sounded like a quarrel from the manner in which their voices rose. When Charles appeared again, he was flushed and angry. He shook a cocktail, and gave one to Peter. He asked him how he had spent the day. Then Angelo appeared and announced dinner, which had been laid at the other end of the terrace.

"Thanks—the Signora won't be coming down—she has a headache," said Charles to the servant. "Come on, Peter, we'll begin."

"I think I'll go back to Venice to-morrow," said Peter, as they proceeded with dinner. "I've had a wonderful time, but I'm sure you've had enough of me—and I want to trot around Venice."

"What's the hurry—when does your friend come from Salzburg?"

"Next Tuesday."

"Then why not wait till he comes?"

"Thanks, Charles—but I think I'll go to-morrow."

They ate in silence for a time until Charles spoke, looking across the table at his brother.

"Why must you go?" he demanded, as if he had been considering something. "Anything wrong here?"

"Wrong? Oh, of course not. You've given me a splendid time."

Peter felt the sweat on his brow and neck. His voice sounded quite false. Charles looked at him keenly and then commented on the storm that was blowing up. A breeze came from nowhere and guttered the candles.

"Sorry about Stefanie. She's got a headache, or the sulks or both," commented Charles, pouring his third whisky and soda.

An ear-splitting clap of thunder shook the heavens. Then heavy spits of rain gave warning. They rose and went into the sitting-room just as the storm broke in all its fury. Suddenly the door opened, and Stefanie, in her dressing-gown and slippers, entered.

"You're very gallant, aren't you? You know lightning terrifies me!" she exclaimed, striding across to the couch, on which she piled up cushions and lay down.

The two men, reading, looked at each other. Charles shrugged his shoulders.

"I think the worst's over," observed Peter, finding the silence unendurable.

No answer came from the couch. The storm went on with unabated fury; then, about twenty minutes later, it began to recede. All at once, in one abrupt movement, Stefanie sprang from the couch, seized a Lalique flower-vase, and screaming, "I hate men!" sent it crashing against the marble fireplace. The next moment she tore out of the room.

Charles and Peter stared at each other, dumb from this sudden outburst. Then a trickle of blood ran down Charles's face. He put up his hand to his cheek. He had been cut by a flying fragment of glass. He sat up, dabbing himself.

"Well—it's mutual. I hate women," he said, cynically, and went over to the tantalus. "You know now what a happy home life is!" The whisky siphon spluttered.

He raised a glass to Peter, his hand shaking.

IV

The skies were clear again the next morning when Peter came down for his swim before breakfast. The shining blue heaven covered the fresh earth like a bowl. There was a promise of heat. After his swim he sat down on the terrace and Angelo brought him breakfast. There was no sign of the others. Charles had arranged to take him into Venice by launch at ten o'clock. His bags were packed.

Busto came bounding along the terrace, and stood by, tail wagging, thankful for all offerings. Peter felt a little sad at leaving; this place was an earthly Paradise to look at. It began to seem a little Hell to live in. Anyhow, he could not stay on after what had happened. He was no good as an actor. How could Charles go on living in this fashion? Something terrible had happened to him. And how would it end? Laura Lanier had a lot to answer for, if only she knew.

Peter drove some wasps off the jam, gave Busto a titbit, and crunched his *gressini*. The delicious sticks of bread were home-made and new. Somewhere, down by the garden-sheds, a mechanical saw made a happy sound. And then, without warning, the peace of the morning was shattered. Angry voices came on the air. A torrent of words, screamed out by a woman, were followed by the heavier voice of a man. Stefanie and Charles were quarrelling again, but with a violence he had never heard before.

Peter got up from the table and walked down into the garden. He felt disgusted by the vulgarity of it. How could they go on living like this when it might have been so romantic? It seemed like a chapter out of a cheap French novel.

After a short walk Peter returned to the house. He went into the library to pick up a book he had forgotten to pack, and was astonished to find Charles sitting at his desk, his head down on his arms. He was sobbing like a child.

Embarrassed by the sight, Peter stood still; then he went up to his brother.

"Charles," he said, quietly, "what on earth's the matter?"

Charles got up without answering and went over to the fireplace, leaning on it, his back to the room. He made no answer for a time, then he turned and spoke, his face distraught.

"I'm coming with you, Peter, I'm getting away from this."

He was shaking, he looked terribly ill.

"You'd better—you can't go on like this," said Peter.

"She'll make a dreadful scene."

"Let her—I'll deal with her. Can you pack now? The sooner the better. Get out, even if you leave things," said Peter, finding sudden courage. "Go and do it now!"

"I will," replied Charles, leaving the room.

Peter waited until his brother had gone upstairs. Then he rang for Angelo, and had his bags brought down and carried out to the launch waiting at the steps. He listened all the time for the sound of voices, expecting an outcry. All was still. Had Charles's resolution come to nothing, was he in Stefanie's arms again?

A quarter of an hour elapsed. He heard someone coming down the stairs. He went out into the hall. It was Charles, with a bag.

"Where's Angelo? Tell him to take this out," said Charles, putting down the bag in the hall. "I've some papers I want—then I'm ready."

He turned to go into the library, when Stefanie appeared at the head of the stairs. She was clad in a quilted dressing-gown. She began to come down, slowly. They watched her come. Her face was a mask. When she reached the hall she looked at the bag, and then out at the launch with other bags already in it.

"So you're going! You mean it?" she said, addressing Charles.

"Yes—I mean it, this time," he replied, quietly, and went into the library.

She stood against the balustrade, her face marble against the marble. Pity for her stirred in Peter's heart.

"Stefanie—I——" he began.

"Get away!" she cried, hate in her voice and eyes.

Charles came out from the library. As he reached the foot of the stairs she stepped forward.

"Charles!"

He ignored her and moved aside. The next moment Peter rushed forward, but too late. Her pistol was levelled. There was a report. Charles stood still, dazed, staring at her. Then he saw Peter stagger. With a cry he went to him.

"I'm—I'm all right," said Peter, as he held him up. "I—— No, there's something——"

He pressed his hand to his side, half fainting. Charles lifted him, carried him into the library, and placed him on the couch.

"Here—here!" breathed Peter, heavily, his hand below his heart. "Charles—I'm done, I think. Say it was an accident, that——"

"Don't talk!" cried Charles, opening his shirt. A red stain had begun to spread over it. He looked at Peter sharply. He was not losing consciousness.

"Can't you let me raise you?" asked Charles. "I want your shirt off."

"Yes—I'm all right," gasped Peter. But his eyes closed and opened again.

Charles pulled off the coat and shirt. He glanced over the boy's muscular brown torso. There was a wound in the left loin.

At that moment, Angelo, with frightened eyes, stood in the doorway.

"Angelo—I want some linen strips—cut up the shirt quickly," commanded Charles. *"Presto! Presto!"*

The gaping Angelo came forward and took the shirt.

"There's scissors on the desk—quick, man!" cried Charles, staunching the wound with a handkerchief. He watched Peter's face, its colour was still good. He slowly lowered him and asked him to half turn. Peter lay on his side. There was no wound on the back. The bullet had not come through. It was still lodged in him somewhere. He said nothing to his brother, and turned him on to his back.

o.s.c.—7

"I can sit up—I'm sure I could walk," said Peter. "It's shock chiefly."

"Don't talk, old boy, and keep still. I'm taking you into Venice, at once—it's the best thing to do."

"If you do that everybody'll know. They'll ask——"

"You must not talk!" said Charles, severely. "Not another word."

A spasm of pain passed over the boy's face. He looked at Charles, a little frightened, and then forced a smile to his lips. Angelo had cut up the shirt. Charles made a pad, and then bound Peter's loin, wrapping him round with a travelling-rug that lay across the couch.

"Angelo, we've to get the Signorino to the launch. You take——"

"No, no, signore. Let-a me carry him. I am very strong-a. I carry him, sure," cried Angelo.

"Gently, then. Let him lift you, Peter—relax."

With very little effort the sturdy Italian picked up Peter and carried him gently out of the room, across the hall, and down the steps to the launch. Charles followed with cushions. They laid the boy on them. Charles started the launch at once, and ordered Angelo to steer, while he went and sat by his brother. He knew they were racing Death across the lagoon. They were in sight of the Riva and the canal leading to the hospital when Peter lost consciousness.

The next four days were a nightmare. The X-rays revealed that the bullet had, by a miracle, missed the abdominal viscera, and lodged itself near the spine.

The first evening, Peter's temperature rose, but the surgeons decided against any immediate operation. Charles telegraphed Uncle Wyndham suggesting Mrs. Woodfall come out at once—there had been a shooting accident. Then, later in that first afternoon, he had gone back with Angelo to the villa to get some things, to see if it was possible to stop any gossip, to deal with Stefanie. With luck they might keep the police out of it, if they could concoct a story. Angelo swore to secrecy, for himself and his wife, Maria, the cook. "She not talk, signore. She know-a I break-a the back if she talk." But when they reached the villa, Stefanie was not there. She had packed all her bags and a wardrobe trunk, and had left the villa before noon.

"How?" asked Charles, of Maria.

"She ordered a car from Mestre. She seemed verra frightened of something. All-a the time she cry, 'Hurry! Hurry!' as I find-a the things."

Charles and Angelo exchanged glances. It was evident Maria had not seen anything, did not know the truth.

"Where did she go?" asked Charles.

Maria spread out her fat arms with a gesture of despair.

"I not ask-a the Signora—she not say, signore. All she cry is, 'Hurry! Hurry!'"

Charles looked in the library, in case there was a note. There was nothing. He went up to their room. It looked as if it had been burgled. Drawers stood open, some of them taken out and on their side. Everything demonstrated hasty flight.

Leaving instructions with Angelo, with renewed emphasis on the need of absolute secrecy, Charles, having collected all he required, returned to Venice, where he took up his lodging in the Hôtel Danieli. There was an answer from Uncle Wyndham. Mrs. Woodfall was leaving at once, arriving six p.m. the next day.

When she arrived, having flown to Milan, Mrs. Woodfall was accompanied by Auntie Janet. Charles had prepared his story before he went to meet them. It was the one which he had told at the hospital, and which had been accepted, so far. Peter, when staying at the villa, had practised revolver shooting in the garden. While cleaning the revolver afterwards, with one of the chambers still loaded unknowingly, it had gone off. The story might get by, if Peter recovered. If he did not, and an inquest followed, the truth would come out. It was a risk he decided to take. Angelo was a temporary servant, of whom he knew little. The man might blackmail him, but so far he had been very co-operative.

Charles was delighted to see Auntie Janet: she was always reliable, and it was in keeping with her character to insist on accompanying his mother at an hour's notice. It was the first time both of them had flown. "I was in a state of exhilarating fear!" exclaimed Auntie Janet. Venice she had not visited since her honeymoon. "It has been improved beyond all protest," was her caustic comment, when she found motor-launches plying on the Grand Canal, and a Bar Americano on the corner of the Piazza.

They visited the hospital with Charles every afternoon. Peter began to improve. On the fifth day his temperature was quite normal. He seemed out of danger. After a conference it was decided that he should be taken to Vienna later, for the extraction of the bullet. The renowned Dr. Flersheim might be secured. But inquiries resulted in the information that that famous surgeon had disappeared months ago into the Nazi concentration camp at Dachau. The equally celebrated Dr. Dornbirn could perform the operation.

One evening, when Mrs. Woodfall had retired early, Charles and Auntie Janet went and sat at Florian's Café. The great Piazza began to empty, the portable bandstand had been packed away after the public concert. Auntie Janet suddenly startled her companion with a question.

"When are we going to have the truth, Charles?" she asked, putting down her Cinzano glass.

"Truth?" he echoed, blandly.

"You don't imagine you can fool your mother and me, even if you've side-tracked the doctors and the authorities. Single young men of twenty-seven don't live in large villas alone. And who is 'we' who slipped into one of your letters? What's happened to the villa—aren't we going to see it?"

"I've closed it. The lease is up at the end of September."

"This is only the beginning. Now don't tell me, unless you want to. I'm full of curiosity, like any healthy woman, but, if we're going to lie when we get back to Henley, we must have the same story. I've a feeling it all goes back to that absurd Twitterwittee, or whatever you call it. You've never been the same since you met Laura Lanier. You're on your way to becoming a scarecrow, my dear Charles. Now tell me to mind my own business!"

Charles puffed at his cigarette angrily and swallowed his brandy. He called the waiter and ordered another.

"Five!" said Auntie Janet, laconically. Their eyes met. "Oh, you poor boy!" Her hand rested on his arm sympathetically. His anger subsided immediately.

"I'll tell you the whole story, I've always wanted to," he said, quietly.

He told her, omitting nothing. When he had finished, she smiled at him, wise and kind.

"You know, Hell isn't a place where the wicked go, it's what the young often create for themselves," said Auntie Janet. "You remember Dante and his Beatrice? Your Laura and your disappointment are a bit like that. There's nothing one can do, except not give way to despair. I've never believed like all those silly people who ignore hard facts, that we're born to be happy. We've got to wriggle our way through to some form of satisfaction. Here endeth the lesson of one silly old woman."

"Not silly," commented Charles.

"No, I agree," laughed Auntie Janet. "I'd like a brandy, and you can have a sixth before you turn over a new leaf."

He called the waiter and gave the order.

"Auntie Janet, you're adorable. I feel better. Anything more you want to know?"

"Yes—one thing. When are you telling your mother?"

"My mother—but should I?" he asked, surprised. "It might upset her."

"I've a feeling mothers never mind being upset by the confidences of their children."

"Very well," he said, quietly.

At that moment, Tony Farnham, going back to the Hôtel Luna, saw them, and came to their table. He was leaving on the morrow, driving Peter's car back to England.

CHAPTER TEN

INTERLUDE IN VIENNA

I

THE leaves were falling in the Ringstrasse. Autumn had come to Vienna, and the Midas touch of gold was upon each tree. Charles and Peter sat outside the Bristol in the early afternoon sunshine, watching the crowd saunter by. It had changed complained Charles. The heavy hand of the Nazi had killed the *Gemütlichkeit* of the Viennese. "They've had the song knocked out of them, poor things. Can these be the feet that Strauss set waltzing?" asked Auntie Janet. No, there was no waltzing in them, either in their bodies or in their eyes. Mr. Chamberlain's spectacular flight to confer with Hitler had electrified Europe, and, after the general rejoicing at the avoidance of war, the betrayal of Czechoslovakia had filled all thoughtful persons with foreboding. The sentence of death hung over Prague. Vienna sensed her fate.

Peter, indifferent to the political scene, enjoyed Vienna, and was sad to be departing in a few days. He owed this city much. He had been restored to health, thanks to the skill of Dr. Dornbirn. The bullet had been located and extracted. After a fortnight he was on his feet again. Now, after a month, he was his young self. But Oxford with the new term called him. There was to be no football, no boxing, he was warned, only moderate exercise. Well, he had got off lightly.

Mrs. Woodfall and Auntie Janet, for whom they had been waiting, came out of the hotel. They were all going for a ride through the Wiener Wald, to see the autumn tints in the sunset. The moment Charles saw Auntie Janet look at him, he knew something was on her mind.

"What is it—something's happened? I can see it in your

face," he asked, as they walked towards the limousine waiting for them.

"You're much too sharp—I'll tell you when you get back," replied Auntie Janet, nor could his pleading move her. It was half-past six when they got back to the hotel.

"I'll come down again in ten minutes and meet you in the lounge," said Auntie Janet, as they walked to the lift.

He was waiting for her when she came down.

"Well?" he asked, having ordered Martinis.

"You have got to be told. I can't keep it to myself, Charles —and you'll find out soon, anyway."

"To be told what?"

"She's here, in this hotel—Laura!"

He sat upright, staring at her, moistening his lips.

"Are you sure—it's not possible!" he said, after a space.

Auntie Janet nodded. "Just before we went out I went to the desk to buy stamps. The register was open, and I casually glanced at the page, and there, at the top, were two names— Paul and Laura Korwienski, Château Golo, Wokolow, Poland. I asked about them. They came in last night, from Munich. He's playing at a concert here to-morrow afternoon. There's a bill up, by the ticket bureau."

Charles sat still. She noticed his pallor. He stared before him, the veins of his clenched hands standing out.

"My God—here!" he breathed at last.

"You'll see them?" asked Auntie Janet.

"I don't know."

"You must, Charles. You'll be tortured if you don't. It might be better for the future."

"What—laying a ghost?" he asked, fiercely.

The waiter brought their drinks. When he had gone——

"You're right, Auntie Janet. I'll see them," he said.

"Good. I want to hear him play—it's the Grieg Concerto, with the Vienna Symphony Orchestra. Can I get tickets for four?"

A smile broke over Charles's face.

"I hope he's foul!" he said, lightly.

When Charles had returned to his room he paced up and down for some minutes; then he picked up the telephone.

"Is Mrs. Korwienski in her room?" he asked the operator.

"Princess Korwienski?"

"Yes—Princess Korwienski, please."

He had forgotten the Princess part. The telephone buzzed.

"Hello?" said a voice.

"Laura!" he cried.

"Charles!"

"So you knew my voice?"

"Why, of course—but where are you?" she asked.

"Here in the Bristol."

"Oh, how wonderful! Can't you come up? We're Suite F, sixth floor."

"I'll come now."

He put down the receiver, letting his hand rest on it, while he sat still. His heart was thudding. It was foolish, utterly foolish, but he could not help himself.

He got up and looked in the mirror, wondering what she would think of him. Two and a half years had passed since they had met, years the locusts had eaten, no, worse than that. It would not have seemed strange if his hair had turned grey. Actually it was still flawlessly black. He had gathered lines around his eyes, but living in the sun might account for that.

Like a somnambulist he walked to the lift and went up to the sixth floor. He walked down the long corridor. Suite F was on the corner. He stood in front of the mahogany door a few moments. Then he knocked gently.

The door opened and Laura stood there.

"Charles! I can't believe it's you! Come in!"

He followed into the sitting-room. It was pleasant, full of flowers, with windows overlooking the Kärntnerring. There was a grand piano in one corner, with music on the stand.

"Paul will be in, in a few minutes. He's lying down," she said.

They looked at each other in silence for a space. She

noticed he was thinner in the face, and his eyes were lined, as if he had been sleeping badly.

"You're well, Charles?" she asked.

"Oh, yes, quite. And you?"

"Well, look at me—the same battered old woman!" she said, laughing. That glint in her eyes, familiar from those Florida days, sent his blood coursing. Her voice, the tilt of her head, they were the same. He saw she was older. Two years and a half, imperceptible in the faces of most women, had wrought a subtle change in hers. It was as beautiful as ever, but it was maturer, the lines had hardened a little.

"Sit down—what will you drink?" she asked, going to a wagon.

"Oh—a Martini, I think," he answered. "When did you get here?"

"Last evening. Paul played in Munich. He's playing here to-morrow afternoon. Why don't you come?"

"We are coming."

"We?"

Her hands stopped as she lifted the bottle. She turned and looked at him, startled.

"We're quite a party—my mother, my brother, Peter, and a friend, Mrs. Cherwell," he explained.

"You're travelling?" she asked, bringing him a glass. She sat down, slim-legged, neat-footed.

"Well—not exactly. My brother had an accident, got shot. We came here to have the bullet extracted. He's all right now, and we're going home in a few days."

"How very alarming—who shot him?"

He hesitated, and wished he had not been so foolish as to mention the shooting.

"Oh—that's quite a story. And you—tell me about yourself. Have you given up acting entirely?" he asked, turning the inquiry from himself.

"Yes, I've done nothing since I married. I look after Paul."

"Lucky fellow! I suppose you travel quite a lot with his concerts?" he said, lighting her cigarette.

"No—we travel very little. You see, Paul's a sick man. He can only play occasionally."

"I'm sorry to hear that, Laura. What's the matter—nothing serious, I hope? He looked very fit, the one day I saw him."

Her eyes opened wide at his remark.

"You've met Paul? Where?" she asked.

"At a lunch at Mrs. Lipvander's, in New York, before I sailed. But he doesn't know."

"You didn't tell him you knew me—but, Charles!" she cried, reproachfully. "And you didn't call on me either. I saw your name in the sailing list the day you left. I kept hoping that——" The sentence went unfinished.

"But, Laura, surely you understood. I couldn't—I didn't think I could ever see you again," he finished, quietly, looking down at his glass.

There was a self-conscious pause. His head, bent before her, had the familiar curve, his hand on the glass was the same she had seen sifting the sand, as he had looked down at her that last day on the beach at Witterwittee. The image of him had never faded. She was perturbed by the faithfulness of her memory. He sat here now. It might have been only yesterday that she had last seen him. The little variation in the line of his parting towards the crown of his head was there, unchanged. His hands, strong and alive, had the same fascination. Dismay and pleasure laid a weight on her.

"I hope you're very happy, Laura—it's nothing seriously wrong with Paul?" he asked, breaking the silence, desperately. As he asked the question he knew the answer from her eyes. She looked at him simply, trying to smile. "Oh, Laura, I'm sorry," he added. "What is it?"

"His lungs—poor Paul," she replied, softly, opening her ringed hand and looking at it. Then, tucking a wisp of hair back from her brow: "He had his first attack on our honeymoon—in Biarritz, a hæmorrhage. When he got out of hospital two months later they said he must go to Davos. Do you know Davos?" she asked, abruptly, and answered herself: "The ante-room of Death. We were there three months.

He seemed better, and went to give a concert in Stuttgart. From there we went to Frankfurt, then Lucerne, and Milan. In Milan, Paul had another attack—the day before the concert. It had to be cancelled. He was a month in bed there, and he went to a sanatorium again—in the Black Forest this time; and I stayed near by at Freiburg. They tried to save a lung, by collapsing it."

"A pneumothorax?"

"Yes—that was it. He seemed better for a time, and left the sanatorium. He insisted, though he couldn't get his temperature down. He never loses hope, you know——"

"They never do—their optimism is a symptom. He coughs a lot?"

"No—not a lot—well, not very often, though it's there; but there's always a little wheezing. Oh, Charles!"

She covered her face in her hands, then, recovering quickly: "You can't imagine how brave he is—how he fights! He's driven to bed, and he gets up again. Always he's had a good night, if you ask him."

"You sleep separately?"

"Yes—it's essential, the doctors say."

"Absolutely—you must take every care, Laura," said Charles.

"Always a good night, always feeling better, always going to give a concert, Charles. The courage of him!" she cried.

"And he gives concerts?"

"Yes—he won't give up entirely. He's played four times this last month. At the piano he's a strong man, Charles. Wonderful, wonderful, but after—he was in bed four days after Munich."

"He shouldn't do it. He should be kept in a——"

"Sanatorium. Charles, do you know those sanatoriums? The awful cold, the snow, those lonely pine-locked villages of the damned, the bare rooms, open windows, the temperature charts, the almost-never cureds, sitting around, telling you they are going back home to-morrow. I've seen them, seen them for eighteen months. I understand why Paul will die rather than live that way. But you didn't come here to hear all this. Poor Paul, he hates anyone to discuss it."

She put a handkerchief to her eyes. Then, forcing a smile to her face, she picked up his glass, and went across to the wagon, filling it.

"Do you hear from Sundown Grove?" she asked, with a cheerful voice that did not deceive Charles, watching her, heavy-hearted.

"No—never. Well, that's not quite correct. Emily wrote to tell me of your marriage. I left under a cloud."

Laura looked at him curiously, and he told her the story.

"I wonder what it is—you don't think Uncle Henry's in the dope traffic?"

They both laughed gaily at the suggestion.

"Perhaps Grandma doped your coffee before the back-gammon," laughed Laura. "Do you think we'll ever know the truth? Is there anything to know, or does the sun and orange-blossom scent do things to one's imagination?"

The sound of a door opening drew their attention. A young man stood there, smiling at them.

"Paul!" exclaimed Laura. "This is Charles Woodfall—and I hear you have met before!"

Paul Korwienski came into the room, and grasped the visitor's hand. "Yes—I remember you now—at Mrs. Lipvander's? How-d'you-do?" he asked, genially.

They sat down. Charles examined him. It was the same fellow, and not the same fellow. He had colour in his cheeks; but it was a deceptive colour, too high, as was the flame in his dark eyes. The face had sunken, the frontal bone was too prominent under the dry skin. He could have passed for a healthy man, helped by his trim figure, youthful in its lines, but under Charles's professional eye the story was plain.

They chatted agreeably until, seeing it was nearly eight o'clock and he was due to dine, Charles rose to take his leave.

"Laura darling—Charles must come to my concert to-morrow—that is, if you can endure piano playing?" asked Paul, smiling at Charles.

"Yes—we are coming, my mother and brother and a friend —we've taken tickets."

"Good—come round after the concert!"

"Paul—I don't think——" began Laura.

"Oh, you see—she's so used to keeping the fans away!"

"You must rest afterwards, darling. Won't you come in for cocktails to-morrow—all of you, at half-past six? Paul will have rested then," asked Laura.

"That will be delightful," said Charles.

They both took him to the door. He went down the corridor. He had come through it much better than he had dared to hope. It was the same Laura, making a desperate fight.

II

Korwienski's playing of the Grieg Concerto in A minor the following afternoon left Charles wondering from what source this frail fellow drew his dynamic energy. He appeared halfway through the orchestral concert, shyly threaded his way between the violinists, bowed to the welcoming applause and to the conductor, and then sat down at the keyboard. The orchestra and the audience waited while he adjusted the piano stool; then, at a slight nod to the conductor, the Concerto began.

It took Laura, in a box on the left, some time to discover the Woodfall family. She found herself wondering which was the mother and which was Auntie Janet, of whom Charles had talked at Witterwittee. She had been forewarned that brother Peter was a big blond Adonis. His curled head and profile fitted the description. He gave no sign of having been dangerously ill. How, wondered Laura, had he come to be shot? Charles had shown no desire to explain.

Laura turned to the platform. She knew every movement, bar, and note of the Concerto, having heard them pounded out through long hours of assiduous practice. He had played it in Munich. He was playing much better this afternoon. Paul liked the Concerto, he was happy with this well-disciplined orchestra. A sense of enjoyment came from performers and audience. Laura closed her eyes. Paul was solo now, elaborating the theme; soon the orchestra would flow in and the great waves of the ensemble would carry him onwards like an exultant swimmer. Down there, in the stalls, sat Charles, a Charles subtly changed, in a manner she could not define, and yet, for her, the same companion as in those happy days at Sundown Grove. She opened her eyes and sought him again, and, taking her glasses, from the cover of the box curtain she trained them on him. She loved him the more for his absorption in Paul's playing. He sat there, his dark head held high, his lips slightly parted, a smile on his face, as though not only the music but kindly admiration of the man at the piano moved him to enjoyment. She watched while Paul crashed out the chords, and the orchestra, as if answering a challenge, swept in, full-toned, and elaborated the piano's theme. How well she knew the line of his jaw, the well-defined arch of the nostril, the wave of one raven lock set back above the sloping ear.

She turned her glasses, conscious of unwilling disloyalty to the man at the piano. She had told herself she could forget, but two and a half years had passed, and looking at him now she knew she had not forgotten. Every detail only confirmed the faithfulness of her memory. With a sinking feeling she knew now she was never going to forget. His voice yesterday, the steady light of his eyes, his manner of lifting a glass, of lighting a cigarette—she knew these aspects so faithfully, too faithfully.

Laura turned away, directing her eyes to the platform. She always grew afraid for Paul as he approached this grand finale. They did not know, these people, how gallant a soul fought Fate to a compromise on that keyboard. They only heard the music he made, watched the passage of his hands, saw the uptilted head, smiling now in a trance of joyous achievement, as the massed orchestra marched on, as if beckoned by an exultant spirit. She watched and listened, a prayer for him on her lips that he would emerge triumphant.

And now it was over, the last sound fading into that brief silence of suspended tribute, soon to be broken by the storm of applause.

The storm broke. The figure at the keyboard advanced, bowed and bowed and bowed. It was the great moment, and she wanted to magnify its recompense, generous though it was. For always she wondered if it would be his last.

He had left the platform now. The conductor had gone, the orchestra was moving. But he had to return again to take the continuing measure of applause, and yet again, while the reluctant audience, standing in aisles and exits, gave its final acclaim. Then he was gone.

Down in the stalls someone waved a programme at her. It was Charles, smiling. A new pride burned in her. He had seen how Paul could triumph, the flame that burned, and but for her might perish.

III

The Woodfalls visited the Korwienskis in their suite for cocktails, and afterwards they all dined together downstairs.

"What a charming pair!" said Auntie Janet. "I like them, they really do things and give themselves no airs."

They were an equal success with Mrs. Woodfall. After dinner they had returned upstairs again, and Paul Korwienski sat down at the piano and played to them for nearly an hour. Peter pronounced him a wizard, his highest term of praise; as for Laura, he said nothing, but he understood his brother's infatuation.

In two more days the family was leaving for England. The Korwienskis were *en route* to Poland. He was giving a concert in Kraków next week.

"Why don't you come and stay with us, Charles?" asked Paul, as they lunched the following day at the *Drei Husaren*. Mrs. Woodfall, Auntie Janet, and Peter had gone off to see the Vienna Communal Housing Estate, under the guidance of an enthusiastic Viennese architect.

Before answering, Charles's eyes travelled to Laura's. She was particularly lovely this morning in a little astrakhan hat and a black bolero jacket, piped with red.

"Yes, Charles—do come!" she said. "We would love it!"

Their eyes met, briefly. Each knew the import beneath this proposal.

"I wish I could—perhaps one day you'll ask me again," he replied, quietly.

"But why not now? We leave for Kraków on Sunday. I play there Monday night. We could show you the city—it's very old and picturesque—and then we'd go on to Wokolow. You'd have a great welcome from all my people. It would be grand to have you with us, wouldn't it, Laura?"

Paul's enthusiasm mounted instantly. He was full of plans. It would be winter, of course, but there was so much to do. And why not stay over Christmas, stay till the spring? People stayed for years at Château Golo.

"Years?" queried Charles.

"Years—Uncle Ivan came for a week, had a carbuncle, and has stayed fifteen years! Golo's a rabbit warren, I warn you, we never know quite how many's in the family. Yes, Charles —you must come!" cried Paul, enthusiastically. "Tell him he must come, Laura—he can write there! There's a book in us—*mon Dieu!* What a book!"

"I'd have to think of libel! It's very attractive—but, alas, I must go home," said Charles.

"Oh, now just say you're coming—why, you're more than half-way now! Laura, he'll listen to you. Command him!" pleaded Paul.

Laura smiled and toyed with her glass.

"I wish I could persuade you, Charles," she said. "Must you go to England?"

"Yes—I must," he answered, avoiding her eyes.

"I shall still hope—there are two days in which to change your mind!" exclaimed Paul.

Later, when he had gone to the cloakroom just before they left the restaurant, Charles and Laura were alone.

"Laura—I couldn't come," he said, desperately.

"I know, Charles."

She looked at him. It was the first time they had ever acknowledged to each other the unnamed thing between them. No self-deception could any more keep from her the truth buried deep in her heart. A thousand loyalties could not strangle it. She would go on, but a part of her, like a woman crying for life, would stare out of a window on a world she could not enter.

They stood now, as lonely as if they were on an island, while the diners chatted, the waiters rushed about. They saw Paul coming back, his pale face smiling, the big dark eyes beaming kindly on the scene.

"Oh, Charles," she said, and it was a cry escaping her that told him what he knew so well. Then she looked up at him, with a loveliness that smote him.

"Laura!" he breathed.

The next moment Paul was with them. They left the restaurant.

IV

He must have been sleeping soundly, for the bedside telephone rang with an insistence he could not interrupt when finally he picked up the instrument.

"Hello?" he cried, switching on the bedside lamp. It was ten past four by his travelling clock. "Hello—hello—hello?" he repeated angrily. The buzzing stopped.

"Herr Woodfall?" asked an operator's voice.

"Yes?"

"A moment, please. You are wanted."

"Charles! Charles!" said a new voice. "It's Laura!"

"Yes, Laura! What is it?"

Her voice had a desperate note.

"Can you come at once! I'm terrified! It's Paul—he's had a hæmorrhage—I think he's dead."

"Good God! Yes, Laura, I'll come at once!" cried Charles.

He replaced the receiver, got out of bed and hurriedly put on a dressing-gown and slippers. In the corridor he waited, impatient, for the lift. It came at last, with a yawning operator. Charles hurried to their room and tapped. The door opened instantly. Laura stood there, in a violet silk dressing-gown.

"Oh, Charles!" she cried. "Paul's dead, I think."

"Dead?"

He followed her across the sitting-room to a bedroom opening off on the right. Just inside lay Paul, on the floor, his face ashen, his eyes closed. Charles knelt and turned him over. Blood oozed from his mouth and nostrils. There was a damp brown patch on the green carpet. He took a wrist between his fingers, and waited. Laura watched, silent, wide-eyed.

"He's alive, Laura," said Charles, after a pause. "Straighten the bed—I'll put him on it."

She flew to the bed, and, lifting Paul, Charles carried him to it. He was astonished by the lightness of the man in his arms. He laid him on the bed, and carefully pulled off the blood-soaked pyjama jacket. Then he covered him with a blanket and looked at Laura.

"Will he live?" she asked.

"I don't know, Laura—his heart's beating anyhow. When did you find him?"

"He came to my door, this is my room. He must have felt ill, he had opened the door and his fall woke me up."

"Did he complain of any pain?"

"No—not really. He confessed he had caught a slight cold yesterday—but he never will admit he's ill. He ran a high temperature just before dinner, but he seemed himself all the evening. He went to bed about eleven."

"I think I should call in a doctor. You see, I'd not like the responsibility in case—if——"

"Oh, of course, Charles."

He turned from her, and began an examination of the unconscious man, then asked for some water and a sponge. When Laura came back, he had a smile for her.

"He's coming round—he recognized me—but he's very

drowsy. We mustn't talk to him. Can you wipe him while I hold him?"

He raised Paul, for her to sponge him. The sick man opened his eyes, and saw her. She smiled at him. Then, the task finished, he was laid down again.

"I shall stay here, on the couch—there's nothing to be done now. In the morning I will find who is the best doctor to call in. Can you go to your room and rest?" asked Charles.

"Can't I stay and watch him?"

"You should rest—there's nothing you can do, Laura. How often has this happened?"

"Three times. First in Biarritz, then in Milan, and also in a taxi one day—about ten months ago—but not so badly that time. Of course we've been warned—any time——"

She broke off. The misery in her face stabbed him.

He patted her shoulder, soothingly.

"I couldn't rest, Charles," she said.

"You'll want all your strength—please, Laura," he urged.

She left him reluctantly. He went over to the man on the bed, and looked down at him. He appeared to be in a coma. It was the face of death. But Charles knew it might not be death. These duels were often so long, and gallant, and useless. For more than two years now the poor fellow had been fighting for life. For more than two years Laura had lived through this battle, through events like this. No wonder there was tragedy in her face. Love and courage could not disguise the strain under which she lived. Love? Was it not loyalty and courage?

Ashamed of the question in his heart, he went to the window to let in the cold air of dawn. In a couple of hours he would ring Dr. Dornbirn, who would know the best specialist. Laura's travelling-rug lay on a box. Wrapping it round his legs, he lay on the couch and kept vigil.

They moved Paul to a nursing home towards noon, after consultation with a Dr. Dallwitz, the recommended specialist. There was nothing to do but watch and wait. The chart over the patient's head began its course. He was now fully conscious, and feebly begged them all not to worry. "I shan't die," he said, in the ghost of a voice.

Saturday came, the day of departure for the Woodfalls. On Friday morning Charles had settled his course. He would stay on in Vienna, he could not leave Paul and Laura in this situation.

Mrs. Woodfall agreed. They could travel home with Peter, who was now perfectly fit.

So, on Saturday morning, he accompanied his mother, Auntie Janet, and Peter to the station. While the ladies were busy in their wagon-lits, Charles and Peter stood on the platform.

"Shall we see you for Christmas?" asked Peter, broaching the subject he had avoided until these last few minutes.

"Christmas! Good heavens, I'll be home before then, I fear."

"Fear?" asked Peter.

Charles made no answer for a few moments.

"He can't last very long—poor devil. Dallwitz says a week or ten days."

"My God—it's as bad as that?" cried Peter.

"It's a miracle he's still breathing."

"And then?" asked Peter, in a low voice.

"Then—I don't know. I—haven't begun to think, Peter."

The younger brother seemed about to say something, but kept silence. Mrs. Woodfall and Auntie Janet came down on to the platform. They all talked until the call came to go aboard. Charles kissed his mother and Auntie Janet.

"I'll be thinking of you, Charles, and poor Laura," said his mother.

That was all she said, but he knew from her glance that she was conscious of the whole situation.

"Good-bye, Charles—and thanks for everything, and come home soon!" cried Peter, with a grip that made Charles wince. His heartiness covered up all the things that had no words in his grateful, worried heart.

The express drew out. Charles waited until it had vanished. Then he walked gravely back to whatever Fate ordained.

CHAPTER ELEVEN

CHÂTEAU GOLO

I

As Paul Korwienski prophesied, he did not die. Despite the gloomy certainty of various specialists who came to examine him and shake their heads, despite the unanimous proof of the X-ray photographs over which they conferred, despite the erratic temperature chart which looked like an Alpine outline, he hung on grimly, day by day. In three weeks, with a food-tray on his knees, he was smiling at the few visitors allowed. He was still deathly white, except for flushes when his temperature suddenly rose, and at all times his eyes were too liquid and bright. The doctors shook their heads. It could not go on much longer. Dr. Dallwitz drew fluid off the right lung, waited a few days and drew it off again.

"You see, there's nothing to hold out with—his strength's drained," he said, confidentially, to Charles, in the odd French he spoke. "Look at this." He drew out of its envelope one of the black X-ray photos on which a skeleton Paul, with blotches like cloud-drifts, lay exposed to the professional eye. "The right's lung's almost gone—the other's extensively infected." He spread his hands despairingly. "Well, another ten days will tell us."

Another ten days told them that Paul Korwienski was coming back to life. There was talk now of getting him to a sanatorium, to Davos-Platz, or——

"No!" said Paul, firmly. "When I can be moved from here I'm going home. No more sanatoriums, Herr Doktor, never!"

The weeks passed. Little by little he gained strength. He was allowed visitors. And then came Christmas, with him sitting up each day in his room.

Charles went daily with Laura to the nursing home. They

came at four each day, when the lights in the shops and a sprinkling of snow on the ground gave a Christmas character to the scene. In the day-time they explored Vienna systematically, until, the sights exhausted, they fell back on concerts, finding new places for lunch, visiting shops to make trifling purchases, meeting everywhere the Austrian kindness breaking through a gloss of Hitlerian stiffness. Their chief anxiety apart, the days passed in an enchanted dream.

The time came for it all to end. Paul was determined to make the journey to Wokolow. There was a through express to Kraków. In Kraków he could rest a couple of days, then take the Lwów express to Jaroslaw. From there it was two hours by automobile to Château Golo.

"Yes—let us go. I shall be a new man at Golo! But I make one stipulation—and you will humour a sick man—I insist on taking my private physician, Dr. Woodfall!" cried Paul.

It was not a whimsical idea, it was something on which his mind was set. In vain Charles pleaded his long absence from home. Failing to gain his way without a brutal refusal, he enlisted the aid of Laura. She had no more success than Charles.

They discussed the matter one morning, walking in the Stadtpark, a bright sunlit morning in January, with everything sparkling in the cold crisp air.

"Very well—I'll come to Golo, and then as soon as he's settled there, I'll go home," agreed Charles.

"Thank you," said Laura. "It will give Paul such comfort."

Her hand pressed his arm. They walked a little in silence. Suddenly, looking at her, the colour in her cheeks heightened by the cold air, he exclaimed, brusquely:

"It's unfair—it's unfair, Laura! If he knew what he's asking!"

"He must never know," she said, and then, as if she were asking the question of herself: "We can be sure of that? Oh, Charles, we couldn't be so disloyal—we couldn't!"

Her appeal for assurance evoked no answer. She watched his face anxiously. She knew that expression on it. He spoke, finally.

"Why should we be tortured like this, why should we!" he protested. "Laura, I am going to say something—you can hate me for it. It's unfair to you. This life-in-death may go on for years! Paul should have died, for himself, for us!"

Her hand fell from his arm.

"Laura, I'm sorry. I'm terribly sorry. Forgive me," he cried.

She looked at him, her eyes shaded with pain.

"All you've said, Charles, I've said in my heart also—it is God who must forgive us. We both know there's only one thing to do—to go on, to let nothing shake his courage. You know how he loves me. Charles, can we make a resolution?"

"What is it?"

"Don't let us talk about it again—ever. We've had these weeks together—wonderful weeks, for all the anxiety in them. I shall always remember them—always."

Her voice trembled, and he saw the tears welling in her eyes, through which she forced a smile. He could say nothing, but she knew his assent, by his arm slipping into hers, and its reassuring pressure.

II

They left Vienna in the first week of February, and reached Kraków, a fairy-tale city deep in snow, with its massive castle, and panorama from the Wawel, its sledges on the promenades, its fur-capped people. Then, after two days of gentle sight-seeing, they took the Lwów express as far as Jaroslaw, where a closed car met them for their two hours' drive to Château Golo.

At the station Charles had his first glimpse of feudal Poland. It was a Republic, but it was still the land of princes, for as Paul came out of the station the chauffeur removed his round bearskin hat and, bowing low, kissed the hands of Paul and Laura.

Wrapped in rugs, they began the journey across the snow-bound country. It was early afternoon, with the sun still above the black forest that broke the flat plain. The road soon disappeared, and they seemed to drive, guided only by ruts, made by heavy sleighs, moving so slowly, and clinging so obstinately to the track, that often they had to make a rough detour. They passed through humble villages, long, straggling places with low, thatched cabins and small windows, and churches that seemed to belong to toyland. The great plain spread out on all sides, with thick plantations of beech and fir. From time to time they passed the gates of a park and glimpsed a large, rambling mansion, the château of Prince This, Prince That. Then, after two hours of rough riding, with the dusk settling over the land, they came to a lodge. A woman, with a coloured kerchief tied over her head, wearing heavy top-boots, swung back the great iron gates. The car passed in. The woman curtsied and shouted a smiling greeting, echoed by two children peering over a snow mound at the door.

"Château Golo—and only a mile now!" said Paul, his face beaming. "I wonder what you'll think of the old place—and its inhabitants!"

They drove down a long avenue bordered with firs, black sentinels massed on the white ground. The half-light gave them an eerie solemnity. Then, emerging, they traversed a vast park and, on a knoll, saw Château Golo, its lighted windows making a cheerful scene in the falling darkness.

The big glass doors, at the top of a flight of stone steps, opened the moment the car drew up in the courtyard. Following Paul and Laura into the hall, Charles saw them greeted by a young woman who kissed them on both cheeks. A footman in a green jacket, with silver buttons, took Charles's hat and coat. Another young footman brought in the baggage. Then strange people came out into the great hall, which was lit by a large swinging lantern with oil lamps. Its walls were covered with antelopes' and stags' horns, mounted on small wooden bases bearing the place and date of the kill.

Charles found himself being presented to several young men and women, but in the general confusion heard no names distinctly. They mounted a wide, stone staircase with an iron railing, past portraits of dead soldiers and statesmen in resplendent uniforms. An odour of burning wood came from the porcelain stove in the hall. Then, on the first floor, they entered a long salon. It was lit with lamps in brackets on the walls. Six tall windows, whose curtains had not been drawn, showed the last glimmer of day. A wolf-hound reared itself from a rug, barked and rushed to greet Paul as they began to cross the boarded floor towards a white-haired woman who rose from her chair. She was Paul's mother, and Charles, duly presented, found himself shaking the hand of a tall, angular woman with black eyes. She spoke to him partly in French, partly in English. Others were seated in the long softly lit room, and one by one were introduced. Charles's head began to reel with so many strange names. He was introduced to some fifteen or twenty, but whether members of the family or guests he had no idea.

They all talked agreeably for a few minutes, about Paul's illness, his excellent recovery, the journey from Vienna. They asked Charles about friends in England, questions he felt he could not answer intelligently, for he knew few of the names mentioned. Then in came a huge man with a long iron-grey beard and shaggy hair. He was dressed in a green shooting-coat with leather shoulder-pads, and black leather top-boots. His voice boomed. He wrung Charles's hand mercilessly. One eye looked in a different direction from the other, and his appearance would have been frightening but for his smile, which was warm and exuded goodwill to the world. His name, Charles did get. He was Prince Ivan Lubirsky, the half-brother of Paul's mother.

Finally, Charles was conducted to his room on the next floor. It seemed to be a tremendous walk along lamp-lit corridors. The footman opened a door and stood aside. The room was enormous but well warmed by a stove. There was a large bed with a hand-embroidered quilt, chairs, a couch, a large writing-desk, an armoire; and skin rugs on the wooden floor completed the furnishings. A large lamp with a yellow silk shade threw a warm pool of light over the floor.

The footman who had followed him into the room asked

him something, but as he spoke Polish, there followed a semi-comic pantomime with the tow-headed lad in green livery. At this crisis Paul came in. The servant wanted to know if he was to prepare the bath, explained Paul. He spoke to the boy, who opened another door. Greatly to Charles's surprise there was a bathroom adjoining. He had expected something more primitive.

"We have supper at eight. Just go wherever you like in the house—it's a wilderness, I warn you. The library's next to the salon, if you want to read. A dressing-bell's tolled at seven-fifteen, and the dinner-bell at eight. Don't think it's for a church service!" warned Paul.

Charles looked at Paul closely. He had stood the journey well. "I think you should have a rest before supper. And to bed early," said Charles.

"Yes, doctor!" laughed Paul. "Now I'll leave you. Your servant, by the way, is called Hans—he's a Ruthenian wood-cutter's son—a bit rough, I fear. By the way, he will feel slighted if you don't offer him your hand to kiss. He's your personal attendant."

Paul left the room, and Charles began to unpack. Hans appeared, smiling, to indicate that the bath was prepared. The boy had a peasant's plump face and round blue eyes. Charles, feeling slightly ludicrous, held out his hand. The boy bent over and kissed it. After all, reflected Charles, even Prime Ministers did that on appointment. Hans assisted with the unpacking. They found one word in common, "cigarette." To celebrate this Charles gave him a box of them. The boy left the room with shining eyes, having delivered himself of what must have been an oration of thanks.

Charles found his way down to the first floor before the dressing-bell had sounded. He began to get an idea of the size of the place. The centre part, built of stone, was probably four or five hundred years old. It had deep window embrasures, with walls five or six feet thick. The floors were of stone, as also the great staircase, some fifteen feet wide. New wings had been built out at a much later period. The salon, in which he had met Paul's mother, had a stone, groined ceiling, painted with heraldic designs. The ground floor, the entrance hall apart, seemed occupied entirely by domestic offices. It was not until the following morning that he learned that the first floor, on which the family lived, was gained not only by the stone staircase, but also by another staircase in the form of a ramp that led up from the back of the hall to the first-floor landing, thus enabling a carriage and horses to be driven up to a pair of entrance doors. This was the old ceremonial entrance. Brackets in which torches had burned were still on the stone walls of this approach.

Charles, on descending, failed to find the salon. A man-servant vainly tried to understand his inquiry. They opened door after door. It was thus Charles had his first sight of the banqueting-hall. Its ceiling vanished into darkness, in the dim light of the suspended lamps. The table down the centre would have seated forty diners. Heavy curtains of green silk damask had been drawn over windows twenty feet high.

A little breathless from this sudden revelation through the opened door, Charles shook his head. They moved on down the corridor, past forbidding figures in polished steel armour. The servant opened another door. It was a square room, striking a note of warmth and colour with its coffered ceiling. Logs blazed in a great open fireplace, with a Gothic cowl carrying a coat of arms. A girl jumped up as the door opened. There was a moment of embarrassment, then she spoke.

"How-d'you-do, Dr. Woodfall? I'm Pauli. You have met me—in the hall, but I'm sure you don't remember."

He went forward. An elderly woman rose from a divan.

"This is Miss Macdermott, Paul's old governess, and Jan's and Anna's. We all call her Smack.'

"Which is short for Miss Mac, and not derived from anything I did to my charges! How-d'you-do, Dr. Woodfall?" said the old lady.

Charles advanced and shook hands with them both. The girl, not more than seventeen, was slender and tall, with flowing black hair and a vivid colouring.

"You're English?" he asked.

"Oh, no—not one little bit. My mother is Paul's cousin. His mother, the Princess, is my great-aunt, and as my father is also Paul's cousin, I'm his second cousin twice—I'm sure you're puzzled, but there it is!"

"I take your word for it," laughed Charles. "You are visiting here?"

"Oh, no, I live here with my mother."

"The Countess Pauli was born here," explained the old lady. "I know it must be very confusing, Dr. Woodfall, but you see there are twenty-three relations living here: Prince Paul's two aunts, unmarried; one aunt, widowed; his younger brother's wife and her two children; his youngest brother; his late father's two cousins, Count Alex and Count John; his uncle, Prince Ivan; Pauli here, and her mother, the Countess Proteki, and her two half-brothers, Felix and Max—— Let me see, where've I got to?" she asked.

"And Princess Wienenski, and Julie and Bobo and Twink and Mitzi, and Ladislaus and Jan, and Zita and——"

The door opened abruptly. A young man strode into the room, breathless, still clad in a dark coat with a black fur collar.

"And Rudi—we'd forgotten him!" exclaimed Pauli. "This is my brother Rudolf, Dr. Woodfall."

The young man clicked his heels together and bowed. He had the same dark eyes and fresh colouring, and was medium in height, and pleasant in expression.

"I'm frozen!" he exclaimed, striding to the fire. "The car was snowed up outside Tarnów. I've been three hours in a cart, getting here."

He spread out his hands to the blaze.

"Well—and what's happened?" asked Pauli, breathlessly.

"I'm acquitted," he said, quietly.

"Oh!" exclaimed Pauli, throwing her arms round his neck.

"Thank you for your prayers, Smack dear," said the youth, addressing the governess.

They saw the bewilderment on the Englishman's face.

"Oh, it's nothing really," explained Pauli, to him. "Rudi shot a student at his university, in a duel, and killed him. We're frightened to death that Cousin Paul might be angry, and stop paying Rudi's fees, and then he couldn't become an engineer—but Paul won't mind now. Smack dear, God must listen to your Presbyterian prayers!"

"Pauli!" expostulated the old governess. "Are you staying long, Dr. Woodfall?" she asked, looking up at him over her glasses.

"About a month or so," he answered.

"Well, I think you should be warned that nothing you see or hear in this house has any basis in sanity. I've lived here nearly forty years, and every day something astonishes me. Oh, I must go and dress—and you too, Pauli."

A deep-toned bell tolled with cathedral majesty. With apologies they all left Charles.

He sat down, a little dizzy with this history, but he was not alone for long. The door opened. A little girl came in. She was not more than twelve, dressed in a white frock, with white socks and patent leather slippers. Her blonde hair was tied with a scarlet ribbon. She surveyed the stranger solemnly for a few moments, then advanced sedately.

"*Bon soir, m'sieur*," she said, and continued in French, "You are the Englishman? I am Zita."

She gravely offered her hand. Charles took it and smiled.

"I am very glad you have come, m'sieur. My grandma says you saved Uncle Paul's life, which is very important because if Uncle Paul does not earn many zlotys we could not live."

"Oh!" said Charles, somewhat overcome by his contribution to the well-being of Château Golo.

"This is a new dress that I am wearing. My great-aunt Oslawa brought it from Lwów yesterday. I must sit carefully, for I must not crumple it."

"It is very pretty," agreed Charles, amused by this self-possessed child. "Tell me more about Aunt Oslawa."

The little girl sat down carefully.

"My mother says Great-Aunt Oslawa is not nearly so poor as she pretends to be. She coughs and coughs to make everyone believe she has bronchitis. And to cure bronchitis she must go to Monte Carlo for the winter. Uncle Paul has to give her the money to go there. My mother says the bronchitis is a fraud. She goes to Monte Carlo to gamble. She is very wicked to gamble because Uncle Paul is not rich. My mother says——"

An opening of the door stopped the garrulous child before Charles could check the exposure of family frailties. Into the room came an aristocratic old lady, dressed in a black velvet dress, far too *décolleté* for one so marked by the ravages of age. She bore down upon Charles with a regal air, holding out a jewelled hand. The little girl stood up.

"Good evening. Dr. Woodfall?" she asked, in perfect English. "I am Countess Oslawa—we are so happy to see you at Golo."

She stooped and kissed Zita, and spoke to her in Polish. Evidently they discussed the new dress.

"Tell me, Dr. Woodfall," said the Countess, sitting down, "what is the real truth about poor Paul? It was a very bad attack, I suppose?"

She coughed, and opened a white ostrich fan. Charles dared not look at Zita, who sat demurely on her chair.

"Well—he is in a fairly advanced stage, as you know," he answered. "He must take great care."

The Countess eased a collar of small pearls binding her neck, and coughed again.

"Of course he must! It's ridiculous for him to spend the winter here. I have to spend the winter here and it is death for me—with my chronic bronchitis. In happier days I always wintered on the French Riviera. I should be there now. Imagine it, we are a hundred versts from a doctor, and two hundred from a good one!"

She turned to Zita and dispatched her on some errand.

"Let me warn you against that abominable child. Her mother has turned her into a spy! I am terrified of her. I was blackmailed into buying her the dress she is wearing. You can't say a word that——"

A fit of coughing interrupted her. The door opened. It was Prince Ivan. He was now dressed in a wine-coloured, plush smoking-jacket. He wore a very large black bow tie on a stiff stove-pipe collar. He advanced and kissed the Countess's hand, and then greeted Charles. One eye looked out across the room, the other straight ahead. His beard, trimmed to a point, had an outward twist. His fine fingers were magnificently jewelled.

He began to describe a boar-hunting expedition they had made that day when two elderly ladies, accompanied by a swarthy youth, came into the room, followed by four Pekinese dogs and a golden-haired spaniel. Charles was duly presented. Their names whistled and rumbled in his ears. A conversation in German began and rose to a pitch of excitement. They were discussing a speech made by Hitler. Suddenly Prince Ivan burst forth into a torrent of Polish. His odd eye shifted its direction and looked inwards. The veins stood out on his forehead, he flourished his jewelled hands. He seemed like a strident cockerel chiding the hens. They stood hushed and apprehensive. The storm subsided as quickly as it had mounted. A charming smile broke over his face. The odd eye went outwards again.

"Excuse us, my dear sir—we were discussing those Nazi brigands. I say not an inch of the Corridor! Not an inch!" he exclaimed.

Half a dozen more people came into the room, and then Laura, who, effusively greeted by the women, made her way across to Charles. Entrancing, young, and pretty in a cream satin bodice and a tulle skirt, with three ropes of pearls on her slender neck, she laughed as she reached him.

"I'm utterly bewildered," he said. "Just who is who, Laura?"

"Don't ask me! I've lived here for months, and I still don't know." The big bell began to toll. "Now you'll see all the animals in the ark."

The room began to fill up, the babel of voices rose. Two

menservants arrived with large trays of drinks and canapés. Feathers, fans, French perfumes, pearls, diamonds, brilliants, the medley spread, overflowed. The women were mostly old, the sprinkling of men were young.

"Are they all relatives?" asked Charles, his eyes roving over this astonishing assembly. Certainly there were twenty present.

"Mostly—and all impecunious and titled. The rich ones stay in Paris. Do you wonder Paul despairs? Oh, there he is, with his mother, thank Heaven. I'm starving! They call it supper. I warn you it lasts two hours!" said Laura.

CHAPTER TWELVE

IN THE NIGHT

I

AT the end of his first week Charles began to accept the extraordinary environment into which he had been plunged. There was order in the disorder of this vast house. It was firmly established that no one was subject to any kind of rules, either of convention, of the calendar, or of the clock. No one seemed to appear before dinner, which was at two o'clock in the afternoon. The women kept to their boudoirs or, if they did not, contrived to remain invisible. The men went off singly, in pairs, or in groups, to various assignments and occupations. There was a stable full of horses tended by Hungarian grooms. Paul's younger brother managed the farming and foresting interests, the chief sources of revenue. There were over one hundred foresters employed on the estate, all clad in a grey-green uniform. A bailiff watched over the farms. The nearest village, with little but a mud track running through it, had about four hundred inhabitants. They were all Korwienski's tenants. There was a school for the children. A priest lived near his church. There was no doctor less than forty miles away.

Charles had been at Château Golo four days before he discovered that a priest lived in the house. Father Josef taught some of the grandchildren and conducted daily Mass in the private chapel of the château. He was a benign old man who sometimes appeared in the dining-hall, but he had his own servant to look after him in two rooms of his own. His French was poor, his English was beyond recognition, but he took Charles through endless corridors to his little suite to show him, with great pride, a complete set of Dickens's novels and a lithograph of Queen Victoria sitting in a pony-carriage, with

Count Oslawa, once a guest at Balmoral, standing at her side.

Paul's sitting-room, where Charles often visited, was a large pleasant room on the ground floor. It was level with the ball-room, which Charles was shown after he had been at Golo for ten days, as if it were a kind of afterthought. The long high room was shuttered up and unheated. It was only opened on ceremonial occasions. Ten enormous crystal chandeliers, covered up in white muslin bags, hung from the barrel ceiling. There was a stage at one end. The decoration was French Empire style, with walls lined with long gilt mirrors, and red silk damask panels between. Under them stood long rows of gilt chairs, with the Korwienski arms embroidered on the backs. At the end, opposite the stage, there was a carpeted dais, with two massive gilt chairs with claw and ball feet. A richly embroidered canopy, surmounted by a golden eagle, with wings outspread, hung over the dais. It all looked very regal. Charles was astonished to notice that every one of the twenty-six great wall-mirrors had been smashed.

"We left them like that—as a memorial," said Paul.

"A memorial?" queried Charles.

"Yes, of the last war. We found them like that after the Russians had gone—they stripped the house of all its movable contents, and broke most of the furniture." He shrugged his shoulders. "Who knows, they may come again—we are a cockpit."

Paul's study had a large bay window, reaching from ceiling to floor. It faced south and looked out on to a terrace and a topiary garden now grotesquely shrouded with snow. There was a large open fire in which great logs were burned, as well as a beautiful porcelain stove, decorated with tiles celebrating the battles of Kosciuszko. The walls were lined with deep shelves and racks holding an extensive music library. In the window bay, so that the light fell across the keyboard, there was a black grand piano. Deep easy chairs, a big lounge in front of the fire, shaded standard lamps, and thick Turkish carpets, made the room the most inviting in the whole château. Its masculine character was denoted by autographed portraits of famous contemporary musicians, University groups, and fencing foils that hung over the mantelpiece. There was a large buhl flat-topped writing-desk, with bronze busts of Chopin and Paderewski.

It was in this pleasant study that Laura, Paul, and Charles gathered when the general company, always in a state of flux, weighed upon their nerves. Members of the household respected the privacy of one another's sitting-room. A week elapsed before Charles was invited into the private apartment of Paul's mother, a perfect replica of a Frenchwoman's boudoir, with its Louis-Quinze chairs, chaise-longue, ormolu mirrors and clock, silk-tasselled lamp-shades, Sèvres vases, and Aubusson carpet. The Princess had none of her son's genial disposition. She never unbent, it seemed to Charles, always remaining the *grande dame*. Flawlessly polite, an aristocrat in every movement, she presented a complete contrast to her boisterous, wall-eyed half-brother. By virtue of birth a lady-in-waiting to the Czarina, she was a memorial to the era of the Romanovs.

"She can never forgive Paul for marrying me. I have three grave defects," said Laura, speaking of her without bitterness. "I am an American, and therefore ill-bred; I am an actress, and therefore a doubtful character, and, being a Hollywood actress without a fortune, I am, therefore, a fraud! We are exasperatingly gracious to each other, but we remain enemies."

When the Princess invited Charles to her boudoir, she began by discussing Paul's health, passed on to French literature, and then reached her real objective, the social background of all the Woodfalls, in England and Florida. As she had feared, and Charles somewhat mischievously emphasized, they were unredeemably bourgeois. Her boudoir tables, he noticed, bristled with portraits of royalties, admirals, and generals.

Charles never invaded Paul's study in the mornings. His own sitting-room being above it, he could just hear him practising at the piano. Paul had been permitted by Charles to play not more than half an hour a day. He kept to his bed until noon, reading and writing. He swore he slept soundly each night, a valiant lie, as Charles well knew, for Paul could only sleep on his back, well propped up, to facilitate breathing, and his hacking cough prevented any continuous sleep.

In the second week of Charles's visit snow fell heavily and blocked the roads, so that only horse-drawn sleighs could make any progress. Winter laid a white blanket over the flat park. The thick woods had a blue haze in the distance when the air was clear. There was a long drive down an avenue of beeches where the snow had not drifted, along which Charles and Laura, always accompanied by a groom, as prescribed by etiquette, rode their horses. The sharp air stung their faces. Foresters, as they passed, doffed their caps. At the end of the avenue, on an eminence, there was a terraced belvedere. Fountains played on the terraces, falling into successive pools, but now everything was frozen. The windows of the château commanded this mile-long vista crowned by the belvedere, with its golden quadriga surmounting the massive marble cupola.

They were riding back to the château one morning, their horses walking abreast, when Laura brought up the subject of Charles's return to England. He was leaving in a few days.

"Paul tells me he has asked you to stay—until the spring," she said.

"Yes," he answered. "I wish I could."

They rode on in silence for a short distance.

"Do you mean that, Charles?" she asked, eventually.

"Of course!" he replied, looking at her.

"Why can't you stay? Paul wants you to stay. He is fond of you," said Laura, leaning forward to pat the glossy neck of her mount.

"I think you know why, Laura," he said, quietly.

She raised her head and turned to him, her face rosy in the sharp air, her figure taut and girlish in its black riding-habit

"So it is—that," she said, solemnly. "Charles, please stay— a little longer. Paul needs you. He feels safe with you here."

"Safe?" he echoed.

"Safe—that was his word. He's talking of working up

another concerto, to play in Warsaw at Easter. He is so sure
he can do it."

"That's folly—it would kill him, Laura."

"But can't he try, can't we let him think he can do it? It
gives him such hope. If you stayed you could watch him, and
then stop him if you saw him getting beyond his strength."

"I'm not thinking of Paul," said Charles, slowly. "I must
go because I am thinking of myself and of you, Laura. How
can we go on like this? All these weeks together we have been
too happy. Soon Paul will see and wonder. Even if he doesn't,
they will—there are too many sharp eyes now, I'm afraid. I
lead a double life, before Paul, before all of them. Laura, you
know I don't want to go, I have never been so happy. I've
come out of a nightmare to—to this. No, I must go, my dear
Laura."

"If I asked you for Paul's sake only, Charles?"

He glanced backwards before answering, to see if the
groom was near. He was too far away to hear.

"For Paul's sake only—are you sure that is the one reason?"
he asked, hoarsely.

She tried to answer, but the words would not leave her lips,
for she knew her face denied them.

"Oh, my dear!" he said, as she turned her head away. "We
should be playing with fire. And to hurt him now—Laura, I
must go, you know I must go!" he repeated, desperately.

She did not answer, for deep in her hidden self the warning
rang clear, beyond denial. She rode on, conscious of his eyes
upon her. Nothing broke the silence of the wintry forest save
the soft crunch of the horses trampling the snow. "Gallop?"
asked Charles. The word was thrown like a life-buoy for her
to catch in desperation.

She smiled bravely and urged her horse forward.

There were guests for lunch. Prince Radziwill had brought
over some of his house-party from Debica. The three Zalewski
sisters, all young and beautiful, dressed in the height of Paris
fashion, came from a neighbouring château, the eldest driving

a tröika sleigh, which swung up to the doors with great verve. They were nicknamed "The League of Nations Sisters" by Prince Ivan, for one was engaged to an Hungarian officer, one to a German attaché, one to a French artist. Their father was Polish, their mother Spanish, and their four brothers had married into Swedish, English, Russian, and American families.

Charles counted the number that sat down to dinner in the great hall. There were thirty-two at the high table. Old Aunt Viktoria dined at a single table in one of the window recesses. It was one of the days when she didn't feel like talking, it was explained to Charles. There was another long table at the end of the hall, occupied by twelve children and three governesses. When their conversation got too noisy Princess Korwienski picked up a hand-bell on the table and rang it vigorously, as a signal for less noise. The strident young voices fell at once, and began another period of ascent.

Prince Ivan sat at the bottom end of the long table. A young chasseur, in the Lubirsky livery, stood just behind the Prince throughout dinner, in case his master desired to send messages down the table to any of the guests. Princess Korwienski, presiding at the top end, sat stiffly, framed between her hand-bell and a bottle of Vichy water. Paul, owing to frequent absence, and out of courtesy to his uncle, had surrendered his position at the end of the table.

The meal began. The bearded old butler, Lodz, kept a keen eye on the footmen, in knee-breeches and buckled shoes, and white-gloved. Six musicians played softly in the minstrels' gallery. They were from the estate, foresters mostly, recruited and trained by Paul. They played well; but no one listened, and their music was drowned by the babel of voices talking Polish, French, English, German, and Magyar.

Charles caught Laura's eye during the meal. They had sat down at two. It was now a quarter past three and they had not reached coffee. Charles had for his companion the fiancée of Paul's youngest brother, who was in the army. She was greatly in fear of a coming war with Germany. More and more men were being called up. A young monocled German in the Radziwill party assured her there was not the slightest possibility. *Der Führer* had affirmed his desire to live in peace with Poland. A little matter like the Corridor could be adjusted.

"But your Herr Forster foments trouble in Danzig," she said. "I have been there. I have seen it!"

"You interpret wrongly, Fräulein, I am sure," answered the young man, gravely. "*Der Führer* would not have said——"

"The Corridor is a forbidden subject—just now!" exclaimed Countess Oslawa. "*Herr Oberleutnant,* do you know Monte Carlo?"

She led him off on to the French Riviera, ending with her bronchitis. For once, Charles admired the old harridan, she had spared them a scene. The Polish Corridor stretched across every conversation sooner or later. He had seen Count Golowski, Paul's brother-in-law, stamp with his riding-boot on a radio, smashing it to splinters because it was blaring out Nazi Danzig propaganda. The aunt of that *enfant terrible,* Zita, Excellency Madame Trun, whose tongue was a byword in Château Golo—the old fishwoman, Prince Ivan called her—carried ear-stoppers which she applied whenever talk about the Corridor made her nervous. The Prince himself terrified her, to his delight. He exulted at the thought of fighting the Nazis. His eye rolled inwards and outwards as he prophesied what the Poles would do to them.

But to-day, of all things, a fierce discussion on annuities sprang up, and raged along the table. Companies, rates, the safest countries, all came into the discussion.

"I'd cash mine to-morrow, if I could. What's the use of only just living!" exclaimed Madame Trun, who had run through two fortunes and three husbands.

"The old fraud!" said Prince Ivan, later, amid the cigar smoke. "She cashed in her annuity ten years ago—that's why she's here. Spent it on a lover who turned out to be a Wiesbaden waiter!"

It was nearly four when the gentlemen joined the ladies. The bridge tables were out in the Blue Salon. Countess Oslawa appeared with a roulette-board and looked for victims.

She found bridge slow. At six o'clock when the company was leaving, they were all driving home in the clear moonlight that sparkled on the frosty snow, the Countess borrowed from Charles a thousand zlotys, to settle her debts with departing guests. "I have the devil's luck always," she complained.

Charles went to Paul's room after the guests had gone. It was the hour when, with a brew of tea in the samovar on a side table, and a great log burning in the fireplace, he sat at the piano and played. He was practising an hour a day now.

Laura and Zaza Wernhoff were in the room when Charles arrived. He liked Zaza. She was a Rumanian actress who had married a cousin of Paul's and, after a successful career, was living in Lwów. Fifty years of age, still retaining her good looks, and always cheerful, she had been quite receptive when Charles struck up a friendship with her. They also, privately, discussed Paul's state of health.

"Is it true you are leaving in the morning?" she asked, as soon as Charles came into the room. "I couldn't believe it when Laura told me. I had hoped you were here for two or three months."

"Yes—I leave at nine o'clock, to catch the express at Jaro-slaw."

"He's deserting his patient! I feel encouraged to fall ill again," cried Paul, filling a tea-cup at the table. He listened a moment. They could hear the wind howling outside. "I hope those people will get back soon—there's a blizzard coming. I know that sound."

He went to the window, pulled aside the heavy curtain and looked out. The moon was obscured.

"It's snowing hard—with any luck we'll have a good blizzard, and then you'll be snowed up here!" laughed Paul, coming from the window.

"Do you get snowed up?" asked Charles.

"Certainly we do—sometimes the roads are so blocked we are shut off for a week," said Paul. He went to the piano, lit two candles, and sat down. "What shall I play to-night?"

"Some Bach," answered Zaza Wernhoff, pulling embroidery

out of her handbag and settling herself into the big easy chair.
Charles sat by Laura on the lounge, on the opposite side of the
fire, facing the piano. Bim, the wolf-hound, lay stretched out
on the rug. The logs crackled, and another gust of the mounting storm struck the windows, emphasizing the warmth
within.

The soft lamplight fell on the busts of Chopin and
Paderewski. At the piano Paul's lean face bent forwards in the
candlelight. Thus seen, Charles was again aware of the deadly
sickness that held Paul in its grip. He had no business to play,
in this exhausting fashion; but to deny him that pleasure was
to deny him life.

The magic began, and the music flowed out from Paul's
quick fingers. Zaza sat back, half closing her eyes, the embroidery in her lap, surrendered to pleasure. He played, and,
the Bach fugue finished, a Chopin nocturne in D flat followed,
like a sigh born of old memories. Charles, listening, found
himself looking at Laura, the firelight on her face and hair.
She must have been conscious of his gaze, for she turned and
smiled at him, and he knew in that moment all that she was
thinking, all that lay unspoken between them in these last
hours.

Daringly, foolishly, his hand stole out and covered hers.

II

Paul's prophecy was fulfilled. In the middle of the night
Charles was awakened by the onslaught of the storm. It
battered the windows of his room. He lay in the darkness
wondering if Paul's playful threat would be fulfilled, if he
would be made a prisoner in the château. The possibility
frightened him. He must go in the morning. He had a feeling that if he did not find the resolution to go now, he would
never get away. He could never be happy here, for the battle
within him never ceased. There were shameful moments
when he looked at Paul and speculated on how long he might
live, since the courage of this battle could not blind him to its

final futility. Paul would go on and on, perhaps a year, two years, three years. The tenacity of the spirit in so feeble a body was one of the mysteries of life. And yet if he were Paul, loving his art, loving Laura——

He started, wondering whether he dreamed or woke. He lay listening in the darkness of the large room. He thought he heard the wind again, and then knew it was not the wind this time. It was music, somewhere in the night.

He sat up, wide awake now, and listened with straining ears. Below him, someone was crashing out chords on the piano. It must be Paul, in his study, practising. The fool! Did he think he could cheat like this and not pay the penalty? The sound swelled into a passage of great vigour and then, as the crescendo mounted, there was a sudden silence.

Charles listened acutely. He should go down and stop him. This was utter folly. There was no sound now. Had he finished then? He waited and listened. Only the storm spoke in the night. The piano was silent. Paul had finished.

Charles lay back and closed his eyes. He lay, pondering on Paul's folly, the storm, his journey in the morning, that look in Laura's eyes as Paul played the nocturne.

He was too much awake now. Leaning over, he found the candlestick and matches. He struck a light. In the feeble flame he saw it was half-past two by his wrist-watch on the table. He blew out the candle, and lay, hearing the gale howl round the château.

It was odd of the music to stop so suddenly. That passage had not been completed. Was it Paul, or was there a secret musician in the house who stole into the study to play unheard? A musical footman, an infant Mozart——

How ridiculous, he thought. He must go to sleep. But the resolution had no effect. He was wide awake, his mind possessed by this mysterious piano playing. Impatient with himself, he struck a light again, got out of bed, and put on his dressing-gown and slippers. Candlestick in hand, he went out into the corridor.

The passage along the high dark corridor, past men in

armour, and life-sized portraits, had a quality of nightmare. His candle only emphasized the darkness through which he moved. He came at last to the grand staircase, with its windows looking out on the long avenue. But all he saw now was a blackness, with the snow piled deep against the sills. He continued down and reached the ground floor, on which Paul's study was situated. He went along the stone corridor until he came to Paul's door. He opened it, and paused on the threshold.

Two candles were burning on the piano, above the keyboard. There was no one there. The player had gone, neglecting to blow them out. A flicker of light on the wall made him step farther into the room, past a screen, and then he saw to his astonishment that a log was still blazing in the great fireplace, its dancing flames sending the light flickering over the ceiling. Charles walked farther into the room. There was not a sound. He crossed by the desk to blow out the candles, and then he started. On the floor by the piano-stool lay a figure in a crimson dressing-gown. At a glance he knew it was Paul.

Charles hurried across the room and raised the insensible man. There was blood on Paul's dressing-gown and mouth, but the heart was still beating.

CHAPTER THIRTEEN

FINIS POLANDIAE

I

IT was high summer in the forests and fields of Poland. Already the harvest was being gathered. The roads were strewn with stalks, fallen from the slow-moving wagons bringing in sheaves from the wheat-fields. All over the Korwienski estate the peasants were busy, still reaping, in primitive fashion, with the sickle. They were mostly women, barefooted, with coloured kerchiefs over their heads, and weather-beaten old men, for the young men were steadily departing. Month after month they had been going, called to the colours as the war-clouds threatened. In the nearest villages Charles had seen these lads and young men, standing patiently, while a sergeant checked them under the eye of a young officer. Then, with some cheers, some tears, and a waving of kerchiefs the motor-trucks had taken them off.

Poland was now moving detachments up to the Slovak frontier. Troops were already massed on the frontiers of the Polish corridor. Yet there was no alarm. Hitler stormed and threatened in Berlin, there were ugly scenes and incidents in Danzig, with charges and countercharges of violence. It was still believed the Germans were only blustering. Last March they had overrun Czechoslovakia, and Europe had shivered, But Germany would think twice before attacking Poland, with a well-organized army and the backing of France and England.

Both Paul and Prince Ivan maintained a stout optimism. Little by little the tide of events reacted on the tranquil life of Château Golo. Paul's brother, Jan, three of his nephews, and Rudi, Franz, and Ladislaus had paid farewell visits to their relations. They were gay and smart in their uniforms, confident, most of them, that they were going to have a somewhat exciting holiday. The effect on the Countess Oslawa was that her bronchitis magically vanished, and along with Princess Korwienski she appeared white and businesslike in her Red Cross nurse's uniform. The two women went daily into the village to conduct first-aid classes.

Things began to look more serious in the second week of August. An official arrived from Kraków and asked how many evacuees could be accommodated in the château. Notices arrived setting forth the regulations concerning food rations, air-raid precautions, and gas attacks. All day long the radio reported the activity in the chancelleries of Europe. The Polish Ambassador and the German Foreign Office were in constant negotiation. The English were now taking a hand.

"The Nazis won't get away with it this time!" declared Prince Ivan. "There's going to be no Munich pact for us."

Six of the ladies were busily rolling bandages. He jokingly called it a labour of blood, and asked who was going to unroll them. But his valet let out the news that the Prince had had his uniform as a reserve colonel taken out of its moth-ball wrappings. It was four inches too small at the belt. A little Jew tailor was spirited in from the village and made to squat in a corner of the Prince's bedroom while he let out the seams and adjusted the tunic.

On the 15th of August the Government requisitioned one hundred and ten horses off the estate. Half of the harvest was in. It began to look serious. Most of the menservants had been called up. Almost a week later, just before dinner, Hans came to Charles's room and said that Prince Paul would like to see him. Hans brought with him some letters.

One was from his brother Peter, dated Paris, August 10th. With Tony Farnham he had set out on a trip to the Riviera, but war rumours had caused them to pause. "You will be interested in the enclosed," wrote Peter. The enclosed was a clipping from the *Paris Soir*. It announced that the Russian Ballet, after a successful season in Paris, had left for a tour of South America. It gave a list of the star dancers who had gone with the corps. Among them was the name of Stefanie Kazinczy.

Having read his letters, Charles went along to Paul's room. For three months Paul, dying, but refusing to admit the fact, had rarely left his bed. This had been moved down into his study, where he lay and looked at the music on the shelves around him, and at the silent piano. Since that night when Charles had found him on the floor of his room, he had waged a losing battle with the remorseless enemy. It had seemed then that the end was only a matter of days. Shut off from all outside medical help by the blizzard, Charles had remained, knowing that the end must come soon. But again the invalid had fought desperately, collapsed, and rallied, and somehow conserved the vital flame.

He was a wraith now, racked with incessant coughing. Minor hæmorrhages, night sweats, erratic temperatures, were followed by surprising rallies, by days when it seemed that he had turned back on that road to the dark valley. These hopes were false, as Charles knew, although the sick man, finding a sudden strength, insisted on being helped to the piano, and began some piece he rarely finished. Often, convinced the end was near, the old Princess, Paula, Father Josef, and himself had waited by the bedside, only to see the sinking man cheat Death and swim back to life.

For six months now Charles had walked this road of racking suspense. Implored to stay by Paul, who was confident it would not be long before he resumed his normal life, he had succumbed to Laura's frantic appeal. Worn and unnerved by constant anxiety, and all the unspeakable details of this relentless dissolution of the body, Laura drew courage from his presence. It was as if Death in sly malice had bound the three of them, to make the triple test of love, loyalty, and endurance. There were moments when Charles, tortured by the fear of himself, vowed he would not continue in the forced role of a hypocrite. The truth had reared its ugly head between Laura and himself. Unspoken, they knew the dreadful prayer in their hearts. Falsely, yet without falseness, they fought for the sick man's life and wished for an end they did everything to delay. There was release in death for all of them, for the dying and the living, and with the knowledge of this she acted to the limit of her strength, he served to the limit of his skill.

There was one dreadful evening when, leaving the sick room after a long vigil, Laura had collapsed in a fit of hysteria. She would not, she could not go on, she sobbed out in Charles's arms. Why wouldn't he die? How could a loving God play with them so cruelly? It might be love had no breaking-point, but she had not even that to sustain her. Her strength had to be drawn from pity. Only Paul's pathetic faith in her could have blinded him to the truth. The living man she could have told, the dying she must deceive.

Charles, sharing her sickness of the soul, tried to comfort her. It could not be long now, he assured her. For Paul's sake they must keep their secret through these last days, he said, seeking to give her new strength. But the assurance had been proved false, for the days passed into weeks, the weeks into months. The end would come, he had repeated again and again.

"It will go on for years, Charles!" she cried out, and then, horrified at the wish implied by her protest, she burst into one of her rare fits of sobbing. Her touch in those moments seared him, while self-restraint held him in an iron grip.

Somehow, through the long cold spring and the hot summer, they had come to August. Two more specialists brought in from Vienna, had declared the end was in sight. Paul was often racked with paroxysms of coughing now, and begged for injections. The dates on his chart marking these were growing more frequent. When, on this sunny August morning, Hans brought Charles the message from Paul, he thought it was another appeal for an injection.

Paul was sitting up, in a dressing-gown, when Charles entered. Surprised, he turned to the nurse, a lethargic creature who would have been sent away long ago but for the scarcity of nurses. Paul, anticipating Charles's reproof, laughed and said:

"It's my fault. I insisted on getting up. I'm better this morning, Charles, a lot better. Can't I sit in the sun a little?"

"The sun isn't good for you—but you might sit in the shade for a while," answered Charles, humouring him.

The desire seemed to vanish suddenly, for he glanced around the room and, seeing the nurse, asked Charles to send her away. When the door had closed behind her, he spoke.

"Charles—there's very bad news just come over the air from Warsaw. This is the end!" he said, quietly.

"The end—what do you mean?" queried Charles.

"Germany and Russia have agreed to a ten-year non-aggression pact. That's our death sentence."

Charles stared at his friend, stunned by the ominous news.

"My poor country! It means war. Russia has given Germany the signal to go ahead. You must get home while you can, Charles," said Paul.

Another paroxysm seized him. The sweat stood out on his brow. When the coughing ended, Charles answered him:

"You may be wrong, Paul. I hope you are—but in any case I shan't go. A doctor doesn't desert his case."

Paul shook his head. "You've been wonderful, but I can't ask you to stay now. Once this thing starts, you might be cut off. Charles, you must go."

"I could get out through Rumania, if the worst happened. I still don't think it will happen. Hitler must know it would set Europe in flames. Anyhow, we'll wait and see," said Charles.

"You won't go?" asked Paul.

"No!"

Paul put up his thin white hand and pressed Charles's arm. Despite his suggestion, there was a look of relief in his face.

"You're an obstinate fellow—bless you," he said, in his thin voice.

The dinner-bell sounded through the house.

"I think I'll go back, Charles," he said. "I tire very quickly."

Charles lifted him and carried him over to the bed.

II

Fate moved her pawns rapidly. Poland declared she would not tolerate the annexation of Danzig. The British Ambassador flew back to Berlin from London. England declared her firm support of Poland. On the 29th Warsaw called up another million men. Hans and all the remaining young menservants departed from Château Golo. Even Prince Ivan became worried. His eye rolled whenever Hitler's name arose. Troops were moving on all the roads in Poland. Five relations, all women, arrived from Kraków, seeking asylum. They brought with them their jewellery and their pets. Old Princess Korwienski could not conceal her contempt. It was the duty of every woman to stand by her post. They would want nurses in Kraków.

When they all retired to bed, on the evening of the 31st, it was announced that Poland had rejected Germany's proposal, but that negotiations would proceed. Prince Ivan spent a long time telephoning Warsaw. He was indignant that, as a colonel on the reserve, he had not been called up. With the butler, he had spent most of the day hiding the silver, and the fire-arms. In 1914, when the Russians swept over the land, the place had been pillaged. It was then in Austria. In 1919, when the Germans had evacuated the country, the Bolsheviks had swept in, destroying and stealing. "The Germans would do it worse, with more system, if ever they got here," growled the Prince. In the kitchen the maids had been busy putting away the extra food supplies that had been brought in from Lwów. The radio from Berlin now filled the air with threats and bombast. Gas masks had appeared and were tried on.

The next day, Friday, September 1st, about noon, the radio announced, "President Moscicki has declared a state of war," following the invasion of Poland. It was not until four o'clock in the afternoon that it reported how the Germans had marched over the frontier at dawn that same morning, and had bombed Warsaw, Kraków, Katowice, Poznan, and other towns.

Two days later England and France declared war on Germany. The first tide of refugees flowed over the roads into the village and up to the château. They had come by every kind of conveyance from Kraków, which was burning. One hundred and fifty evacuees, billeted on the estate, arrived that night. Ten more relations sought refuge in the château. The next day four planes flew over and bombed the village. It was soon in flames from end to end. There was now a ceaseless trek of refugees on the roads. They arrived with only small parcels. They told stories of trains bombed, of lines of carts being machine-gunned on country roads, of the woods being bombed in which they sought shelter. The old Princess, the Countess Oslawa, Paula, and six other women in the château worked from morning until night. Charles found himself attending over a hundred sick and wounded people lying in the village temporary hospital, on straw in the stables and barns, or in cottages on the estate. The problem of feeding them became desperate.

Warsaw, shelled and bombed, was holding out with desperate gallantry. "Although under constant bombing, we will not yield," declared the Mayor. The Germans rolled on over the land. Warsaw was surrounded. Then, finally, no signal came from the city. German news now poured out from the Kraków radio. The roads were clogged with refugees. They slept in ditches, they fainted with hunger. Cars, wagons, hand-carts, perambulators, the slow, sad trek never ended day or night. They were going to Lwów, bombed and burning, *en route* to Rumania. Planes flew over by threes and fours, bombing indiscriminately. One bomb shattered the ballroom wing, killing five servants, Madame Trun, Countess Proteki, three children, and Father Josef. Miss Macdermott, bleeding from a face wound, rescued three children from flaming débris.

Princess Korwienski and the Countess Oslawa had made a temporary hospital for the wounded and sick in the village church, which had miraculously survived the bombings. "The Holy Mother guards us!" proclaimed the little priest, passing from bed to bed. Here Laura and Charles worked day and night. Without medicines or instruments, Charles did all he could. On the tenth day the morphine ran out, and he could give no relief to patients screaming in pain from their wounds. On their way to this temporary hospital the helpers from the château passed a wood where refugees, machine-gunned on the roads, had fled for shelter, only to be bombed. The wood was now a shambles of human beings and splintered trees. The stench of putrescent bodies filled the air and drew large flocks of carrion crows. The long steady procession of cars, wagons, and trucks passed by, making detours into the fields to avoid bomb holes.

Charles had left the hospital to attend some patients in a barn, where Laura was working, when a tremendous explosion shook the ground. Two planes zoomed overhead, dropped bombs, and then flew off. When the cloud of smoke and dust had settled, the church had disappeared. Charles hurried with Laura to the scene and joined the rescuers at work, lifting the wounded out of the débris. They had left Princess Korwienski and the Countess Oslawa there. A rescue-party toiled for an hour, but there was no sign of the two women. Along with some forty sick people, they were buried in the débris of masonry. There was no hope now of their having survived. The old doctor from Lwów, in charge of the hospital, was dug out unharmed. He crossed himself. It was his second burial.

They carried the surviving wounded on improvised stretchers across a field to a barn, already overcrowded. Some were carried to the château and laid on the floor of the laundry. Charles attended to them briefly. He was kneeling by one man, in a barn, whose arm and leg had been crushed, when the man's face evoked a memory. Where had he seen that face before, with its shaggy head and bushy eyebrows? In a flash, he recalled this man with the Dantesque features. He spoke to him in French, as he attended him.

"Were you ever in the United States, in Florida?"

The man looked up, startled by the question.

"Why, yes, m'sieur—several times," he answered.

"Did you go in a plane to Lake Witterwittee, early in 1936?"

The man did not speak for a few moments.

"Why do you ask me?" he said, cautiously. He was in pain, and beads of perspiration stood on his brow. He was a man of about sixty.

"I stayed on an island there, Sundown Grove. One night I saw an aeroplane descend. The fellow who got out of it was taken down to the lake, and he set off in a canoe with a man named Henry Woodfall."

"Who are you?" asked the wounded man, hoarsely.

"I'm his cousin and I have always wondered why you came there like that, and went up the lake to a motor-car hidden in a creek."

"Why should I tell you?" asked the man, suspiciously, after a pause.

"There's no reason at all, except that I recognize you and wonder who you are, and what you were doing that night. You needn't tell me," said Charles, curtly. He cut away the man's trouser and examined the crushed thigh. The man winced. Charles proceeded with his work. He had been machine-gunned before going to the bombed hospital.

"Later, m'sieur, I'll tell you—I'm in too much pain. Can I have a drink?"

"Yes—I'll see you again, later," said Charles.

He ordered a nurse to fetch some water, and turned to the next figure on a nearby stretcher. It was a young woman with a baby in her arms. She had a terrible gash on the shoulder. The baby was dead. After an hour's exhausting work, shared throughout by Laura, he came back to the strange man. He was shocked at the change in him. He was slightly delirious but he recognized Charles.

"I shan't live through this," he murmured, as Charles attended him. Then after a pause: "Those people at Witterwittee, m'sieur—it was an old woman, an alien smuggler."

"A what?" asked Charles. "Don't talk if it exhausts you.'

"I want to tell you—it's strange to meet like this. Witterwittee—an odd name! You can't forget it." He closed his eyes, then opened them. "She was an alien smuggler. For five hundred dollars she had you fetched by night from Cuba, got you into the States, and put you on the train—it was a regular traffic. They'd got it all nicely worked out, at a price."

He paused, asked for a drink, and was silent for a while. Laura looked at Charles, wondering if he had finished, but the man began to speak again.

"You're curious to know why I went into America so secretly? There was a reason, m'sieur. I am an art dealer in Warsaw—I was, that is, until my business failed. Then I got into an odd line. Some Bolsheviks, who stole pictures and jewels out of palaces they had looted, asked me if I could dispose of them on the side. America was the best and safest market. I heard of the Woodfall gang—that was the name of the old woman's people who collected the money—they were first of all in the liquor racket, smuggling it by boat from Cuba to Tampa and up the canals to Witterwittee, so I heard. Then, when Prohibition ended, they turned to smuggling anybody or anything in by aeroplane. I liked that fellow, Henry—he was always scared; but the old woman, m'sieur, she was a hawk. She'd raise the price on you if you didn't watch. She tried it once on me."

He took another drink, and looked up at Charles.

"I left that game two years ago, m'sieur. I'd made a nice little fortune, opened a shop in Warsaw. Now it's all gone— all gone and my—my——"

Tears streamed down his face, and he covered his eyes with a trembling hand.

"You mustn't talk any more," said Charles, gently.

"My wife and boy—were killed the second day. Everything's gone—our poor Poland," he cried. "M'sieur, you are kind. I shall be gone in the morning, I'm finished. Will you accept this, please."

He pulled a large signet ring off his finger.

"It once belonged to the Grand Duke Boris—it's got his arms on it—beautiful work! It mustn't be buried."

Charles hesitated, but Laura, seeing the desire of the dying man, spoke.

"We will take care of it for you," she said. "Now you must sleep."

The man smiled at her, his eyes travelling from face to face.

"You know Shakespeare, m'sieu—*Hamlet*?"

Charles nodded.

" 'The rest is silence,' " he quoted, softly.

III

They went back to the château. Somehow they must break the terrible news to Paul. In the courtyard there was a great commotion. Three cars and two carriages were there. In them sat seven children, two governesses, two of Paul's second cousins, and Zita and her mother. The Princess Wienenski came out of the hall and down the steps, struggling with a large bag, and Mitzi, carrying her dog.

"You have heard?" cried the Princess. "The Russians have crossed the frontier!"

"The Russians—it isn't possible!" exclaimed Laura.

"Yes! Good-bye. You must follow quick!" called the Princess. Mitzi got in with her. She gave an order to her Hungarian chauffeur. The car moved off. A servant was piling more luggage into another car. Bewildered, Charles and Laura turned to enter the house. Lodz, the old bearded butler, met them on the threshold. Yes, it was true. Prince Ivan had come back from Lwów with the news. The Russians had crossed the frontier, from Latvia to Rumania, and were advancing to meet the Germans. It was the end of Poland. The Prince had given orders for every able-bodied man to make for the Rumanian frontier, out of the clutches of the enemy. He had gone down to the hospital to warn them.

"Down to the hospital—when?" demanded Charles.

"Oh, three hours ago, m'sieur."

Charles and Laura looked at each other, then entered the hall.

Just before they went to see Paul a messenger arrived from

the village. They had recovered the bodies of Princess Korwienski, the Countess Oslawa, and Prince Ivan, crushed almost beyond recognition.

Paul was sitting up in a chair when they entered his room. He saw Charles's disapproving look and laughed. It was obvious he had a high temperature.

"I've lost my jailer—she's bolted, but I don't blame her!" he said, referring to the nurse.

Charles told him of the bomb on the hospital, and the news they had just received. The sick man listened to their account, then crossed himself, saying, "My poor mother!" Presently he turned to his wife. "Laura, my darling—will you fetch my mother's crucifix? It hangs above the *prie-dieu* in her bedroom." As soon as Laura had left the room he spoke to Charles.

"You've heard the Russians are advancing? There's no hope now. This is the end of Poland. President Moscicki and Colonel Beck called here an hour ago. They are fleeing to the frontier. Charles, I've one wish in the world now. It's useless to move me?"

"Well——" hesitated Charles.

"We agree on that. Now, you are to leave at once, with Laura. If you travel all night there's a chance you can reach the Rumanian frontier before dawn," said Paul, "through Lwów and Sniatyn."

"That's impossible. Neither Laura nor I would think of leaving you. We shall stay and see it out," answered Charles.

"But can't you see? You're English, you'd be taken a prisoner by the Russians or the Germans; then Laura would be alone," urged Paul.

"Warsaw hasn't yet fallen. Help may come from England, from France. In any event I'm not going to desert you—I'm certain Laura is of the same mind," said Charles.

"Very well," observed Paul, quietly. "Now I must say something. I'm of no account any longer. The end should have come long ago. I'm nothing but an obstruction to the happiness of you both."

Charles looked at him with startled eyes.

"My dear Charles," he continued, smiling, "do you imagine I haven't seen? You love each other. You must live on and be happy—there will be an end to these horrors one day——" He broke off, seized by an attack of coughing which left him breathless, and blue in colour.

"Paul, do go back to bed!" insisted Charles, perturbed by this scene.

"No—no—Charles, you must go—get Laura away," he pleaded, "and take care of her."

"Paul, tell me—how long have you known this?" asked Charles.

"I wondered for some time; then—there was a moment when I knew beyond any doubt. I watched you both suffering, but I wouldn't admit the truth to myself. Then one night, the night I played to you and Laura and Zaza, I knew for a certainty. You were sitting on the lounge at the side of the fire. You covered Laura's hand with yours——"

"You saw that!" interrupted Charles.

"Yes. It confirmed everything. You remember I got up in the night to play, you found me on the floor? I went to the piano to drown my agony. I wanted to die then, for all our sakes."

"I'm sorry," said Charles, shaken.

"Don't be sorry. These things happen. We can't control Fate. Charles, you'll go now?" he asked, looking up, appeal in his sick eyes. "You'll take Laura?"

"No, Paul—I won't go. Send Laura, if she'll go. I am staying with you. Nothing you say——"

He stopped. Laura had come back into the room. She went to Paul and gave him the crucifix. It was of Russian workmanship, a cross of diamonds and rubies on a platinum chain. Paul took it in his thin hands, looked at it for a few moments, and then kissed it.

"I'd like you to have it, Laura," he said, raising his trembling hands and holding out the loop of the chain.

Laura slipped to her knees at his side. The drone of planes

invaded the room. He passed the chain over her head. Then, holding her face to his for a moment, he kissed her brow.

"My poor *Maman* would have wished it," he said. "Are they—buried yet?"

"No—not yet, Paul. They've only just been found," replied Charles. "I think you should go back to bed now."

"What time is it?"

"Nearly six o'clock, darling," replied Laura, holding his hand.

There was a sound of more explosions. They looked at each other in silence.

"I've asked Charles to take you away, my dear—you can still get over the frontier if you go at once," said Paul; "but Charles refuses."

Laura glanced up at Charles.

"Of course! I won't leave you, Paul," cried Laura.

"Come, Paul—you should be in bed," said Charles.

He let Charles lift him and carry him to his bed.

"Have you eaten anything?" asked Charles, seeing no tray on the side table. "I'd shoot that nurse!"

Paul shook his head. "I'm not hungry. Poor Uncle Ivan, he was here three hours ago. He was going to organize a guerrilla band."

Charles looked at Laura.

"We'll leave you to rest awhile now. We've not eaten since ten o'clock. And I'm going to find you a nurse. We'll come in again soon," he said.

Paul smiled, and put out his hand to take Laura's.

"Bless you both—don't worry about me," he said, kissing Laura's hand. Then, looking out through the open French window, beyond the piano, on to the terrace: "You know, the bombing's driven all my birds away—they don't come to feed any more. I miss them."

As soon as he had closed the door, and they stood in the passage together, Charles looked at Laura.

"He knows everything, Laura," he said, quietly, and saw tears welling in her eyes. "It was no use denying it. He said he wanted us to live on—and be happy. There's nothing to hide now."

She tried to speak, but could not. His arm went around her, holding her to him, while the pent-up tears flowed. It was the first time through all these days of horror she had given way to tears.

They had just sat down to eat something, before another visit to the sick and wounded, when Lodz, the old butler, appeared at the door, white-faced and breathless. Prince Paul had shot himself! Lodz had heard a report and, on running to his room, had found him dead on the floor.

Charles and Laura followed the old man. At the side of the piano, still clutching the revolver with which he had done the deed, lay Prince Korwienski. The white silk pyjama jacket was scorched above the embroidered crest where he had shot himself through the heart.

With the aid of a couple of servants Charles carried the dead man and laid him on the bed. His face was quite tranquil. There was nothing to be done. Laura fell on her knees and kissed the thin hand, with its emerald ring engraved with the Korwienski arms.

"We'll bury him with his mother—they've dug a grave in the paddock. Get me a big curtain or something to wrap him in," said Charles to the butler.

There were no coffins, no ceremonies these days. The graves themselves were but shallow holes hastily dug to take the swelling company of the dead.

Charles glanced round the room. A drawer of the writing-desk, half open, attracted his attention. In it he found the case out of which Paul had taken the revolver. There was a small box of cartridges. He replaced the revolver he had taken from the dead man's hand, and shut the drawer. It was only then that he saw, prominently placed on the writing-pad, and pinned down by a miniature bronze bust of Mozart, a letter with 'Laura' written on it. He picked it up and took it across to her. She stood up and took the envelope with a trembling hand. Then, giving it back to him: "Read it," she said, in a quavering voice. He opened the envelope and read the message written in Paul's flourishing script:

> *There is nothing to stay for. Good-bye and God bless you both.*
>
> > *Always your loving*
> > *Paul.*

IV

The crimson sunset burned over the woodlands and across the flat plain. The blue sky of a perfect September day darkened, and the first star shone clear in the amber glow of eventide. In the dim courtyard of Château Golo, windowless, unlit in its long façade, a car waited. It was Prince Ivan's, and his chauffeur, a young Rumanian, by good fortune, was packing away into the luggage trunk the bags belonging to Laura and Charles. Old Lodz came out with rugs and Thermos flasks. There was also a box of food. Then, the task completed, the chauffeur waited by the car. Almost everybody had left the château in the past twenty hours, joining the long trek to the Rumanian frontier.

Charles and Laura came in from the paddock where, in the shadow of the silver birches, a group of peasants hastily dug graves and brought simple crosses made from two pieces of wood. In the unconsecrated ground, with no service, the dead, some unnamed and without mourners, were laid to rest, a few inches of soil only on the poor uncoffined bodies. It was here amid their own people, mourned by those who had lived their lives in the shadow of the great house, Prince Paul, Princess Helen Korwienski, Prince Ivan, and the Countess Oslawa were placed in their temporary graves. When a new day came to Poland and she rose again, with due honours paid, they would join their ancestors in the Korwienski vault in the cathedral of Kraków.

Three old servants waited in the hall while Charles and

Laura made their final preparations. As they came into it they kissed the young couple's hands, weeping, then, with old Lodz, followed them down the steps. It was almost dark. A dog howled dismally. It was Bim, Paul's wolf-hound, by the French window of his master's room.

"Oh—Bim, what shall we do about him!" cried Laura, moved by the hound's distress.

"I'll look after him, Highness," said Lodz. "We'll watch here together."

They got into the car, the farewells said. It went forward cautiously out of the courtyard, for no lights could be shown, into the silence and darkness of the road across the park. The lodge gates passed, they soon came to the main road leading across the fir-clad plain towards Lwów. The road was crammed with a procession of cars, wagons, trucks, wheel-barrows, anything by which the flight from death could be made. Tired children slept in their mothers' arms, old men and women lay exhausted in farm wagons drawn by weary horses. All along, on foot, each with a pitiful bundle contain-ing his or her sole possessions, trudged the silent multitude of refugees. Some had not made the journey safely. Wounded and roughly bandaged, they were the suvivors of bombing and machine-gunning. They had left relations and friends dead along the roadside, in the fields across which they had run terror-stricken, in the woods which had failed to protect them.

The night was warm and dark. The procession moved by night, for darkness was their friend against the winged death that harassed them. Here and there, in a clearing or a village, the light of a fire, still burning over ruins, silhouetted gaunt walls and roofless cabins. The stench of dead things sometimes hung in the air. It was like crossing the plains of Hell.

In their car Charles and Laura dozed for a time as the chauffeur crawled in line. They were utterly exhausted, physi-cally and mentally. Could it be only a month ago they had dined and laughed in that lively concourse gathered in Château Golo? Perhaps they would wake from the nightmare, and Paul at the piano would be playing Bach or Chopin.

They woke, but the nightmare was reality. For some reason the car had stopped, the long procession of vehicles had come to a halt. They could dimly see and hear the trudging pedestrians who flowed by them. The chauffeur got out and went ahead. He came back to report that everything was held up by an overladen lorry that had collapsed on a narrow bridge. It would be some time before they could move. People began to get down from their vehicles. They talked in whispers, as though the dreaded planes might hear them and come back, raining death.

Charles and Laura got out to stretch their legs. They had halted at the side of a small churchyard. The little church loomed ghostly in the darkness. They walked down a path above a stream murmuring in the night. There was peace here. A slim moon had risen over a fir wood. Charles looked at it.

"Strange to think they see that moon in England," he observed, thinking briefly of Henley, the old house by the river, and his mother, reading now, probably, in Uncle Wyndham's study. England at war, but not like this. Pray God, never like this.

"And over the orange groves at Witterwittee," added Laura. "With Grandmama waiting for a client!"

They laughed quietly at that. One seized any reason for laughter.

Laura slipped her arm over Charles's as they stood there.

"I'm sorry to have brought you to this," she said, softly. "If I hadn't come to Sundown Grove you would not be standing here."

Charles made no answer for a few moments. Then he spoke, slowly, after looking up at the starry night.

"Do you imagine I regret it, Laura? I never believed in life as I do at this moment. Once, when I was walking home one evening, with Auntie Janet, we found a little memorial stone set up on the roadside. It was to somebody's pet that had been killed there. We read the inscription. I've never forgotten it— I never shall."

"What was it?"

"*There is not enough darkness in all the world to put out the light of one small candle,*" he quoted, softly.

"How beautiful!" cried Laura.

"And true! I believe that. It must be true, otherwise there's no meaning in anything."

They stood in silence and listened. Voices sounded distantly. There was a movement along the road.

"I think we should go back," he said, taking her hand.